Praise for
A Deathly Irish Secret

"A murder disrupts the perfect vacation in the Irish countryside. Cozily delightful."

—Marilyn Levinson aka Allison Brook,
author of the *Haunted Library Mystery Series*

"Escape to the Irish countryside with Bang Murningham and her sister-cousin Haasi Hakla in A Deathly Irish Secret, a delightful cozy filled with colorful characters and a captivating mystery. Cozy fans will enjoy the close bond between Bang and her cousin and their shared humor as they explore Ireland on the hunt for a killer."

—Michelle Hillen Klump,
author of the *Cocktails and Catering Mysteries*

"A fun mystery that takes you to an Irish castle where a cast of likeable characters weave you through the twists and turns of a captivating whodunit."

—Christina Romeril,
author of the *Killer Chocolate Mysteries*

"The Irish accent, phrases, and the bog scene, especially, are fun, and the description adds delight to this rollicking mystery."

—Sandra Young,
author of *Divine Vintage*

A Deathly Irish Secret

A Blanche Murninghan Mystery

A Deathly
Irish Secret

A Blanche Murninghan Mystery

Nancy Nau Sullivan

Light Messages

Durham, NC

Published 2023, by Light Messages
www.lightmessages.com
Durham, NC 27713 USA
SAN: 920-9298

Paperback ISBN: 978-1-61153-503-7
Ebook ISBN: 978-1-61153-504-4
Library of Congress Control Number: 2023934763

This is a work of fiction. All characters, organizations, and events portrayed in this novel are either products of the author's imagination or are used fictitiously.

To my little queen maeve

For thyme it is a precious thing
And thyme brings all things to my mind
Thyme with all its labours, along with all its joys,
Thyme brings all things to an end.

—Traditional Irish folk ballad

One

Letter from Heaven

THE CALL CAME from her grandmother's lawyer: "Good morning, dearie!" He was annoyingly chipper.

Blanche held the phone away from her ear and looked at the clock. It was after nine. She threw off the tangled covers and struggled to sit up.

"Sam, I haven't had coffee yet. Wait. I've hardly opened my eyes." Blanche Murninghan was not an early riser.

"Well, open up those peepers. I've got news!"

She squinted through the porch screen at the sunlight dancing on the turquoise water in front of the cabin. The birds chittered away. It looked like another lovely day on Santa Maria Island, but it was too early for *business,* especially loud business.

"Are you there, Blanche?" Attorney Sam Gustaitis almost shouted into the phone, rattling papers. He was usually so calm.

"Yes, I'm here, Sam. What's going on?"

"Something interesting has come up. A letter from your grandmother—Maeve Murninghan, herself."

"Sam! Maeve's been gone almost five years. And you're calling me about this *now*?" She missed her grandmother, and this news stirred up the memory of her face and voice and a heap of sadness at losing her. Blanche's emotions flip-flopped. An intense curiosity shook her awake.

A letter?

Sam's voice pitched louder still. "Oh, Blanche, I'm sorry for the oversight. We came across some of Maeve's papers, buried in a packet

1

of notes with a draft of the will after we moved offices. We'll review it all, for sure, and get back to you with what we find. But for now, the *letter*. You need to go look for it."

"*Go look for it?* Don't you have a copy?"

"No, I do not. Let me see here …" More paper rattling.

It was hard to deal with lawyers and all the *detail*. Blanche needed patience. Sam Gustaitis had been a real sweetheart after Maeve died. He'd tied up all the loose ends of the will, except for this, apparently. Now he was still taking care of Maeve's final wishes.

"Maeve had notes and accounts *everywhere*, it seems," he said. "We got to most of it, but, well…"

"I know. I'm still finding little surprises. She was a packrat."

"She was," he said, as if that put the capper on it. "Blanche, listen. It says here, the letter's hidden in the cabin. You need to go to the southeast bedroom and look behind a strip of baseboard, next to the closet on the back wall." Gran's old friend and confidante was normally not given to such urgency. But in the space of about a minute he'd gone from amused, to somewhat agitated, to downright *excited*.

Blanche's mind raced. She'd solved some mysteries and had an adventure or two. But a secret letter from her grandmother? This sounded like another adventure in the making. She could feel it as if Maeve Murninghan were standing right there.

"You're calling to tell me to look for a secret letter. Under a strip of wood." She confirmed the instructions, per Maeve Murninghan.

"That's what it says here in these notes."

Blanche put the phone on speaker and headed for the spare room in the back of the cabin. Sheltered in the pines, it was dim this time of day. Her eyes adjusted to the light as she ran a hand over the weathered door jamb and looked around at the old cedar walls. Somewhere a treasure was hiding—a message from Gran!

Sam was still talking. "Seems like Maeve had ideas all her own. You know her better than most."

"Well, I wouldn't have guessed this. It sounds like a treasure hunt. Secret letter and stuff?"

"I'd say so," he agreed. "The letter is of a personal nature, she says here. I may have a copy of it somewhere, but most likely not. I'll be danged if I can find it in all this paperwork. Your grandmother was a complicated woman…"

Her grandmother might have been complicated. Her lawyer was messy, and Blanche wondered if that had added to the delay in finding this new information. She pictured his office, a wreck of documents and folders littering the desk and one barely surviving fig tree in the window.

"I'm back here in the bedroom right now," she said.

As he waited and mumbled, she walked around the small, square room, probing the baseboard next to the closet with her toe, feeling for loose boards.

Oh, Gran.

"It says here in these notes there's more to come. This is the first chapter…"

"Really? Sam!"

"I know, I know. I'm sorry for the delay."

"Do you want me to get back to you—if and when I find anything?" She was delighted at the prospect of "hearing" from her grandmother after five years.

"I don't know if that will be necessary. Like I said, there may be a copy here. We do have some *other* matters to clear up in the near future, and they may be related to the letter, or not. I don't know. For now, *look.* We'll be in touch." Rustle *mumbled swear word* click.

Blanche put the phone in her pocket and began to search in earnest. Soon enough, she found it: a loose strip of wood, just as Maeve had directed. It came away from the wall easily. A piece of folded note paper, tucked into a plastic bag, was wedged behind it.

So like Maeve. Couldn't leave without stirring it up a bit.

Blanche didn't wonder for a second where she got it.

Dear Blanche,

When you read this, I'll be gone. Don't be sad. It's the circle of life. Ha Ha…

Blanche clutched the letter and tried not to cry, or laugh. Here was her grandmother, reaching out of the grave, making a joke of it. Nothing seemed to faze her, not even being dead! Blanche closed her eyes and remembered her Gran's booming laugh and that white hair flying in the breeze.

Still holding the letter close, Blanche went for a Miller Lite. It was a little early for a beer, but she figured coffee would make her even more jittery. The Gulf pounded the beach, and the parrots screamed in the Australian pines. She smoothed the rumpled pages and gave it another go:

> You've had a visitor, and most likely a phone call. That's how you found this letter! Did Sam get hold of you? Sam's good at handling things, and I trust him. If you ever need any help, with anything, he's the one. I'll bet he did a nice job of wrapping up my little details. Carry on with your future now and remember all the things your Gran told you. Well, most of it anyway. You have the job at the newspaper, and that's fine and all, but extra help doesn't hurt now, does it? I left a tidy sum for expenses. You know about that already.
>
> This here letter is something else. I want you to go on a TREASURE HUNT! Yes, that's right! Oh, I'll bet you get a good laugh out of that. Good! I can hear it all the way to heaven! HA HA!
>
> Go into the other spare bedroom now, the one painted blue. Ninth floorboard from the east wall in the middle of the room.
>
> (I can just see you, my darling Blanche. You know I'm watching you.)
>
> There it is. Look under that board—yes, that's it—and you'll find something.
>
> You'll know what to do.
>
> I love you.
>
> Gran

It didn't sound like a suggestion; it was more of an order. Blanche was puzzled. *You'll know what to do. Do what?*

She held the letter up, read it one more time, and then hurried into the blue bedroom. She paced off the floorboards from the wall and bent down, her fingers tracing the rough planks. Sure enough, the ninth one was loose. She dug her nails into it, and it came up easily enough with a great deal of dust and grit. She set the board aside. Peered into the dark slot. What could be down there after a hundred years—besides spiders and a nest of black snakes?

She poked around in the opening, and there it was—a package sitting askew under the floor. Blanche reached in, carefully. It was taped and wrapped in plastic and brown paper and string. No name, no markings.

She turned the "treasure" over, wiping away the dusty layers of years. Then she hugged it. The last person to touch it was her grandmother. She held it to her nose, nostalgic for that old familiar lavender scent, but all she got was a musty sea-like smell. She fell back on her heels and picked at the tape and string. *Funny Gran. She just loved surprises.*

The wrapping was crusty with salt and cobwebs, and loose. Blanche peeled it off easily to reveal a grey rectangular box. It was well preserved under the plastic, and the lid wasn't locked. It sprang open. Inside were neat bundles tied with green satin ribbon.

Money? Lots of it.

Frantically, Blanche picked out a stack of bills and yanked at the bow. Fifties and hundreds fluttered onto the floor. She took out more, her eyes disbelieving, her fingers trembling. Handfuls of it!

For God's sake, Gran!

Blanche dropped the box like it was on fire and stared at it. Then she counted. There were thousands and thousands of dollars here—well over fifty thousand. *At least.* She clutched the bills and went after the other bundles.

She had to think, but think about *what?* She drew a blank, shocked at this surprise out of nowhere. Her mouth was dry. She finished the beer and sat. Dumbfounded.

How did Gran get hold of so much money? Did she rob a bank? Why would I think such a thing?

Blanche wanted answers. She had no idea where she'd get them. The only person who knew about this was Gran, and though Blanche looked to heaven and talked to her almost every day, she'd never get an answer for this.

Sam managed the estate. She should talk to him. No, she wouldn't talk to Sam about this. Not yet anyway. Maybe he knew about the money, maybe he didn't. He'd never said anything about it—only about the existence of "the letter."

She had to *think*, dammit. She began stuffing the contents back into the box. After she thought this through, maybe some clue would come to her, some past hint from Gran about the source of this windfall. But the hole in the floor stared back at her, dark and empty. She slumped back against the double bed.

Her thoughts skipped over the possibilities. Her grandmother was eccentric, but crooked? She immediately denied *that*, especially in light of all the righteous talk Gran had dished over the years. Blanche only had love and respect—and now a great deal more curiosity—about her grandmother, who had raised her since Blanche's mother Rose was killed in an auto accident and her father went missing in Vietnam. Gran was caring and frugal. They'd been comfortable, Blanche and her cousin Jack, who'd occasionally come to live at the cabin. Jack had gone on to own a hugely successful trucking and construction company and travel worldwide. He'd made it clear to Maeve he did not want nor need any inheritance from her.

Maeve gave no sign of amassing a small fortune. Blanche had always wondered about the hefty inheritance, too. But Sam had assured her that Maeve Murninghan had invested wisely. During the energy crisis of the '70s, oddly enough, Maeve had gotten a tip and made a killing in Armstrong stock. The demand for insulation had, literally, gone through the roof.

So, this?

Who knew? Who was this person she had loved all these years? Blanche still found notes around the cabin, instructing her on its ancient plumbing, the history of Bean Point, what not to eat in Lent, and a recipe for sweet potatoes with pecans and brown sugar. These reminders drifted out of books and from under sacks of flour. One was hidden in a long-forgotten drawer in the shed. Blanche had discovered them, one after another, for months and months. Each time she did, she felt her grandmother was conquering death; it was a recurrent warm feeling, the briefest respite from missing her. But domestic concerns and a bit of local history seemed to be the extent of Gran's world—weather, food, and religion; she had a caution for every corner of their island universe. Finances were not a topic. In fact, Maeve had a distinct diskregard for institutions, in general, and that included banks and the government. She'd rarely ever mentioned money, and she certainly never brought up anything related to the source of this treasure trove.

That old saying of Gran's rang through Blanche's brain: *Don't think ya know all there is to know about a person—'cause ya don't. Ever. Everyone has secrets.*

Blanche looked up, her eye drawn through the cabin, past the pines toward the beach. The water lapped gently a hundred feet from her porch. She had to get out there to the Gulf. It gave her a fresh start every time.

I didn't know my own grandmother?

The box sat heavy in her lap. She'd stow the money in its hiding place. She'd leave it there until she sorted out the mystery—if it were possible.

She finished tying the bills into some kind of order. It would have to go back just the way she found it. She stacked it, tied it up neatly. It was the oddest feeling, and a nice one in a way, but really … so much damn money!

Then she saw it. There, in the bottom of the box, a white square. She would have missed it had not the corner curled up like a beckoning fingernail. Blanche peeled back the paper. It was a leaf of stationery folded in half, and she recognized the heavy vellum. She opened it. Another note. From Gran.

Blanche stared at this new message: A picture of a shamrock, hand-scrawled in green ink, and underneath it: *Ireland!*

Two

My Wild Irish Home

BLANCHE FIDGETED with a stack of receipts and invoices, including those from Amos Wiley for repairs to the roof. She wasn't thinking about any of it as she shuffled paper into piles. Her mind was on that mysterious box of cash—the pot of gold discovered under her floorboards and the odd note in green from Gran.

She hadn't slept a wink for a week, and she couldn't get a thing done, while her deadline at the *Island Times* loomed. Her boss, Clint Wilkinson, wanted her to write a series of articles on the disappearance of coquinas and sand dollars along the Gulf coast. Blanche was less concerned about the shell population and more concerned about the influx of tourists who were rampaging over the turtle nests and raging through the canals on speed boats, causing the banks to collapse and the mangrove to fall apart. But sand dollars were not tourist dollars, and so the slightly more negative stories didn't get the attention and response they deserved. It set Blanche's teeth on edge. And the dollars under her floorboards drove her to further distraction.

She got up from the table and poured herself another cup of coffee. It only gave her more jitters.

Ireland!,

All right.

She set the mug down on the glass top with a click. Obviously, Gran meant for her to take the money and book a trip to Ireland. What else could it mean?

Maybe she would do just that and get her cousin Haasi in on the act. Gran had talked of making the trip herself and mentioned the family history a time, or two: The Murninghans and McLoughlins were from Limerick, Cork, Kerry. There were horror stories of British-owned bailiffs and the eviction of Irish from their lands, the famine of the 1840s and dire poverty. But she'd also told Blanche stories of the unparalleled beauty of the Celtic Sea and the River Shannon, of green so pure it rivaled heaven, and people full of cheer and goodwill.

A plan to visit popped into her head now with regularity. Where to begin? She had no idea, but she should go, she *would* go. Meantime, the cash and the notes bugged her.

She drained the last of her coffee and pushed the piles of bills out of the way. She sat back in the rattan armchair. The humid air from the Gulf blew onto the porch, damp and enervating. She opened her notebook, then closed it. She considered getting a beer. It was too early for her walk to the point. Slumped down, her chin lifting to the occasional breeze, thinking and wondering and enjoying. Springtime on the island was great, a respite from snowbirds and a break before the start of ninety-degree weather…

At first, she didn't see him coming across the beach. The short, little man picked his way over the sand burrs and pinecones. She slid the papers into a folder and watched the visitor walk toward the cabin. His gait was jerky, spritely. He avoided the prickly dune grass, and he didn't seem to take to the hot sand or the humidity. He kept fanning himself with a brown fedora. *Fedora? What the heck?* He wore a light brown suit, and the polish on his cordovans, clearly, was losing its sheen.

If this was yet another developer offering her a ton of money for her Gulf-front cabin, she was going to dispatch him immediately. She'd rehearsed, and used, her get-the-hell-off-my-land speech a number of times. She had it down pat, and she had no qualms about using it, but it was getting to be a drag. They could offer her a gazillion dollars. She wasn't going anywhere unless the gods and hurricanes prevailed, and, except for a few hiccups in the weather pattern, so far, so good.

"Miss Blanche Murninghan?" He stood outside the screened-in porch where Blanche had set up her little office—with the one-word note from her grandmother propped against a pink geranium. The visitor's face was beet red. He had sparse little tufts of white hair above his ears and kindly, sparkling eyes. Blanche lost all her wary feelings.

"That's me." She got up from the table and opened the door for a closer look. "What can I do for you?" She joined her visitor under the pines.

"Malcolm Sagus of Gustaitis, Sagus, and Malo, the firm that's been handling your grandmother's estate." He held out a small business card, and Blanche read it, shifting her feet back and forth on the pine needles. She'd forgotten her sandals.

He fanned himself. "As you know, Sam Gustaitis is the lawyer for Mrs. Murninghan's affairs, and I do research and accounting when called upon." He had a high, tinny voice and delivered the introduction quickly. Mr. Sagus juggled his briefcase and hat. "I believe you spoke with Sam Gustaitis, and he told you we would be in touch further about Maeve Murninghan's estate?"

"He did mention that," Blanche said, reminding herself to hold back and not start blabbing. "But five years? Seems like an awful long time."

"A bit unusual. But as aforementioned, your grandmother scattered accounts and also put some things in storage. We found a key among the notes and papers." His voice drifted off.

"A key?"

"We thought it was an old house key, but it was a safety deposit box. Again, I am sorry for the delay."

"Well, that's all right. Gran was a bit of a case."

He chuckled. "I'd like to talk with you if it's convenient. I'm sorry I don't have an appointment. We tried to call."

"That's all right, the reception out here is iffy, at best."

He looked out over the white sand toward the glistening water. "Well, I guess it's worth it. The bad reception, I mean."

Blanche hesitated. He seemed an odd bird, but sweet. And she knew Sam well and trusted him.

Now there's more Gran stuff? Oh, boy.

She'd forgotten her manners. "I'm sorry. It's hot. Won't you come in? Up to the porch? We can talk there." She turned toward the steps and pushed open the screen door. He followed. She pulled out a wicker chair.

"So grateful." Again, he fanned himself with his hat, murmured something unintelligible, and plunked down in the chair. "Whew! Another hot one!"

Blanche hovered. "May I get you something to drink?"

"Oh, that would be splendid. Water? Tea? Whatever is cold."

"I was about to have a beer. Would you like one?"

His head shot back. "Oh, my, gracious no." He checked his watch.

Blanche veered into sober territory. "How about some peach tea?"

"Oh, peachy." He chuckled, his face disturbingly red.

Blanche grinned and went off to the kitchen. She poured them tea in tall goblets, and added ice, lemon, and a sprig of mint. Mr. Sagus was smiling and staring out at the Gulf when she returned to the porch. "Lovely spot you have here. Maeve talked about it like it was paradise, and I guess it is."

"It is."

He took a large swig of the tea and smacked his lips. He settled the briefcase on the table. All business. "May I?"

"Please."

He studied Blanche as he opened the case and riffled through a stack of papers. "You have the light of your grandmother all about you!"

"Thank you! You knew her?"

"Only briefly. Sam handled most of the estate, but I was given a special assignment. On the side, so to speak. Sam and I work together, but you know your grandmother's papers were...awry. And that is why I've come out to see you today."

The money under the floorboards seemed to pulse and yell at Blanche from its hiding place, like a line out of an Edgar Allen Poe story. Now she caught herself again before she blurted something she'd regret. *Let him talk, see where this leads.* She had a feeling Mr. Sagus might know about Gran's secret. Would he unravel the mystery of it? It did not seem so. For one thing, his partner, Sam Gustaitis, apparently hadn't located his own copy of the letter. She hadn't heard from him.

"Really? You've come here about an assignment? What sort of assignment?" Blanche folded her hands neatly.

"It has to do with your Irish heritage. You know something of that? Maeve was keenly interested ..."

Blanche was not aware of a *keen* interest, but an interest, yes. She wished that she could see her grandmother one more time, look into those deep baby blues, and ask: *What the heck is going on, Gran?*

"Gran knew some family history. She shared that. I guess my blood is practically *green*. Murninghan and McLoughlin on my mother's side, and my father was Fox. But, beyond that, I'm not aware that she was driven to get into all of it."

"Maeve and I had some dealings. Some chats. It was that lineage that I spoke with her about. She wanted me to trace your ancestors and other connections in Ireland."

Blanche listened attentively, and she was sitting down, but she would swear later on, when looking back at that moment, that a ghost flitted by and lifted the curls on the back of her neck. "Gran did tell me stories. She wished, no, she probably longed for information about the family, but she'd lost contact years ago."

"Well, I have good news. I've found your relations. I've been aware of the family tie for some time, but I wanted to confirm the whereabouts and background of these relatives. And now I have it." His cheeks puffed out. "These connections are almost exactly where your grandmother suspected they might be."

Blanche sat up. "They are? You did? She never seemed sure. Many died during the famine in the 1840s, or left Ireland. They just seemed to drift away."

"That's so, but some were planted firmly and were highly successful. Do you know of the late Colonel William McLoughlin?"

"Who?"

"A relative of yours. No doubt of it. The colonel seems to have kept a low profile, you might say. A good measure Irish chieftain. Anglo Irish. Descended from traders and a prominent Dublin solicitor." He mulled the history, his fingers tented. "Colonel McLoughlin was British military and wielded quite a bit of influence."

"British?"

"Yes, not uncommon among the old Irish families. He spent his early school years in London and later joined the military, mostly as a staff officer. He chose his battles judiciously and won those he fought. A righteous man, it seems."

"Well, that's good to hear."

"He once ran a British soldier through who kicked a pregnant farmer's wife in the stomach. The colonel had seen a skirmish or two and always carried a sword."

"Oh my. This was …"

"I would say, a grand uncle on Maeve's side of the family. The colonel died in the '50s."

"Gran wants me to go to Ireland. I just found a note from her." She didn't mean to sound so abrupt, but shoot-from-the-hip Blanche "Bang" Murninghan couldn't help it. *So much for patience.*

"That's a splendid idea, and I'm sure you will want to make plans *tout de suite* when you hear this," said Malcolm Sagus. He took a sheaf of papers out of his briefcase and thumbed through them. "Allow me: Colonel McLoughlin did not have children, but he was close to his nephew, William. The nephew was the last to occupy the family castle, Dunfaedan, near the village of Ballycill, County Limerick. Sadly, the young William passed on some years ago, in the '70s. Tragically, it seems. You are not to meet this member of the family." His eyes cast heavenward.

"Tragically?" Blanche did not like the sound of that. "What happened?"

"There was an accident. I'm not sure of the details so I would not wish to speculate. Perhaps you will find out more. When you visit…"

Blanche straightened in her chair; her curiosity tuned up.

Sagus's words rushed together. "William the nephew was a generous person, like his uncle the colonel. The family had the best interests of the village in mind, finding employment and supporting the local residents in any way they could. Finally, the nephew left instructions in his will to look for heirs. Now, after all the paperwork has settled, *you,* Miss Murninghan, are determined to be the closest heir." He took a deep breath, tapped the papers on the edge of the table, and thrust a packet toward her. "As such, you are now owner of approximately one-sixteenth of an Irish castle. It stands in Limerick on the Shannon estuary, not far from Cork and Kerry where many of the Murninghans and McLoughlins have lived after moving south from Ulster and the Burren."

If he'd had a feather, he could have knocked her over with it. All she could say was: "*Owner? Of an Irish castle? Huh?*"

He eyed her over the rims of his glasses and smiled broadly. "It is a rather nice piece of news now, isn't it? It's a small share, but still … It entitles you to some usage of the property." He chortled and looked around at Blanche's rough but cozy, weathered log cabin, bright floral cushions, an abundance of geraniums and white candles. A far cry from *castle*. "The majority of the castle and grounds are part of a legal entity, organized to pay for its upkeep and to benefit the village. You needn't worry about the upkeep. It manages itself quite well."

Blanche glanced at the blur of gray legalese that Malcolm set on the table. She murmured, "You were searching for them, and they were searching for us? *All this time?* For, like, twenty-five years since the nephew's death?"

"Something like that. But, actually, the search had long gone dormant. Maeve kindled it once again. The Irish end of it suffered a lack of diligence on the part of the estate handlers, I'm afraid. But now there is some resolution after our research. It was the hope of your grandmother that one day you would go and renew a connection to the auld sod. She made it happen, but I'm sure she didn't envision it quite this way." Here he stopped and mused.

"This means I can go to Ireland and stay in a castle? Which I partly own?" Blanche was incredulous, but it sounded very cool.

His eyes sparkled under those bushy brows. "Well, yes, your castle, in a manner of speaking. Your time to visit depends on whether or not it's leased to help pay for maintenance. At present, you have two weeks a year during which you may occupy Dunfaedan, at leisure, or lease it. As you wish." Here he stopped, looking over the terms. "But, yes, you may go to Ireland…for a brief reign?" He chuckled. "It'll be grand, I should think. I do wish I had pictures. We should have some soon."

"Grand. That's the word for it. I'd love pictures, but better than that, I want to see for myself." *When do I pack for Ireland?*

"You'll need to come to the office to finalize some of the details. We'll be in touch." He stood up with a perfunctory bow and gathered his briefcase and hat. He started toward the door and turned. "You know, Miss Murninghan, I can't help but think that your grandmother was determined that you go to Ireland. One way or another."

"Oh, I know she was. That's Maeve Murninghan for you. *Determined.* Just full of surprises."

He digested that observation, thoughtfully. "What if this search for distant relations had been fruitless? Would you have gone anyway?"

"That's a good one, Mr. Sagus." Blanche looked away, and then squarely met his gaze. "Have to say, yes. One way or another I'm meant to visit Ireland."

"I believe so." He murmured and clapped the fedora on his head.

"Thank you." She grabbed his free hand and shook it. "Really, I can't thank you enough for finding this connection. It'll be an adventure of a lifetime."

"I should say. Goodbye, then." He said, cheerily, then retraced his steps over the sand and was gone. *To where? Was all this an apparition, a ghost, a dream?*

Blanche was thrilled at the news. She stared out at the water.

Ireland. It's meant to be.

Three

Key to the Castle

"WHAT ARE YOU TALKING ABOUT, Blanche? You are part-owner of a castle? *In Ireland?* Does that mean you're a duchess or something?" Haasi Hakla sat cross-legged on the beach in front of Blanche's cabin. She twisted her gleaming black braid until Blanche was sure she'd spin off like a top. Cousin Haasi always had a way of putting a fine point on it.

"Jeeeez, Haas! No! Well, maybe." She took a swig of beer and suppressed a laugh. "You want to call me Duchess Blanche?" The pelicans were diving for dinner, and the sun was setting orange over the silvery Gulf. The sand was still warm in the late afternoon.

"No, I do not."

"All right. And I can't call you *Princess Haasi*?"

"Nope."

"We're a royal pair, aren't we?" Blanche looked down at her salty T-shirt and ragged cut-offs. "The duchess and the princess." Blanche laughed and gave Haasi a gentle poke in the rib. The sun lowered into the Gulf with a flash.

"Well, we sort of are," said Haasi. She and Blanche shared the same great-grandmother who'd had a fling with Miccosukee royalty, a chief on Florida's west coast; Haasi was descended from the love child of that affair. Blanche and Haasi were sister-cousins and about as different as the sun they'd been staring into and the moon that was about to rise. Different, and at once nearly inseparable. Haasi's successful charter fishing business had lately taken her to Aruba, but she and Blanche always ended up sitting in the sand in front of the cabin. Two gulls on the beach.

Haasi squinted at Blanche. "That is crazy! My cousin, the castle owner! Do you have pictures?"

"No, not yet." Blanche grabbed Haasi's arm. "But listen, how about we go over there and have a look. Don't you want to see the real thing? I do."

"Oh, sure, let's just book a plane to Ireland and go live in your castle. Blanche, what is up with *that*?"

"I mean it. Gran intended it. I gotta tell you what happened. What she left."

And so she did.

Blanche sat across from Malcolm Sagus in his office in downtown Bradenton, Florida, not five miles from her cabin on the beach. She might as well have been five hundred miles from that leaky, loveable cabin; this was the *city*, and Blanche was wearing a skirt and a blouse. A hibiscus with huge pink flowers bloomed over Malcolm's shoulder, and a coffee pot sent a heavenly scent from the tray on the corner of his desk. Blanche perched on the edge of one of the red leather armchairs, listening to every word as more details—and paperwork— emerged about Dunfaedan Castle, the former home of Colonel William McLoughlin and his nephew, William. And now, one-sixteenth *hers*.

"The last to occupy the castle, the nephew, left instructions for the structures and grounds to be maintained and self-sufficient. Occasionally, the property is leased to help pay for the roof. The farm production adds to the upkeep, and it provides employment to many of the village residents," said Malcolm. "All in all, I've received reports that the business end of it is in pretty good shape."

"And there are no other owners? Besides me and this company, or corporation, of sorts?"

Malcolm shifted in his seat and mumbled, "Well ..." Blanche raised an eyebrow. He poured them more coffee. She didn't need any more caffeine.

"This is the situation." He hesitated. "There is someone. An aunt, a cousin, perhaps? Very far removed. I believe she is related to Maeve's grandmother's brother, but that is for another deep dive."

"*Family?*" Blanche was now out of her seat, a taut arm on the edge of Malcolm's desk. "You found living relatives?"

"Indeed. Mary Ann "Maggie" Fitzpatrick McLoughlin. She lives in Ballycill near the castle. Maeve didn't know of her, or about any present family connection. Maggie does not inherit the McLoughlin property."

"But she's a relation, and she inherits none of the castle?"

"As regards the will, it was specific about the line of inheritance. Due to some quirk of legalities—and her own quirks, if I may say. No disrespect intended. According to the reports, Maggie is a lovely person and happily ensconced in a cottage in Ballycill. She seems to have no interest in the castle, after inquiry, and is quite the celebrity of the village, shall we say. Colorful, and she knows a good bit of history."

"Colorful?" This development added a new layer of curiosity. Plus, Maggie was a local historian. What might she know about the family? What could she tell Blanche about the "tragic" death of the nephew?

"You'll meet her straight away." He stared at the ceiling, tapping a finger on his chin. "The whole situation is rather complicated, if you ask me. But, heh-heh, my personal opinion is of little consequence. The landscape is for you to explore."

"Complicated?"

Malcolm's shoulders shook with a deep laugh. "A thousand years of Irish history and ancestry? It's a tangle, all right, Miss Blanche. And you're tied to it. A *colorful* tangle."

She sat back in the armchair, eager for details.

Malcolm tented his fingers. "The villagers work the farm and benefit from produce and other products from some four hundred acres of grounds and livestock at the castle. Some proceeds go to charity. The McLoughlins were acutely aware of how the British treated the Irish, and the colonel, and his nephew, were determined to provide a suitable and profitable atmosphere at Dunfaedan."

"Sounds like the colonel was generous—and in a precarious position. As a British officer?"

"Precarious, and fortunate. The colonel was a powerful man, all the way to the Crown."

"And now? What's the situation … with the Crown?"

"Relations with the British are on an even keel, more or less. A hands-off policy. The castle enterprise is fully an Irish entity and not a burden to you to run, but it does come with some responsibility. Sam and I will assist you with details."

Blanche mulled this over. "I don't know the first thing about running a castle. I've enough here on my island to keep a roof on the cabin." She was secretly grateful for the complication and thankful to her generous relatives.

"Ah, don't worry. It does quite well, run as a company with a board and good management. It seems the agent in charge has matters in hand."

"Does Maggie know about me? Will she be expecting me?"

"Oh, yes, she's just learned about you, and she's looking forward to a meeting." His eyebrows shot up, hands crossed over his ample stomach. "Now the matter of finances. There are funds should you need assistance to make the trip."

The pile of money under the floorboards kept calling to her. "I'm all right for now, thank you."

"If you need help, we're here for you. We can move residuals around so it's no burden for you to go."

Blanche grinned. "No burden at all! Maeve was frugal, and I don't spend much." She smoothed her new cotton skirt with a print of green parrots and palm trees. *Green, the wearin' of the green.* "But, Maggie. What can you tell me about her?"

"You'll discover for yourself. The agent for the castle, Declan O'Brian, has told us she's a lively character. *Ahem.* But then there is talk of this Declan O'Brian…" He smiled, a bit tightly, as if he were holding back, then added, "But it's nice to find old family connections now, isn't it? You'll enjoy this reunion with Miss Maggie, I'm sure."

"I'd like to go soon."

"That should not be a problem. You need your passport, and I can secure the vacancy, alert the staff, that sort of thing. And then these various documents I have here for you to review and sign. Sam will be here shortly to go over them with you."

The gray lines on the sheaf of papers swam before Blanche's eyes. "Unbelievable."

"Perhaps, and a fine piece of Irish luck." He sat back and laced his fingers over his vest. "If anyone could pull this one out of a hat, I'd say Maeve Murninghan is the one. If it weren't for your grandmother, you'd never have known of this property. Unless the colonel came out of his grave and told you himself."

Blanche's imagination ran off with that one. "Only in my dreams."

He popped forward in his chair. "I'd say the dream is just beginning, Miss Blanche. Pack your bags. Enjoy it! It'll be there for you until the place crumbles away. Which, I expect, won't happen any time soon."

Four

At Your Service (Maybe)

IT WAS TWELVE HOURS to Ireland's Shannon Airport from Tampa with a stop in New York City. Enough time for Blanche to drink two Coronas, read one quarter of James Lee Burke's *Purple Cane Road,* and eat a dinner of mashed potatoes and a square of unidentifiable meat the size of a pack of cigarettes. Haasi had devoured all of her dinner and most of Blanche's because that's what she did; the woman was an eater from dawn 'til dusk and still maintained her hundred pounds or so.

Blanche marveled at her sister-cousin, curled up sound asleep in the seat next to her. A sense of déjà vu swept over her. It wasn't long ago that they'd flown off to Mexico City, on the adventure of a lifetime that included a mummy, a kidnapping or two, and the meeting of several inestimable Mexican friends—including Blanche's new love, Emilio Del Sierra. She was still waiting for him to leave Mexico for a fellowship at the University of Florida and complete his training as a doctor. She missed him all the while she regretted getting him shot. By accident, of course. At least, she hadn't gotten him killed. He'd smothered her with kisses and taken her in his one arm, the one without a bullet hole, and promised he'd see her one day.

Blanche sighed. *They don't call me Bang for nothing.*

She stared out the window at the clouds zipping by. Yes, someday, after a trip to the castle and back to Santa Maria Island, some day she would see him again. If it killed her.

In the meantime, Blanche indulged in a premonition. It was going to be hard for her to keep her promise to Haasi. The trip to Ireland aimed to be uneventful, but the details tugged at Blanche. Maybe Blanche had painted too rosy a picture. She hadn't mentioned all she'd learned from Gustaitis and company. The nephew William's tragic death under murky circumstances was disturbing. And then there was the "colorful" cousin, Maggie, and a rather "complicated" history. And what about this castle agent, Declan O'Brian? Blanche figured she'd save all the details for later and hope for the best. She was determined to make it a nice family visit to an Irish castle with a drive or two through the green hills and valleys and a lot of stops at pubs for beer and local food. If only …

"No bodies, no murders," Haasi had said when agreeing to the trip. "Nothing but idyllic tunes and that pot of gold at the end of your rainbow."

Blanche had looked at Haasi sideways. She couldn't help but hear the sardonic tone in her voice.

"Promise," said Blanche. "I guess."

"What do you mean, you guess? Is something shady going on over there?"

"Shady? Well, no. Not that I know of. But there are a lot of questions…"

"Blanche, with you, there are always the questions."

They landed at Shannon with no hassle at customs and the distinct feeling of being in a new land. They made their way through the airport past round-faced redheads and bustling workers and tourists. It was a busy place that offered a warm welcome and a distinct smell of diesel mixed with the scent of bread and beer. Blanche called Declan O'Brian, the castle agent, and told him they were on their way.

They climbed into the small rental car. Undaunted, Blanche started it up and yanked at the stick shift. She was sufficiently rested after a short nap on the flight; she could sleep standing up, like a horse. Haasi studied her and then leaned in from the passenger's seat: "Drive on the left side of the road, drive on the left side of the road."

Blanche fiddled with the visor and the lights, turning them on and off. Fortunately, it was the middle of a sunny day. "I *heard* you. What am I? An incapable klutz?"

Haasi remained silent, then added, under her breath. "I'm sorry. Just reminding you."

"Well, thanks. Where would I be without your reminders?"

"You'd be dead?" Haasi's defense skills, spy tactics, and plain old getting after it had been the perfect complement to Bang Murninghan's impulses—and crazy ideas—to search out culprits and solve murders. Blanche had to hand it to her. They were a good team, and they were still alive.

"Point well taken." Blanche grinned and lurched out of the parking lot.

Haasi wrestled with a map to Dunfaedan as they headed toward Ballycill. "Says here we should make it in under two hours, if we don't stop."

"I'd like to stop on every corner. Look at this place!" The sky had been sunny but suddenly reflected a brilliant gray light over the green land and the neat cottages and fields of yellow gorse. She could almost smell the endless expanse of ocean with a zillion secrets of the living and the dead that had separated her from the land of her forbears. Now here she was. It all swept over her in a wild moment. She shook her head and concentrated on driving on the left side, flapping against the thick, abundant hedges that hung over the roadway and watching out for the sheep who had the right of way.

Blanche was not tired; she was wired.

"We turn right after the rise ahead." Haasi hunched down in the seat and smoothed the map on the dashboard. Her head bobbed back and forth at the vast sky and the brilliant green hills dotted with the tiny white humps of foraging animals.

"The directional signs are awfully vague. You got this?"

"*We* got this, B." They threaded their way over narrow roads along stone fences, past lakes in the valley, and few houses on the stretches of pastureland. "Isn't it cool? Wow, I thought Florida was green."

"It's a rather different sort of green, isn't it now?"

"My god, Blanche, are you talking with a brogue? Already?"

"Something is coming over me."

"Well, just make sure it helps you …"

"I know. Stay on the left side of the road."

The vista opened up to the town of Kinleithe with houses all stitched together like a quilt; the doors were painted bright red, blue, green. They canted up a hill to a small-town square with a fountain in the middle. O'Blakely's Pub reigned over this block of houses, and stout women walked briskly along the street with leafy bundles and loaves of bread.

"I like this place."

"You would. It's got a nice pub," said Haasi, peering through the windshield at the flower boxes and gold lettering over the door. "I like it, too." She poked Blanche. "Duchess."

Blanche took her eyes off the road and gave Haasi a look.

"Hey, I have a thought," Blanche said.

"You often do."

"Why don't we have that be our signal—our keyword? On the trip, I mean."

"To mean?"

"Be careful. Heads up. I smell danger. That sort of thing."

"*Duchess.* Could be. I like it." Haasi eyed Blanche. "But, danger? No, thank you. We'll have none of that, please."

"Oh, Haas. How could anything bad happen here, far from the madding crowd?" Blanche waved a hand over the lovely green hills. "Just look at this place. We're on the edge of heaven."

"OK, Duchess. Remember that."

"Once we're off this island, I do not want to hear *duchess* again," said Blanche. "Agreed?"

Haasi rolled her eyes. "Right on, Dutch."

Blanche parked the car at an angle near the fountain. "You thirsty? I am."

"I love your sense of adventure."

"Yeah, trying out the local beer."

They got out and stretched. It was another hour or so to the castle, and they needed sustenance. They walked into O'Blakely's pub, into a dim woody interior, nearly empty of patrons except for an old gent in a cap hunched over a beer. Geraniums grew leggy and wild on the deep-set windowsills. A blackboard offered the pick of the day for lunch: boxty and bangers and mash, colcannon and blood sausage.

"Will you look at that menu. What planet did we land on?" Blanche mused.

"It's all delicious. Boxty is pancakes, bangers are sausages, and mash is mashed spuds. Colcannon is cabbage and mashed potatoes," said Haasi.

"How do you know so much?"

"Where the stomach is involved, I'm a walking cookbook."

A large-bosomed woman smiled and clinked beer glasses onto a shelf behind the bar. She turned around. "Ah, good day to ye ladies."

"Hello." Blanche climbed onto the barstool, Haasi next to her.

Blanche sighed. Ireland. *We made it, Gran.* The brass and glasses and bottles shone; the bar gave off a yeasty smell mixed with a whiff of clean pine.

"What can I do for ye?" The woman produced a towel and wiped the bar, which appeared to be spotless. She smiled a bright gap-toothed smile, her face ruddy as a ripe peach. She had a wild fluff of white hair.

"One of those lovely beers?" Blanche looked over the array of drafts and beer signs.

"That'll be *foin*," she said, grinning. "I'm Mabel McGlory."

"Blanche Murninghan and Haasi Hakla. Nice to meet you."

"Ye look like you've come a long way."

"Indeed, we have. And we are thirsty!"

"Yer at the right place."

"Surely. How about the Smithwick's?"

"Smithwick's." Haasi lowered her voice. "Blanche, I have no idea what that is, do you?"

"Well, no. But we're in the land of beer…"

The barkeep busily poured. She set the beers on the counter and stood back, hands on hips. "Now, where could ye be from?"

"Florida. West coast, Tampa area."

"Aye, the land of the Great Mouse. Why would ye be leavin' that nice sunshine to come here, to this gray place, lovely as 'tis?"

"We're going to Ballycill. To the castle Dunfaedan?" Blanche did not feel compelled to give details.

25

"Is that so? Ah, *such a place.*" Mabel McGlory's expression dimmed a bit, her thoughts straying. She clucked and, with vigor, resumed wiping the same spot on the counter. "Will ye be havin' a bit of bread and sossage with yer beer?"

The offer of food made Haasi perk up while Blanche's radar flipped on. She leaned over and planted her hands on the bar. Haasi knew what was coming; she nudged Blanche before she could shoot off her mouth.

"Bang? How about that sossage?"

Blanche moved the beer glass around in a circle. She remained cool, and deaf to Haasi's question about food. Her journalistic gene, working. She couldn't resist. "*Such a place?* The village, and the castle? Why do you say that, Miss McGlory?"

Mabel narrowed her eyes. "Well, it's all beautiful and grand, to be sure, but the shenanigans of that Declan O'Brian who runs the castle and them loovely grounds. Sure and it's said, they can't keep the kitchen maids a cause of him." She stopped, squinted at Blanche, and whipped the towel onto her waist. "And other *tings.*"

"What other…things?"

"Oh, now, it's all gossip. It's a country that keeps secrets, and because of that, no one can keep a secret. We're a bubblin' lot." She set steaming plates of mashed potatoes and sausage on the counter. Blanche did not look at the food; she studied Mabel McGlory while Haasi dived in.

"Bubblin'?" Blanche was intrigued—and confused.

"Ye go and see for yer foin selves," said Mabel. "The two of ye *loovely* Americans. I'd like to see the look on the face of that Declan O'Brian when he meets the two of ye."

They had one beer each and the bangers and mash. Blanche was raring to go, her curiosity in high gear. She had enough adrenalin to power them all the way to the castle. *Shenanigans…and other 'tings'?*

"Are you all right, Blanche?" Haasi buckled her seat belt. "You seem awfully wound up."

"Who me? I'm great. I'm quite fortified with my first Irish meal though I hardly know what it is I ate." She clutched the wheel and breathed in the fine air.

"Well, we did it justice. Those spuds were the creamiest. Yum."

"Haas, you haven't met a potato you don't love."

Haasi seemed oblivious to Mabel McGlory's comments. *Oh, just as well. We'll have the details soon enough.*

Haasi resumed wrestling with the map. The quiet, hilly street with its neat little storefronts and dogs keeping watch looked ripped from a postcard. Blanche stared straight ahead out the windshield, her mind going round about Declan O'Brian and the *bubblin'* and *'tings.'*

"So interesting, don't you think, Haas? What Mabel said about Dunfaedan and that agent?"

"It's all grand and interesting, B. Just drive." She smiled but didn't look up, her finger tracing a line on the map.

The small car rumbled over the cattle guard at the entrance to the grounds of Dunfaedan. Blanche steered between the enormous leaves of elephant ear and rhododendron, a tunnel of green delight. The wheels crunched down the raked gravel drive and around a bend to a circle in front of the great Georgian castle.

"Wow," Haasi murmured. "Very un-Disney-like—but it sure is a castle, all right."

"I'll say." It was imposing, an elegant white stone apparition with a crenelated roof line. Rounded towers balanced the façade, one on each side. Its tall, narrow, rectangular windows were dark, the straight lines broken by a riot of climbing purple flowers and sculptured topiary trees on either side of the great carved door. The grounds were a manicured green carpet.

As soon as the car stopped, the door sprang open, and a tall, dark-haired man strode toward them. He stuck his hand up in greeting. His form-fitting shirt, top button undone, revealed muscles, and his stride was purposeful. *Like he owns it.*

He approached the driver's side, and Blanche stared up at him. The window was rolled down to take advantage of the fresh green air and all the sights. She got a good look. She'd never seen a man quite so dangerously handsome: He wasn't young, for sure, but his hair was thick and black, his skin smooth and white and freshly shaved (she noticed a small nick under his chin). His eyes, well, his eyes were the windows to … heaven? The deep, cerulean, icy blue of a cloudless sky.

"Good afternoon. Miss Blanche Murninghan, I presume?" He opened the car door and stepped back. He said her name like it was—a private joke? "Declan O'Brian, agent at Dunfaedan." He smiled a devilish smile. "At your service."

From the passenger's seat, Haasi let out a breathy, "Wow." Blanche turned, briefly, raised her eyebrows, and quickly resumed staring at Declan.

"Yes. It's me. I mean, it's *we*." Blanche gestured at Haasi. "My cousin, Haasi Hakla. Here all the way from Santa Maria Island, Florida. We're so happy …" The last words fell off as she climbed out of the car.

"I am definitely at your service." The grin was wide, revealing perfect white teeth. Of course. There didn't seem to be anything imperfect about this guy. He held her gaze.

"My service? I'm not sure what that means, Mr. Declan O'Brian." She didn't mean to sound playful, but there she was.

"We'll figure it out now, won't we." It wasn't a question. This seemed to amuse him further. He chuckled while he went around and opened the door for Haasi, grabbed a couple of bags, and came back to the front of the car. Haasi was her implacable, dignified self; no doubt she was sizing up *all* of her surroundings. She definitely liked to know where she stood.

"Una Mullins awaits your arrival, ladies. I've alerted her to be ready for you." Declan inclined his head toward the castle door and hefted the bags. "We want everything to be *grand* for your stay with us."

"Well, so far the scenery here is more than grand," murmured Blanche.

Haasi stifled a laugh.

Just then a short little woman appeared at the entry, gray hair pulled back severely, a tweedy cardigan buttoned all the way and pulled taut over her ample hips. She had a dour expression—until she and Blanche exchanged looks. Una's face transformed like the sun coming out. Blanche stepped forward and offered her hand. "Miss Una? So nice to meet you."

"Sure and yer so welcome, Miss Blanche. And Miss Haasi. 'Tis grand to see ye."

Blanche was surprised at Una's grip, the strong fingers and broad palms, for one so small and elderly. "I've looked forward to this visit, and I hope we haven't inconvenienced you on such short notice."

Una tipped her head, still smiling. "Why, no, 'tis lovely yer here! Declan will see to yer bags now, and then we have a bit of refreshment for ye in the salon. Ye must be *parched*."

"Great! Yes, we're a bit parched." The beer and food at McGlory's, plus Mabel's bit of gossip about Declan and the castle, made Blanche thirstier than ever.

"Miss Haasi?" Una greeted her. Their serene expressions were a match across all differences.

"So lovely to be here in your home," said Haasi.

How typical of Haasi to pick up on that. Blanche had relayed some family history. Una had been a resident at the castle for sixty years, lest anyone forget. She had been nanny and tutor to the late William, last in the line. In his will, he had stipulated that Una was the "heart of my home" and should remain there until she decided to leave, or the Lord decided it was time. She'd been like a second mother to him.

Apparently, Declan hadn't gotten the memo about Una's connection. He stepped in front of her, rather abruptly. "Now, I'll just see to the bags and meet you in the drawing room," he said. "We have a bit of business, and a tour—of your castle." He flashed those white teeth and winked. "But tea first and then you can get settled."

Blanche's head was spinning, trying to figure out what was behind those crinkly blue eyes. But, yes, of course, tea! That should reveal all.

Una looked up and gave Declan a bland look. Her face was hard to read, but Blanche didn't see much love there. Una stepped forward. "This way, please, Miss Blanche and Miss Haasi," she said, all of her attention firmly directed at her guests—the brand-new castle owner and family.

Five

What's up with That?

BLANCHE WALKED INTO THE CASTLE entry and caught her breath. A spray of pink lilies, yellow roses, and ferns shot from a crystal vase on a round table centered on a lovely Oriental rug. Her eye followed a double-flying staircase curving up to the second floor, each polished wing, to the left and to the right, suspended above the stone floor. A large marble bust on the connecting landing shined in a beam of light. Gold-framed officers and ancestors hung on the walls, and Blanche wondered which were the Williams. Somewhere among the portraits, her relatives were looking down at her. She smiled back at them.

Una led the way over the polished slate and thick runner into a room that opened to a garden of topiary and white stone benches. A gravel path extended out into the demesne. She stopped next to a glass coffee table between two loveseats in front of a fireplace glowing with a low peat flame. Blanche shivered from an overwhelming sense of discovery, curiosity—and gratitude. "This is so lovely, Una. Thank you."

"The thanks is mine to give, for it is good to welcome ye to Dunfaedan." Her hands were clasped in front of her pearly buttons, her head bowed slightly.

"Well, and here we are then." Declan appeared on cue, announcing himself heartily. *The "lord" of the manor has arrived.* Blanche raised an eyebrow. Una shuffled around Declan and poured the tea while Blanche sat down on the edge of the loveseat. Haasi whispered a thank you and stared stonily into her teacup.

Blanche sighed. Haasi had already made up her mind about this Declan person, and Blanche was not far from agreement. He seemed to be a bit of a boob. Handsome, but clueless, and rude, clomping around and interrupting.

"That'll be all, Una," he said, dismissing her. Una resumed her original dour expression, threw Blanche a look, and retreated on her soundless carpet slippers.

"Mr. O'Brian…" Blanche had every intention of getting on the right track with the agent, but her prospects were dimming. His loud, brash approach was off-putting.

"Please. *Declan*," he said. "And may I call you Blanche? And Haasi?"

Haasi remained stone-faced and didn't respond. Blanche nodded. She was at a loss for words, which was rare, but then she delicately cleared her throat. "I was about to say, *Declan*, that I wanted to talk with Una a bit further."

He seemed to get a kick out of that. He leaned back on the blue silk cushion and laughed, his fingers laced around a knee. He wore a gold signet ring on his pinkie, his nails had the sheen of a fresh manicure. "Ah … and you'll have plenty of time to chat up the help since you are the *duena* of the castle. How do you like it so far?"

"What's not to like? It's beautiful. And once I have this tea, I'd love a tour." Blanche decided to push on. She'd be as pleasant as possible. A business approach would be most appropriate—cool, with a touch of let's-get-this-done. "Declan, what can you tell me about the colonel's nephew, William McLoughlin?"

"Una will be able to tell you about him, I'm sure." His tone changed, forcing the words as he grit his teeth. "Perhaps later? After dinner?"

What an odd reaction.

Haasi placed her saucer and cup on the table with a decided click. "Of course. I'd love to talk with Una further, too." A slow smile crossed her lips. She gave Declan a level look. "You mentioned a tour?"

They stood. Haasi leaned into Blanche's ear. "Shall we, Duchess?"

Uh-oh, something's up. I have radar, and Haasi's is bone deep.

Declan laughed. "Duchess? You Americans are *cards*. Is that how you say it? I'm glad you came to visit. We need a bit of Yankee cheer about the place."

"We are not from the North," said Haasi. "We are Floridians."

"Oh, sorry." He ignored the frosty tone and made a little bow. He seemed full of mirth—and full of himself.

Haasi was peeved, but her dry tone didn't do a thing to deflate Declan O'Brian. He didn't seem to get it. Blanche could only wonder where they were headed with this Declan O'Brian. She determined to keep her "wits about her," as Gran would say.

Blanche wanted to go to her room. She needed a bath and a nap, and Haasi needed to get away from Declan before she strangled him. Maybe they all needed a break—already—and they hadn't been at the castle an hour.

"You must be tired. Come this way. I'll take you on a short tour now and then show you to your rooms," said Declan.

"That would be good," said Blanche, smiling. She coaxed a grin out of Haasi.

They ascended one wing of the flying staircase. Blanche ran her fingers over the polished rail and looked up at her ancestors. "Which of these portraits is William, the colonel? And the nephew?"

Declan stopped midway and pointed to two large portraits. One, a dignified officer with a weary eye, a white mustache, and a high forehead. "The colonel. We will meet him and his nephew again in the dining room." Hanging next to the colonel, a smaller portrait showed a young man with black curly hair and a spritely, suppressed grin. He wore a high white collar and black formal attire. Blanche liked him instantly. She wanted to know more, and tomorrow she would surely get to know both of them better when she met her new-found relative, Maggie Fitzpatrick McLoughlin. The faces in baroque frames smiled solemnly from the cream silk walls. *My ancestors. They had been right here. On this staircase, going up, up to their rooms. Like me and Haas.*

"Well, let's see about those rooms," Declan said, briskly. He didn't elaborate further about the McLoughlins as he rattled on. "Here, the Pink Room, and down the hall, the Green Room and the Blue Room. The jewels of the place."

The Pink Room was all that, outfitted with a rose-colored quilt and lacey pillows and vases of blooms the size of cabbages. The rug on the polished floor featured a splash of rose, blue, and green. And more green: The window framed the dewy green afternoon rolling away amid the yews and conifers under a blue sky.

"This, of course, is quite nice." Declan sidestepped out into the hallway. "But I think *this* one is most appropriate for the *owner* of the castle," he said, pointing the way to the Blue Room.

A gold crown on the canopy of the bed clasped a drape of blue silk. It flowed to either side of the bed, next to exquisite gilt nightstands topped with crystal lamps. Across the room, a walnut desk on delicate legs displayed paper and ink and blotter and an armchair in gold brocade. Vases of pink lilies on pedestals stood on either side of the tall window. The room was many shades of blue, and somehow, it worked, like looking up to the sky and seeing the different layers of light. Blanche peeked at the bathroom, at the claw-footed tub, black and white tile floor, and brass fittings. She wanted to sink into that tub and stare out that tiny window into heaven.

Thank you, the William McLoughlins and Maeve Murninghan.

Declan's chest puffed out like he'd swallowed a lot of hot air. "The McLoughlins dabbled in trade. The colonel traveled in France and Britain, and he recovered many pieces of furniture that had been sold off during the early years of Dunfaedan. This desk, for instance. He carried it on his horse from the train station." Declan suddenly seemed amused, a smile on his lips as he tilted his head toward the desk. Blanche was surprised at the warm burst of nostalgia from the agent. For a moment, a proud, familial attachment shined through—when he talked about the furnishings.

She studied the small desk with fine inlay and brass fittings. It had gouges but was highly polished. She imagined her relative, back straight, leather and stirrups, riding a horse as big as a truck, the desk strapped to the side. Did he carry it up the flying staircase on his back? She wanted to sit down at that desk and write something. She looked at his picture and imagined him striding through the castle. She was glad to be here. In his home. *Our* home.

Haasi smiled and nodded. Blanche had a hundred questions, but she reserved comment for now; her brain was a jumble. Besides, it was nearly impossible to wedge a word into the one-sided, walking travel brochure that was Declan O'Brian. There would be time for questions, and soon. Haasi was taking notes in her own way; she had a brain like a computer.

Declan pointed the way toward the Green Room. He seemed better at describing furnishings than being a perceptive host; he was all business about the contents, fabrics, décor. The material things. He fingered the draperies of celadon silk, a gleaming silvery green. The fur rugs and wall tapestry that were near medieval. Haasi's disdain for skinned animals as pure decoration was evident, but she kept smiling. "It's lovely," she said. "Thank you."

Their bags were already in place on luggage racks. Declan bowed. "I'm going to leave you now, and we can have a more extensive tour later. Dinner will be at eight, if that is to your liking." He almost smirked. "But you will let us know during your stay what hour you prefer, and, of course, you will advise the cook of the menu…each day you're in residence.…"

Haasi raised her eyebrows.

"That'll be fine." Blanche composed herself. "Thank you. We'll see you later then?"

"Oh, yes, indeed. At eight. And if you need anything, please ring the bell." He pointed at a long silk tassel on the wall, turned with a dramatic flourish, and left them.

"'each day you're in residence,'" said Haasi. "Really."

"What? We *are* in residence." Blanche twirled and stumbled onto a chaise lounge. "And what's up with the *Duchess* business? I heard you, and so did he. What're you thinking?"

Haasi put her hands on her hips. "Blanche, this guy. I don't know… We need to be careful. Something of the con man about him. He's so *smooth*. Don't you think?" She went to her bag, lifted small squares of clothing out of her suitcase, and dropped them into a drawer.

"He does seem full of himself." Blanche adjusted a velvet pillow and crossed her arms. "I don't have that much info on him, at least the personal stuff. Guess we'll find out. Mabel hinted that he's a piece of work."

"What's the extent of his…reach?"

"He's a manager. Has to answer to a board—bunch of finance types at the bank and accounting firm the McLoughlins dealt with. Sam is handling that end for me, but he wants me to take some *responsibility.*"

Haasi looked at Blanche quizzically. "What does that mean?"

"Not sure. I told Sam and Malcolm I'd keep an eye out. My castle-keeping skills are in short supply."

"Well, I'm not leaving you here."

"Thanks."

"You're good with him when you put your business hat on. Just hope he stays in his corner—with his damn hat and his pants on."

"OMG, Haas. He's gotta be pushing fifty, and he's a dope. An awfully handsome one, but still a dope." Blanche stood up and stretched.

"We agree on so many things."

"I can't wait to meet Cousin Maggie. She might have more of a scope on *tings*, as Mabel McGlory says."

"Yeah, when do we meet her?"

"Soon. Have to call. In the meantime, we'll manage Declan." Blanche hesitated. Impressions of the castle agent indeed were unsettling. She blurted: "Don't you think it's funny he didn't answer my question about the nephew? He immediately went to Una…"

"Not really, Blanche. We just got here, and there's so much to see and do."

"Hmmm." Blanche noted the firm set of Haasi's jaw, the wry smile.

"We'll figure it out," Haasi said. "Let's just have a good time."

"Yup. So much for Declan. I say, keep him at arm's length. He's a pushy type." Blanche headed toward the door. "I'm going for a soak and a nap. You?"

Haasi was already tucked under the green silk quilt, her black braid flung over a white lace pillow. "Ummmmm. Yeah." She yawned. "We'll talk. Love you." And her lips parted in slumber.

Blanche tip-toed down the hall in the ghostly silence. The floor creaked at every step. The sun had gone in again and clouds of mist scurried past the windows. One leaded pane swung open to the whisper of leaves and the chitter of live things all around the castle.

In her Blue Room, the afternoon light cast a silver patina on the silk and wood. The bed covers were turned back to brilliant white linen. She went into the bathroom, drew a fierce jet of hot water into the tub, and slid into the bubbles. Her chin rested just above the foamy surface. She gazed at the brass fittings, the sparkling porcelain, the small rectangle of blue in the window. It was delicious, like a cotton candy dream. "Ah, the castle …" She closed her eyes.

Peace. They were situated on acres of land. Cattle were lowing not far off, a dog barked, and a rooster crowed. She'd have to investigate the livestock. *Well, why not?* Sagus had mentioned her "responsibility," which she hoped didn't extend to milking cows and hauling manure. She chuckled at the notion, an island girl, down on the farm. She hardly knew one end of a cow from another.

She'd only been handed a vague outline of what was involved in running an Irish estate of this sort, but she wanted to learn. Be useful. Keep her ears open. *Later.* She sank down into the warm, soapy water. Let the hour tick by until it was high time to get up and rinse off. She'd nearly dozed off. *That's what I don't need, to drown in my castle bathtub.*

She grabbed hold of the curved sides of the tub and stopped right there. A loud rumble of voices broke the silence, the muffled sound close by. But from where? Outside, or downstairs? She sank back and lay perfectly still. It was definitely a male voice, and it was getting louder. Soon it became a one-sided rant.

She got out of the tub, and covered in soap bubbles, wrapped herself in a towel, and stood on the cold tile. She was shivering, but the yelling—now it was yelling—overtook the discomfort of goosebumps. She dried off, scurried into her room, and grabbed her robe before heading out into the hall. It was empty. She crept along toward the sound of voices. There seemed to be a pause in the ranting, but not the stomping about. She stayed to the edges of the passage, careful to avoid the creaking floorboards. If there was one thing Blanche had learned, it was this: Stealth mattered. She could be quite good at listening, and creeping.

She crouched near the top of the staircase and looked through the railing. Now she heard Declan's voice: "I don't care if you were nanny to Prince Albert, this is the way we are doing it now. You're much too forgiving of staff—and I want to see receipts for the last delivery of salmon and beef. Seems way overpriced to me." Boots pounded the floor far below. A door, or drawer, slammed.

"Well, it's not as you say. Tony Costello delivers the same and the prices are just." Una's voice was strong, belying her years.

"Tony Costello? That wanker. He's all about pulling the wool over."

"I find this insulting. I know what I'm about, and I won't be takin' any more from the likes of you, Mr. O'Brian." Gone was the soft brogue, replaced with hard English.

"Excuse me? I am in charge here." He hammered down each word.

Una, again, ignoring his pronouncement: "Perhaps we need new guidance in management. Of the property. Your temper tantrums are wreaking havoc." Her message was firm and measured. "I'm after approaching the board to have you replaced."

"You'll do no such thing."

"I shall. You can't hide anymore…"

Declan stopped, abruptly. "What do you mean by *that*," he thundered.

Silence. "You know exactly what I mean." Her chilly, cutting response serrated the air. Blanche crouched still as a mouse in the upper hall. They moved from the drawing room to the kitchen, their voices rising and falling with each step and slam of a door. Trouble was brewing, or it was already at full strength. Una and Declan sounded like old hands at this sort of thing.

Then, nothing. The silence was ominous. Blanche didn't breathe for fear of missing a word, but the yelling seemed to stop.

Declan stomped away. His parting shot: "Bollocks!" She could only imagine the durability of that door through which he left; it either withstood the agent's mighty blast, or it was surely off its hinges.

Blanche sat on her heels and wrapped the robe tighter. The late afternoon filtered into the entry below. The eerie, bright gray light threw shadows onto the bouquet in crystal, across the lustrous silk rug, and over the faces of officers and ladies hanging on the walls. The color seemed to fade; the calm beauty contrasted with the deep rancor between the agent and the housekeeper.

Welcome to Ireland. I wonder what all that was about. It just can't be good.

Six

A Tour de Force

BLANCHE NEEDED TO THINK this one over. She'd have liked to confer with Haasi, who was out cold, for sure. Blanche pulled up the duvet and snuggled into the down-soft mattress. She stared at the draped canopy over her bed, into the folds of blue silk, her eyes wide. She was tired. She needed a nap, but she couldn't sleep. Declan was hiding something, and Una was deeply disturbed with the castle agent.

Blanche had planned a nice castle vacation—minus drama—and now this. She'd have to get to the bottom of it; it was an itch she had to scratch. She'd promised Haasi an uneventful, quiet time, all the while knowing how her curiosity somehow ended up pulling them into one *adventure* after another. *Adventure* was preferable; mess was more like it. Now she remembered Mabel McGlory's words again. She was beginning to get a sense of the "ting" she'd mentioned about this Declan. He was a self-important cad with a volatile side, and everything about him seemed bad business.

She couldn't do anything about it now. She needed to sleep on it, and, often, upon waking, she'd see the trouble for what it was. This was a tall order, and despite her nice bath and tea, she was frazzled by all the yelling. She made herself relax, turned over into dreamland, and dropped off that cliff. *To be continued…*

Haasi wrapped the long thick braid around her head like a crown and stuck pins in it. She was almost ready for dinner. Blanche sprawled on the chaise lounge. The day had gone, leaving a velvet dusk on the landscape and shadows in the room. The crystal lamps sparkled.

"Well, you look like a princess." Blanche sat up, ready to go, while Haasi checked herself in the vanity mirror. They both wore sheaths and sweaters to match. Blanche had tried to tame the curls, gave up, and now wore a beaded headband.

"You're looking pretty spiffy yourself, Miss Duchess." Haasi said into the mirror. She turned from the skirted vanity and buckled one sandal onto a golden-skin foot. "You hungry?"

"Not in particular." Blanche had slept on it. The argument she'd heard was still bothering her, the details troubling and confusing. She leaned forward and clasped her knees tightly. She tried to maintain her cool but was not succeeding. "We need to talk."

Haasi's eyes narrowed. "What's up?"

"This Declan. I heard him berating Una, and I don't like it. You are right about him. Something funny there."

Haasi stiffened and put her hands on her hips. "What's happened now?"

"An argument. I heard it from downstairs this afternoon while you were sleeping. I'm telling you, Haas. It was *chilling*." She recalled the goosebumps and bubbles as well as the yelling.

"Hmmm. I know you feel some sense of involvement, Blanche. But I'm sure Una can take care of herself. Think she's been doing it, pushing eighty years now. You know what I mean?"

"Yes, I know. But I just don't like the things he said, accusing her of mismanagement and excessive spending. Throwing around veiled threats. He was very rude."

"I hear you." Haasi bent to fasten the other sandal. "I just don't want to see you, you know, getting into a fix around here. Let's just *enjoy*."

Blanche stood up. "I know. I promised."

Haasi sighed. "Sometimes you can't help it, B. Well, most of the time you *don't* help it. I understand. But we're only here a short time, and I don't think we can change the course of Irish history by getting mixed up in Una and Declan's arguments."

"True." Blanche fell silent, thinking it best to hold back and get merrily on with the stay. But she couldn't do it. "Listen. Get this. Una had a zinger of her own. She accused him of hiding something, and that set him off even more. I'm telling you, that guy is a piece of work."

"Oh, brother."

"Now I'm wondering. *Hiding what? A secret?* Mabel McGlory hinted around. About things and such. He's got quite a reputation."

"Blanche. Relax. Let's keep the guy at arm's length. Two arms, at least."

The dining room had seating for thirty at the long, carved Jacobean table and padded leather armchairs. The walls were deep red silk and hung with gold-framed portraits and landscapes of horses and dogs and hunters in little round hats and tight red coats. Sconces threw buttery light around the room. White roses quivered on a pedestal next to an open window.

Una shuffled toward the sideboard with a tureen. It smelled divine. "A bit of creamy potato-leek soup. 'Tis from the garden," she said. She set it down next to an assortment of china and silver and bustled off to the kitchen. Mae, the little kitchen maid, appeared with a large platter: salmon and dill sprigs. Small boats of sauce sat on the table set with linen and heavy cutlery. Mae delivered the platter, carefully, and clasped her hands. "This fish is fresh out of the Shannon, he is, and I hope ye enjoy the sauteed greens and berries. They were just wee sprouts in the greenhouse not so long ago. And the cream and butter are from the lovely cows, and, of course, our own brown bread. From me, and Nancy, our cook…" She blushed from the outpouring of delicious facts. She seemed so eager and proud of helping to produce this grand dinner.

Declan swept into the dining room. He'd changed into a dinner jacket with a red satin handkerchief in the pocket and a sparkling white shirt. He planted himself in front of Mae, cutting her off in mid-sentence, and put his hands behind his back. "Good evening, Miss Blanche, Miss Haasi. Trust you had a good rest?"

He didn't wait for an answer, preening and fussing with his collar. He smoothed back the damp-looking shiny black hair. "Shall we?"

Shall we what? He'd caught Blanche off guard. *Bop you on the head and knock some manners into you?*

Mae stood there, clearly flustered.

"Thank you so much, Mae," said Haasi, ignoring Declan. "It looks *delicious.*"

"Well, then, let us know if you need anything." Mae blushed furiously, turned on a heel, and disappeared back into the kitchen.

They advanced on the sideboard after exchanging subdued greetings and pleasantries. Between bites, Declan went on, and on, about the cultivars of grapes from Normandy (at the castle winery) and the breeding of cows. Blanche listened politely. Haasi hardly said a word, which wasn't that unusual when Haasi sat down to dinner. It was food heaven. The mayo was homemade, the fish pink and flaky, and the rest of it so fresh Blanche would be spoiled for life.

While Declan entertained, mostly himself, Blanche's eyes wandered to the colonel and the nephew, and to the other McLoughlins in their framed portraits, each with serious expressions wearing uniforms and sashes and medals. She saw no resemblance to her fluffy-haired, smiling grandmother, not in the slightly aquiline noses or high cheekbones and prominent foreheads. She wished they looked a bit more cheerful. She'd heard they were warm, generous, and kind to their neighbors. At least, this knowledge was something she would cherish. She peered at the younger William, so formal and handsome. The hair flat and shiny, the black coat resplendent with red braid, and an expression not quite as playful as in the painting on the stairs. She liked *that* one better.

"Yes, the colonel was a well-loved chap, so they tell me," said Declan, looking up at the officer in an enormous portrait, which hung on gold cords from the molding. Blanche chafed at Declan calling the colonel a "chap," like he was a ruffian on the loose. But she kept quiet. She'd have a word with Mr. O'Brian in the near future; it was coming. She'd find the appropriate time. She had a feeling there'd be nothing appropriate—and friendly—about it. She'd have to get her mind right, and then choose her words and the moment, carefully. *That'll be a first.*

"And William, the nephew?" Blanche asked.

"Ah, yes. William. Last in the line, so to speak. Except for you, Miss Murninghan." He turned his blue eyes on, full blast.

Once again, changing the subject.

"But you knew William, Declan. What can you tell me about him?"

"Ah, he was a sport." Declan chuckled and swirled the last of his wine. He tossed it back, forgetting all the affected lip-pursing and sipping he'd been doing during dinner.

"A sport?"

"Yes, the ball. Polo, the horses." He grinned. "The ladies."

"Hmmm. That doesn't tell me a great deal about my long-lost cousin."

"Did you say you were meeting this Maggie McLoughlin tomorrow?"

"Yes," said Blanche. "Another long-lost relative."

"Well then, you're sure to get your fill of *deceased* McLoughlins by then." His voice was low, and his tone changed. There was something calculating about his remark. Something cold and hard.

Haasi and Blanche exchanged glances. "You were going to show us more of the castle, Mr. O'Brian?" Haasi stood and delicately placed her napkin on the seat.

"As promised. And, *please*. Declan." The agent bounced up, chipper and ready. "I will point the way. The kitchen should be put away, except for some deliveries. I asked Una to have a fire in the grate should you like to have a drink later."

They followed Declan down a hallway into a marvelous greenhouse off the kitchen. Everything from basil to orchids grew in profusion. Rows of ferny carrots and leafy sprigs of new berry plants. "Nancy and Mae keep a fine house here, starting off the seeds for replanting in all the beds," he said. Blanche had to hand it to him; he seemed heartfelt—showing off *his* gardens.

A green-felt billiards table glowed under a Tiffany lamp in the center of a game room. There were chess and checker boards set up in bay windows, and a scattering of leather armchairs in front of a stone fireplace. The hearth opening was as tall as Declan. In an adjoining sitting room, over-sized yellow-and-cream chintz sofas sat in front of a white marble fireplace. Books lined one wall to the high ceiling with a rolling ladder. Blanche stared at the brown and red bindings with gold lettering; she'd have to spend some time here, perusing Irish history next to the cozy fire. Another smaller drawing room with chinoiserie bowls of flowers on pedestals on either side of a French door led to a garden path. The chairs were covered in floral and stripes, ottomans to match, amid blue glass tables and various rugs with a *fleur-de-lis* pattern.

"Who decorates?" Blanche was in awe of the richly appointed rooms with lovely color and generous seating, certainly not feminine but discreetly decorated for any taste. Classic comfort was a theme; the faded chintz was soft from sun and wear, and slightly shabby, and the rugs wore the patina of age.

"The colonel, and his nephew, had fine taste, as did the colonel's wife. He was married briefly to Caroline Marintette, a French noblewoman. They dedicated themselves to restoring many furnishings that had gotten into British hands. They rebuilt the gardens and farm." He ticked off the facts like a tour guide.

"Well, they did it nicely," said Haasi.

"And I keep things in order." He rocked back on his leather (Italian?) loafers.

Of course you do.

"I'm sure Una is a great help around here." Blanche said, loudly. Haasi gave her a gentle nudge. But Blanche couldn't let it go. *I might irritate him, but so what?* The argument she'd overheard nagged her like a toothache. And she was bursting to know more about the McLoughlins. That information never seemed to be forthcoming. All the better to see Maggie soon.

She was not surprised that Declan didn't answer. He stomped ahead, back down the hall toward the kitchen, and they followed.

The white-tiled kitchen sparkled with cleanliness and order. The lights glazed the marble counters and polished floor, and the wind gusted from an open door, sending a stack of linen towels into the air like ghosts. A delivery man unloaded crates from the back of a truck.

"Ah, Tony is here. That'll be fine. Let's have a look about." Declan peered toward the back door and turned around. He showed off a pantry lined with glass jars of preserves, copper pots and ceramic bowls, mixers, blenders, racks of plates of all sizes. He proudly pointed out the reserves of wine in a separate cooler built into the wall. "This," he announced with a flourish, "is a retro-fitted ice box."

Declan opened a drawer full of utensils. Blanche glanced at it. All sharp and gleaming, neatly arranged. "Una and the staff certainly *do* run a tight ship, I see," she said.

He yanked at a shallow drawer to reveal rows of black-handled knives, each secured in red velvet grooves, and then he stood back, arms crossed. "These are the finest German blades. Just pick one up and feel the heft of it. Fine ebony handles, the sharpest honed steel." He leaned over the drawer, looked up at Blanche, and waited. She wasn't sure what she was supposed to do. Pick one up and start chopping peppers and onions?

"Go ahead. Select one, get the feel of a fine piece of wood and metal."

Blanche drew a knife from the drawer and held it. The knife was a perfect balance on the tips of her fingers, the handle and blade light but formidably strong and beautifully crafted. Haasi eyed it. Blanche shivered, and not because she thought of vegetables. She was reminded of Haasi's skills. If anyone knew how to use a knife—throw it directly, and accurately, at a target—it was Haasi. She'd given Blanche lessons, and they had come in handy in the past. Now Blanche lifted the knife, up and down, and smiled again. She placed it back in the drawer.

Declan hesitated before he shut the drawer. He turned then as Tony dropped a crate of vegetables on a counter near the back door. "Tony. Still at it, mate?"

Tony grunted. He didn't smile. "Another delivery. I'll finish this one. Others on the way. From the vintner and baker, I believe."

"At this hour?" Blanche was surprised at the late industry in the kitchen.

"On the farm, Miss. We work nearly 'round the clock," said Tony, not unkindly. "Jim will bring the bread around by and by."

"Say, Tony," said Declan. "This is Blanche Murninghan and Haasi Hakla. From Florida. You may see them around here later."

"Good evenin' to ye," said Tony, pulling at his tweed cap, his expression grim. He gave Declan a glance and headed back to the truck. The lack of warmth for Declan O'Brian was chilling, and Tony's abrupt departure left no time for discussion. The back door remained open. The cool air gushed around Blanche's ankles. She caught Haasi's eye.

44

"That concludes our little tour." Declan's cheer seemed forced, but clearly the agent had an agenda.

"Lovely," said Blanche. "Thank you."

Declan rubbed his hands together. "Ladies, why don't we adjourn to the drawing room for a brandy? Staff keeps the fire going there. Should be quite cozy." He moved a step closer to Blanche. Haasi took a frigid stance.

"Thank you, but I think we'll just go up." Blanche moved out of his space but not out of his aura of charm. Declan seemed clueless as he pressed on—a hand on Blanche's elbow. Blanche smiled and withdrew. "Been a long day," she said, "and we want to see Maggie tomorrow, first thing. It's all arranged."

"Of course. Sorry to miss that drink and a bit more chat about the castle." He tipped his head. "But are you sure? We have a fine stock of brandy … Would help you sleep." He winked and leaned casually against the counter, arms crossed. His gaze rested steadily on Blanche. She stared back at his smarmy expression.

Haasi moved in. "Yeah, Blanche, we need to get an early start. So much to see and do."

"Declan." Blanche concentrated on her painted toenails. She composed herself and looked up. "I heard you arguing with Una earlier today. It was very unpleasant. Is there some problem between you two?"

"Why ever would you think that? We do have our disagreements, but it's nothing serious. Really." His smirk took on a bit of an edge. He dropped his arms and bounced forward.

Blanche stood her ground. "Una seems like a lovely person, and she's put in so many years here. I'm told she's an invaluable staff member, more of a family member than staff, if my information is correct."

Haasi stared at the ceiling. She put her hand on Blanche's arm, surreptitiously, and murmured, "Duchess."

"You may think she's a lovely person, but even the loveliest have their place," said Declan, stiffly.

Why do I feel like he's directing that remark at me?

"Well, I suppose, but …"

He blathered on. "Una is not the most adept at managing the kitchen and other affairs. She's beginning to slip. You've noticed, she is, ahem, quite elderly." He did have a temper. With each word, his voice got louder, his face redder. He planted his feet wider apart.

"Nonetheless, she deserves respect. And, for the record, I don't see much *slippage*, as you call it. She runs this house, and the staff, and it seems to be in perfect order. Not only from the looks of it but from what I hear from the law firm …"

"With all *due respect*. You are new here, and you don't know what is going on."

"In any event, Mr. O'Brian, Una should be treated with a certain amount of deference, given her dedication to this beautiful…home? And her devotion to the McLoughlins?"

"Respect? Devotion?" He scoffed, his lip curling in derision. "Excuse me, Miss Blanche. Once again, I don't think you understand. You appear from across the ocean, and just like that…"

"Well, I don't mean to upset you."

"You're not upsetting me, you're being…" Here he stumbled, his ire getting in the way of his thoughts. He fished for the right word. "Oblivious? Obtrusive?" He pounded the counter and the lid to the sugar bowl flipped off.

Haasi stifled a nervous chuckle. "*Duchess.*" She shook her head, teasing. "Ob…ob…"

Blanche stared at her cousin. She turned to Declan. "It's been a long day. We probably should just go up and relax. We can talk tomorrow."

Footsteps in the back entry off the kitchen drew Blanche's attention. The door had been open all the time. Tony Costello stood framed in the dim light, holding a leafy pile of greens in a wooden crate. Clearly, he'd heard the testy exchange. He paused. His face was set in stony silence, his lips in a tight line. He walked into the kitchen and clapped the box next to a sink. He nodded at Blanche and glanced at Declan. "That's it then." He turned and stomped off, slamming the door.

Seven

Crunch

BLANCHE AND HAASI bid Declan a hasty "good night" and left him and his bad mood in the kitchen. He was clearly angry after his exchange with Blanche—and Haasi's mild but firm dismissal. Blanche couldn't help thinking of a petulant child as she bid him *adios* for the *noche*.

"That went well," said Haasi as they climbed the flying staircase.

"Ugh. Couldn't wait to get away from him."

"Me, too."

"What's up with chuckling at that dolt?"

"I know. Sorry. Couldn't help myself. You were being nice and sincere, and he's so…ob…ob…obnoxious!" Haasi started in again. "I can't wait for breakfast to hear what crap he comes up with next."

"I hope he doesn't eat breakfast *here*. And if he does, he can eat a big crow pie for all I care!"

"Oh. Duchess."

"I want to have a chat with Una about this guy. Maybe Maggie knows what's up with him. It's no wonder Mabel in the pub called him a cad." Blanche followed Haasi into her room, talking the whole time.

"Good one. Talk to Una. If it'll make you feel any better. And Maggie." Haasi sat at the dressing table and started pulling pins out of her braid. "But, really, Blanche. Let's just see if we can avoid him. We've got other stuff to do, like, hike around the grounds and go out to the sea and hit up all the restaurants and pubs in town. That brown bread is like biting into heaven. And what about that salmon? Where did he swim in from?" She yawned and unbuckled her sandals. Her bed was turned back, a small lamp burned, and a single rose had been set on the nightstand. She grinned. "I could get used to this place."

"Una does think of all the little things … and the big ones. And to think Declan says Una is slipping."

"The only thing slipping is my approval of Declan."

Blanche gave her a hug. "See you in the mornin'. May the road rise to meet ya and the wind be at yer back." She headed for her room.

"So Irish of you," said Haasi, who snuggled into the lovely sheets. Her two dark eyes were all that was visible above the silk cover. "See you, Dutch."

Blanche went off to her royal blue suite and tucked herself in. She had a hard time falling asleep.

She tossed and turned and couldn't figure out why. She was dead tired. She began counting seagulls and finally drifted off, fitfully, but she didn't last the night. She awoke, startled, without a clue as to her whereabouts.

Ireland!

It came to her. Yes, here she was, and something was not right. She crossed it off to travel fatigue. It was the wee hours; the room was pitch black, and it was time to go back to sleep. But the unsettled feeling persisted. Now she was fully awake, and the cause of the wakefulness was not the shock at being across the ocean or jet lag. It was the sound of crunching outside her window. It reverberated in the night, steady and regular over the gravel, and because of the quiet all around, each crunch hit a nerve. She lay rigid under the covers.

The dragging finally petered off around to the back of the castle. A faint expletive. Boots or wheels? A bike wending slowly…? *Now, what's that all about at this hour?* It was certainly hard to tell. The night was empty, and the sound was over before she knew it. She waited. The quiet was more unsettling than the crunching and the dragging. She should go have a look. No, she was not about to go outside and stumble around the grounds in the dark. A cow mooed softly far off near the barns, a dog barked, and then it was still.

She stared into the night at nothing, and finally threw back the covers. She went to the window. The sliver of a moon cast an eerie pattern on the lawn, but she could see little in the shadows. She stood there, arms taut on the sill between the heavy damask curtains. The air was humid and soft. A light mist hovered among the arborvitae and low evergreens. Nothing. Not a soul. She finally gave up as the silence hung on. She got back into bed.

Then she remembered. Tony Costello had said the deliveries were coming. They work "round-the-clock" on the farm, he'd said. Didn't he? The thought comforted her, and she relaxed. Breathed in some of that Irish air and curled up in the feathers and silk. She soon fell into a deep sleep.

She was solidly adrift in dreamland when the sun sent a shaft of light between the draperies. The warmth on her face, the silky sheet under her chin, the plump feathers of the pillow. It was heavenly, and she burrowed deep into the covers, floating off on a cottony cloud of lovely thoughts …

A scream pierced the early morning quiet. It was a woman, definitely. The scream hit a high note. Then it turned to wailing.

Blanche shot up in bed. She shivered at the blast of cool air from the open window just as voices pitched higher still. Was the commotion coming from outside, or downstairs? It seemed to come from different directions. She threw off the covers, dropped to the floor, and ran into the hall. She froze, barefoot, wearing only shorts, strangling the dolphin on the front of her favorite T-shirt.

Good morning, Ireland!

Mae ran across the entry and back into the kitchen. Her heavy shoes sounded like rifle shot. She yelled, "Nancy! OH MY GOD IN HEAVEN!"

Blanche fled toward the stairs, rubbing her eyes.

Haasi was right behind her, wrapping her robe tightly, and mumbling. "Now what."

They made their way to the source of all the yelling and huddled in the doorway of the kitchen. At first, all seemed to be in order. The clean white tile and bright lights, the wooden cutting boards and windows open to the early gray morning. The sun had risen and just as fast gone in. Not a sound came from without or within.

Blanche's vision focused on Mae and Nancy. They framed, like bookends, a strange scene: Declan, draped over the edge of the sink, his arms hanging loosely on either side of him.

What is he doing? Washing his hair?

Blanche stepped closer. The tile underfoot—and now the sight of him—sent cold waves through her. Declan was not moving. Blood pooled around the soles of his shoes. A knife stuck out of his torso. Blanche crouched down and stared into the face of the agent. One unseeing eye was open. "Is he ..."

"I'd say so," said Haasi, her voice a low whisper of dread.

A sweat broke out down Blanche's back. *Why?* But she could think of several reasons why Declan had ended up this way, and she'd only been in Ireland a day.

Mae had stopped yelling and was now moving in small circles, shaking her hands and praying to "the Virgen Mary."

Haasi stood at Blanche's ear. "A lot of good that'll do."

Nancy, the cook, had not moved at all. She seemed frozen in place. Disbelieving? They all were disbelieving. *How could this happen in their lovely castle kitchen?* Nancy pressed her hands against her red cheeks, her eyes large and terrified. She'd obviously been about to prepare breakfast, but she'd not gotten far. Her hairnet was askew, her apron bunched on the floor. "I'm after calling the gardai, they should be here straight away."

"Yes, seems to be no need for a doctor," said Blanche, frowning. She clamped her lips in a tight line.

In record time, a blue-uniformed pair arrived at the back door. Mae ushered them in with a frantic wave. A tall, thin young garda seemed to be in charge, and he knew the territory. "Aye, mornin' to you, Miss Nancy. It's not such a fine one now, is it." His eye went to the sink, and he murmured, distractedly. He stood straight at attention, looking around the kitchen. Several more gardai clustered at the back door with police tape. "Please step back to the other room, ladies, and no one is to leave the premises. I'll be takin' names. Ian Handley here, and the investigators will be on the way." He nodded at Mae and Nancy, and took in Blanche and Haasi with surprise, but introductions didn't seem necessary. The staff knew Garda Ian Handley.

"Ye mustn't touch a thing now." He extended his arms and motioned them through the door to the interior of the castle. "Step out if ye will, and we'll be with ye presently. I repeat, no one of ye should leave the grounds." He was grim as his gaze shifted to Declan draped over the sink.

Another garda held a clipboard, and without looking up, said, "There'll be questions for ye. Ladies, step out like Garda Handley has instructed. If ye please."

Blanche wasn't pleased in the least. She was shocked. She grabbed Haasi's arm, and they headed toward the door with the staff as the garda had instructed. Everyone was present and accounted for, except for Una.

"Now who would want to kill Declan?" Blanche whispered to Haasi all the while thinking of the possibilities.

"Who wouldn't?"

"Haasi! That's pretty cold."

"Think about it, Blanche. The guy was pissing everyone off, and he acted like the king of the walk. And he wasn't." Her whisper had the ring of truth.

Una appeared at the doorway, fully dressed in the gray cardigan with pearl buttons, and an especially grim look on her face. She clasped her hands. "Now, what do we have here." She eyed the agent in his deathly position and looked away, quickly. "Jesus Mary and Joseph." She crossed herself and breathed. "What the devil."

"Precisely," said Haasi.

The garda, Ian Handley, turned then. "Now, ladies…Aw, Miss Una. It's a bleary mornin' for sure. We're just in the preliminaries, but the detective will be here straightaway to take statements from ye all. And no one is to leave. We have the grounds surrounded. The murder squad will eventually make a sweep of the property. *I've asked that ye all step into the other room.*"

He'd seemed like the calm patient type, but he wasn't now. He was dealing with a disparate bunch who were shocked in place and barely awake. Una's mouth formed an O, but nothing came out. She joined the clucking Mae and Nancy and the astonished Blanche and Haasi. "There, there." Una snapped to. "The authorities will have it all in hand soon enough."

Blanche noted Una didn't seem particularly upset. She was calm and contained. Her complexion was nearly as gray as her sweater. *Was she in shock, or, God forbid, glad of Declan's demise?*

"I'm so sorry, Una," said Blanche. She didn't know what else to say as they shuffled toward the drawing room.

"Sorries are not to be bandied about now. Some things we bring down upon ourselves, doncha' know." Her expression was flat, the cloudy blue eyes revealing nothing.

Blanche and Haasi exchanged looks. "Save your sorries, Blanche. We might need them later," said Haasi.

Blanche plopped down on a sofa and stared into the dying embers of a peat fire. The room was cold as death, the air outside suitably gray. She wanted to be as far away from Declan as she could get. And at once she was overwhelmed with an intense curiosity to see what was going on in the kitchen. Nancy and Mae and Una huddled together, sniffling and lamenting. Haasi had excused herself.

Blanche crept up to the kitchen doorway. A gowned and uniformed crew had already entered from the back of the castle and begun to examine and photograph and finally unbend the remains of Declan O'Brian, knife still stuck in his side. Blanche was aghast as the once flirtatious, pompous, lively agent was unfolded from the rim of the sink. Cold and dead.

She felt a chill. The damp early morning was getting to her as the special team from the district traipsed back and forth with grim purpose. She was half-dressed and fascinated and horrified at the scene. Haasi appeared next to Blanche and held onto her arm. *"What are you doing, Blanche?"* she croaked.

"What does it look like I'm doing? Creeping around, of course."

"Well, come on back. They don't want us around here. I don't want to be around here."

Blanche let out a big sigh. "Oh, all right."

Declan was trundled off and the rest of the team continued the painstaking, detailed—and boring—work. Blanche and Haasi retreated to the drawing room with the rest.

Mae scurried over with wool shawls. She shyly offered them to Blanche and Haasi. The little maid stood back, nervously clasping her fingers, glancing at the doorway.

"Thank you," said Blanche. "Why don't you sit, Mae?"

The girl didn't move. "Oh, it's a terrible thing, but I can't help but think Mr. Declan brought it upon himself." Then, aghast at her own remark, she slapped a hand over her mouth and crossed herself. "Oh, I'm sorry, Miss."

"No need to apologize, Mae. Don't worry. Seems like the police have things under control," said Blanche. "We'll all sort it out soon enough." She didn't believe any such thing.

"*We?*" Haasi sat up straight and gave Blanche a level glance.

"You know, Haas. We're all in this together. For truth and justice…"

"OK, Super Woman. *We* don't want anything to do with this."

Blanche sat up straight and reserved comment. She wrapped the shawl around her shoulders. Haasi's stony expression said no more, her face sticking out of the tweed wool shawl. They sat silently and watched and waited.

A garda came to the door of the drawing room and beckoned to Mae who'd set off the alarm. She was shaking and nodding. She could hardly utter a word to respond, but he persisted, taking notes as Mae told him how she'd found Declan.

"That poor thing. What a mess." Blanche nudged Haasi.

"Haas, I heard something. In the night. I should go over there and tell him." She gestured toward the garda with her chin.

Haasi whispered. "What? You heard what? The *murder*?"

"No, don't think so. It was a crunching sound outside my window. In the wee hours. And *dragging*. Could have been a dog or another animal. Or wheels? I don't know."

"A human animal? Dragging? What?" Haasi sighed. "Oh, Blanche. No."

"Yes, I've got to talk to them. Now. Before they walk all over that driveway."

She hopped up and approached the garda, just as he flipped a notebook closed. Mae sat. "Sir, I need to talk with you," said Blanche.

He tipped his head, kindly interest animating his expression. A shock of unruly red hair matched the eyebrows that worked up and down over green eyes. He wore a rumpled white shirt and a raincoat and carried a small notebook. "Detective Leary, madam. From district." A man of few words.

She took a deep breath. "I heard something in the middle of the night, or the early morning. Can't say when, exactly. It was so dark. But I need to tell you before the place is trampled about out there. It was the sound, I believe, of someone, or maybe an animal, on the gravel drive under my window. A crunching, and dragging." She peeked around his wide shoulders toward the kitchen, but it was no use. She saw nothing. She heard stomping back and forth and gruff voices talking at once. Orders and organization. The kitchen had gone from a quiet, comforting station of providing deliciousness to a hive of investigation in the space of an hour or so. Blanche was amazed at how fast "the district" had sent a team and taken over the castle. *The Irish are warriors, all right.*

"You did, did you?" He turned and called to another policeman, a taller older fellow with thick, white hair. He wore a tweedy jacket with leather buttons. He had a solid, respectable air of authority about him.

"Morning, Miss." He carried a clipboard. "Detective Inspector Nobegly. You are staying at the castle?"

"Well, yes, in fact, I'm an owner of said castle."

His expression lifted in surprise. "Indeed. You are Miss McLoughlin then?"

"Yes, well, Blanche Murninghan. The colonel and his nephew were distant relatives. I've just been informed of my very minor place in ownership."

Haasi stood at Blanche's elbow. "Good morning. I'm Haasi Hakla, Blanche's cousin," she said, cheerily. "*Not* an owner."

"*Fáilte!*" Nobegly nodded and his expression changed from surprise to confusion. "I am sorry for this welcome to Ireland. Not a fine sight for ladies such as yerselves."

"First time to Ireland. First time to a castle … not my first murder, however," Blanche offered. "What I mean is, we have had experience in running into unfortunate occurrences in the past." The heat crept up

Blanche's neck. "But the police have always been gracious and thorough and able in solving the cases. Bringing the threads together, so to speak. Putting the bad guys away, you know."

"Jeez, Blanche." Haasi breathed. "Duchess."

"And these murders? In the United States?"

"Yes!" Haasi chimed in quickly. Blanche relaxed. She decided not to mention their adventures on Santa Maria Island and in Mexico City—and her side trip to Vietnam!

"I trust the authorities were involved?"

"Oh, very involved." Blanche and Haasi agreed in unison.

"Now, then." Inspector Nobegly cleared his throat. "You have something to report? As regards the situation at hand? I heard you say there were strange noises in the night?"

"I heard something," said Blanche, "possibly a person moving around, and wheels. Maybe a light vehicle, like a bike. Dragging and such. Might be tracks out there now, and it would be a good idea to check around. Before they get wiped away."

"Time? Approximate?" He was writing down Blanche's words.

"Well, I don't know. Stupid of me. I didn't look at the clock, but it had to be three, maybe four. We went to bed late, and I had difficulty falling asleep."

"Seems you should have been tired after your trip. Arrived, just?" He eyed her sideways, looking right through her. "Staying up? Partying, perhaps, with the ... deceased?"

"Excuse me." Haasi stepped forward, all five feet of her. The inspector stepped back. "That fellow was a party of one. He got a real kick out of himself, and certainly not with our help."

"Hmmm." He busily scribbled on the clipboard. He finished the notes and tapped the sheaf of pages with the pen.

Leary hadn't said a word, and now he spoke up. "We did find some narrow tracks in the gravel," he added.

"That would be irregular," said Una who had been quietly listening. Blanche eyed her. "The drive is raked, routinely. Should not be mussed, especially under your window, Miss Blanche. There's little traffic on that side of the castle."

The inspector pulled at his sideburns and pursed his lips. "Except for last night, perhaps." He looked at Una and turned to Blanche. "Will you think that one through, Miss? Exactly what you heard in the wee hours? The time, especially? Try hard to remember."

"I can't be sure. But the more I think about it, I'll bet it was a bike. What else could it be? A wheelbarrow? A scooter? A cart of some sort? It wasn't a car or a lawn mower or a tractor. No motor sounds." Her mind went round and round with all kinds of wheeled things. "Just churning and grinding and dragging. And it had to be between…three and five o'clock? It was very dark, and I was awakened from a deep sleep."

"That's somewhat helpful." The inspector made a little bow and tucked the clipboard under his arm, his movements crisp and final. Blanche almost expected him to salute. "We did take photos, and we'll be checking into it further. Sure, and there'll be more questions." He walked away with a curt nod.

"We'll be here." Haasi forced a grin, waving her fingers genially.

"Thank ye then," said Leary. "Have a good day, such as it is."

Blanche squinched her eyes, her arms taut at her sides.

"Bang, what are you doing," said Haasi under her breath.

"I'm thinking. Hard."

"About?" Haasi watched the door, expecting more fresh hell to walk through it. The voices were still rising and falling off in the kitchen.

"This gravel. Seems so fine, not like your run-of-the-mill pebble. I don't think it's common. Might be imported or treated or something."

"Blanche, who cares about *gravel*." Haasi attempted to draw her to the fireplace to get warm and as far removed from the investigation as possible. She resisted.

"It makes me think. Wouldn't those teensy tiny stones get stuck in tire treads?"

"Could. So?"

"So, it's worth a look around."

Haasi sighed and stomped over to the sofa. "Come on, Duchess. Sit, and stop thinking."

Eight
Ride a Fine Horse

LATER THAT MORNING, after a hastily assembled breakfast, baths, and some deep breathing exercises, Blanche and Haasi borrowed bikes at the castle and rambled down the drive and through Ballycill to Maggie McLoughlin's cottage. A wild growth of red and purple fuchsia rose to the eaves under a thatched roof. The blooms shook mightily when the door swung open. Blanche and Haasi set their wheels against the low rocky border at the edge of the property as Maggie hurried down the path, waving her arms in welcome. A halo of white hair fluffed out around her happy face.

"Now, here ye are! Finally!" Maggie called out. She wore an outlandish gown of purple velvet, the long sleeves flapping like wings.

Haasi hung back, grinning, while Blanche clasped hands with Maggie.

"Ye must be Blanche," said Maggie. "If ye don't have the map of Ireland written all over yer lovely face!" She held Blanche by the shoulders and made little clucking sounds. Blanche had never seen such twinkly eyes—except maybe in the face of her beloved grandmother. She felt such ease in that grip, and thoughts of the ill-fated morning flew out of her mind. At least temporarily.

Maggie hugged Blanche, her cheeks a peachy velvet, and then she turned to Haasi. "And this must be the darlin' sister-cousin, Haasi!"

"'Twould be me. It's so nice to meet you, Maggie."

She wrapped her purple wings around Haasi and Blanche and led them over the stone path toward the cottage. A tiny dog yipped about

Maggie's heels. She untangled the wings, scooped up the dog, and kissed him on the head. "Robert, behave for our guests now." Robert immediately calmed down and burrowed under his mistress's arm.

"Robert?"

"Why, yes. Doesn't he look like a Robert?"

Blanche wasn't sure. The dog's huge brown eyes were sad but loving. "Hi, Robert."

"Yip!"

Robert and his coterie of women paused on the wide stone stoop at Maggie's open front door, painted bright red with a brass trim. "These flowers are delightful, Maggie," Blanche said, commenting on the profusion of blooms.

"Aye, there's been a lash about and now the dingleberries are burstin'."

"Lash?" Blanche asked. "*Dingleberries?*"

"Ah, yes, rain on the fuchsia. In Flar-da I know ye have a bit of it there."

"Sure do." The two-toned bell-like flowers crowded Maggie's door. They also heaped in enormous hedges over the narrow roads.

"The blooms love the soft mist, day on day. Just drink it up, they do."

The cottage was warm and inviting; the peat fire burned steadily in the grate and weak sunlight beamed in through the deep-set windows. Steam rose from a china teapot on a shiny tray piled with cakes and biscuits. A bottle of brown liquid sparkled in a crystal decanter. The room smelled of cinnamon and fire.

"*Fáilte!* God and Mary to ye!" Maggie moved around the room, patting pillows and scooting chairs closer to the fireplace. "Ye will be comfy here. Now sit and tell me all about yerselves." Maggie descended on the tea things with a great deal of clatter and hospitality.

"This is de-lightful! You shouldn't have gone to all this trouble." Blanche sat on the edge of one of the chintz-covered chairs while Maggie poured the tea.

"Indeed," said Haasi, her eyes bright and fixed on the array of sweets. "But, I confess. I love this Irish tea custom—with cake!"

"It's such a treat to have ye here! *Family* from so far away!"

The words thrilled Blanche. *Family*. She squinted at Maggie and definitely saw shades of her dear dead grandmother Maeve in this new-found relative. Now she longed to know if there were any further connection. "Maggie, did you ever hear from Maeve? Did she ever call or write?"

"Oh, no, sadly, it never did happen though I longed for it. I saw a picture, lovely she was. Why, I didn't even know she existed all these years." The blue eyes shone. "Sam and Malcolm were in touch not long ago but sometime after dear Maeve passed on. They told me about ye and the family and the serendipitous reunion of ye two darlin' sister-cousins."

Serendipitous. That it was. It struck Blanche once again how lucky she was to have found Haasi—or was it that Haasi found Blanche? That was probably more the case. It didn't matter to Blanche because she knew they were meant to be together. Haasi had landed in Blanche's life during a low point. Blanche had always thought there had been some spirits at work to bring the two of them together—the long-dead Indian chief who'd had an affair with Maeve's mother, and Maeve, the grandmother, whose presence Blanche always felt. She wouldn't be on this adventure to Ireland without Maeve and the rest of them reaching from the grave.

"Now! Let's celebrate our reunion! *Uisce Beatha!*" Maggie lifted the crystal decanter. *Water of life. Whiskey.* Maggie poured them each a splash into stemware, and held up her glass. "*Sláinte!*"

"This family circle reaches far, now doesn't it." Maggie pinned her gaze on Haasi.

"Yes, it does," said Haasi. She sipped and smiled at Blanche. "If it hadn't been for our dear great-grandmother straying, we wouldn't be here."

"We wouldn't be here. Together." Blanche definitely would not be here without Haasi, given a mishap or two they had both fortunately survived.

"To *family.*" Maggie lifted her glass.

The whiskey raced to the tips of Blanche's toes and fingers. The troubling thoughts of Declan stayed away, out of mind. He would circle back soon enough, but for now, he was gone.

"I have so many questions—about you and the colonel and his nephew," said Blanche.

"And that we will attend to. Such grand ones, they were..." Her words drifted off, and she didn't stop smiling. It erased the lines of years. "Now, then, let me look at ye. Just the sight of ye brings a smile to me."

"We could certainly do with some cheering up." Haasi smiled, too. "What a morning!"

"And so, I did hear." Suddenly, she frowned, and the eyes lost their sparkle. She set the glass down with a decided clink. "Hardly a warm welcome for ye. Tell me, who would do such a thing? Declan was not the most popular person, yet this was a cold deed." She pulled the purple wings tightly around her ample middle.

"Wow! How did you hear about Declan's ... demise? So fast," said Blanche.

"Word flies faster than a virus hereabouts. Everybody has heard of it. From the garda station to the grocer to the butcher and baker. It's a small place, ye know."

"I was hoping you might have a clue, Maggie. *Why?*" Blanche held back discussion on the deficient character traits of the late agent. She was anxious to hear Maggie's version of Declan O'Brian's life and times.

"He was a *desperate* fellow," said Maggie. "God rest him, in any case." She took a sip thoughtfully.

"Desperate? How do you mean?"

Maggie chuckled. "A manner of speaking. A cold, gray wind off the sea, he was. Had an expression like a cow shite on a frosty morn. So disgusted was he with anyone who crossed him. Few people did, mind ye."

"Hmmmm." Blanche thought of the argument he'd had with Una. She hadn't seemed the least bit hesitant to cross him. "We had dinner together the night before the, er, accident. It was a pleasant enough time, but he seemed to be awfully full of himself, I'm sorry to say."

"That would be Declan. He had a way about him. And there was some talk he had his way with more than one of the maids in town—and at the castle. That would not be the extent of his nefarious deeds, I'm afraid."

"The extent?"

"Oh, talk, ye know. About the management at the castle. He did seem to make it work for himself, the hours he kept. The clothes he wore. The money he spent about town, and it weren't on the upkeep of that castle, I can tell ye."

"Oh?"

"Them shopkeepers are none too tight-lipped. He ordered the finest wines and brandies for himself."

"So, we did hear from Mable McGlory about the girls," said Blanche.

"Mabel's a lovely person, one of our top grapes on the talky vine, so to speak. But the vine is long and twisty." Maggie stared off into the peat fire, shaking her head.

"We had a beer at her pub. She mentioned Declan, and his reputation," said Haasi. "He didn't strike me as the sincere sort."

"That would be right, then. Love 'em and leave 'em. Left broken hearts throughout the townland, he did."

"But something else, Maggie. I overheard him and Una talking on the day we arrived. Or, rather, arguing. She said she knew something."

"He did seem ill tempered." Haasi's scone paused midway to her mouth, and she shook her head. She added, quickly, "I'm sure the police will consider all the facts, and Declan's whereabouts, and have the matter wrapped up nicely in no time."

Maggie sat back. "It is a bit unusual for Ballycill. A peaceful little village, it is. Haven't had much controversy since dear William died."

"William? The colonel's nephew?"

"Yes, our kin, and it was a sad, sad day when he shuffled off this mortal coil." She put a gnarled finger to her lips and coughed lightly. "Rather, he didn't exactly *shuffle*."

"I heard there was an accident…" Blanche probed lightly.

Maggie bustled over to the fireplace where she poked at the embers. "Sure, an accident it was reported." She turned and raised an eyebrow. "But there's been gossip, and that gossip has long legs. Oh, dear, the place seems to run away with it now, doesn't it though."

Blanche leaned forward. "Gossip about?"

Maggie sighed. "I suppose it might be more than gossip. Declan O'Brian was lacking friends, especially on account of the people who work about Ballycill had little trust in him."

Blanche stood, too. She put her cup down and kept her mouth shut, for once, listening intently. Haasi balanced a mound of clotted cream on the rest of her scone. Nothing kept the Haasi eating machine at bay, and Blanche did not want to disturb the process. Sister-cousin seemed determined to downplay their involvement in the whole Declan matter while Blanche determined to dance directly into the middle of it.

"What's the gossip, then, Maggie?"

"Ah, I suppose ye never did hear it." Maggie sighed and resumed her seat, the cake she'd been nibbling forgotten.

Blanche sat down and picked up her glass, her eyes riveted on Maggie.

"It happened years ago, the drowning in the river," said Maggie. "Declan and the lot of them were lads then, not but in their twenties. The colonel's nephew and the bairns of Chandy, the barber's son, Hermie. And the butcher's boy, Tony, of course. They were a-playin' as lads do, but somehow, young William got away on the current. Drowned, he did. Some blamed Declan."

"What do you think?"

"It makes no matter what I think. Never been a fan of that Declan though I wished him no harm. We didn't get on, I must admit." She sat back, her lips set in a tight line, the eyes clouding over once again. Robert leaped up for the remainder of the cake in Maggie's lap. "Aye, down boy. Yer a pig of a dog." But she laughed and patted his head.

Blanche waited, hoping patience would open up Maggie's memory of the day of the drowning. "You weren't close?"

"Never been. There was always something off about that boy, Declan." Maggie's voice took on a bitter edge. "It was never clear to me. The lads in the town didn't talk. Some moved on. Or they said the fault was with Declan, but they would never say exactly how. I always wondered. Someone had to know more …" Her words trailed off. She poured herself a bit more whiskey. "Just a child's portion." She sipped. "It would all be gossip then. The gardai never said otherwise. They couldn't prove a thing."

"Tony was one of the lads? He was making a delivery the night before Declan was … murdered."

"Didn't seem the friendly sort," Haasi added. "Polite enough, but never cracked a smile."

"Ah, yes, that would be Tony Costello. His da is hard on him, always has been, lugging them carcasses of pig and such up from the fields, all the hacking and blood. The boy was too young for such gory work, but work he did. Was always handy with the tools, doncha' know." She looked off into the fireplace and tickled Robert's ears, much to his delight.

Handy with tools? A knife, maybe? Blanche hesitated as the thought occurred to her. Tony had been there, and he certainly was not a fan of the dead agent.

Maggie's attention returned from wherever it had drifted off to. "Tony was indeed among the crowd that day. The Costello butcher shop is up the river from where poor William drowned. With all the hullabaloo following the death, Mr. Costello was at the point of shutting down his shop. The authorities hounded the surrounding residents and businesses, and then the incident blew up into something of a local mystery." Maggie sighed. "Sure, it did, and then it died away. What actually happened, we'll never know. Doesn't seem anyone has visited the circumstances of the drowning in years."

"I'm not so sure we shouldn't take a look. Especially with the death of Declan O'Brian," said Blanche. "Seems to raise a question or two."

Haasi had been smiling, eating, and sipping. And now she stopped abruptly. "How's that? *We should take a look?* There you go again, Blanche." Haasi turned to Maggie, deadpan. "If anyone could think of a question—or two—it would be Blanche. The girl's a regular question machine."

Maggie laughed. "The episode does make one wonder. And I've often posed a question or two about it meself."

Blanche nudged Haasi. "I can see *your* wheels turning over this whole Declan-Tony thing. Don't kid me, Haas."

"Can't hide from you." Haasi grinned and drained her whiskey.

Blanche leaned toward Maggie. "You know Una at the castle. Do you think, after all these years, she'd talk about the drowning? I'd like some details, especially anything to do about Declan's possible involvement."

"It does seem ye would be entitled, being William's long-lost relative and all," said Maggie. "Una knows a bit about every little thing. You can ask her. I'm sure she'll have something to say on the matter!"

"Can't imagine what we'd do with those details, but it wouldn't hurt." Blanche was already mulling what she would do. She threw Haasi a quick glance.

Haasi resumed her interest in the scones and cream.

Maggie said, "Sure and it's a sad affair, the killing of the agent."

"Any death is. Especially a murder," said Blanche.

"You might say that. And it is a sad time for this to happen in our little Ballycill—to one of our own." She frowned. "Though I can't say many wanted to claim him."

"Did he have any friends at all?" Haasi asked.

"If you'd call it that. Not really. I think most of the people in the village put up with him and his demands."

"I can understand that." Blanche exchanged a look with Haasi.

"Well!" Maggie clasped her hands "I'm sorry for the sadness that's crept into our little meetin', but I must say, it is a happy thing to have ye lovely sister-cousins come visit."

"It's rare, isn't it, Maggie? I'm so glad to be here—to be part of this beautiful place. *Your* place." Blanche couldn't help it. Her thoughts strayed again to the question of why Maggie was shut out of inheriting the castle. Blanche chose her words carefully.

She had to know. It didn't seem fair. "Maggie? I have to ask. You're related to the colonel, you're a McLoughlin. Why are you not part of this castle business?"

Maggie patted Blanche's knee. "Dear one. Why would I want to be mixed up in that fine kettle of fish? I'm happy right here in my bitty cottage. Wouldn't ye be, too?"

Along the walls piles of books, nearly to the low ceiling, tipped over precariously. A mountain of them. *Death by book. What a lovely way to go...* Despite the decidedly crooked arrangement, and haphazard décor, it was a comfortable and cozy room with its white-washed walls, wood timbers, and deep-set windows crowded with pots of flowers. The old leaded panes with beaded glass opened out to the fresh air, and the front door stood ajar in permanent welcome, typical of the Irish cottages. All seemed welcoming here. "I love it." Blanche smiled. "It's awfully nice, Maggie."

"'Tis, and I thank ye both for blessing the place with yer lovely presence," she said. "I'm happy. The lawyers did come a-calling after the nephew William died, but I declined to be involved with the estate. Ye can have at it, my dear. I'm a cousin of the colonel's brother, distant indeed, by marriage. Ye are in direct line through Maeve to the colonel's sister. Ye must know what a generous lot they were, the colonel and the nephew. They took care of the village—and the young nephew made sure I was set up here. I have no worries. No regrets." She sipped, and savored, and lifted the bottle for a refill.

"That's good. But this business with these deaths. It's disturbing," said Blanche.

"I'd leave it for now. Enjoy yer young selves!" She stood up and went to a side table where she picked up a framed photo. "I suppose ye saw enough likenesses of that handsome young William over at the castle. But they're a stiff bunch of prints and paintings on those fine silken walls. This one here is my favorite."

She thrust a photo of a handsome young man on a grand horse. William's hair was a mass of unruly black curls, his smile from ear to ear was radiant—a striking resemblance to Blanche's mother, Rose Murninghan! He wore a white shirt with billowy sleeves and high, shining buckled boots. Around his neck, a Celtic cross on a long chain fell against his chest as he reined in the horse.

"'Twas Paddy, his lovely horse." Maggie shook her head. At that, Robert's ears perked up from his bed near the fireplace, and he yipped. Blanche and Haasi laughed. They huddled together and studied the photo. "Inseparable, the two. William was a fine horse rider. It's a pity he couldn't swim."

Blanche didn't take her eyes off William. She absently fiddled with a black curl on her neck. "Troubling."

"And so 'tis. *Trouble*." Maggie put the photo back gently and went to poke the fire. She resumed her seat. Clapped her hands on her lap. "Now, ye listen to an old lady. Know that it'll all boil over for sure should ye stir the pot. Stay well away from it!"

"There's one heck of a truth if I ever did hear one." Haasi's eye lingered on the photo of William. "Right, Duchess?"

Nine

Simmering Stew

BLANCHE AND HAASI PEDALED away from Maggie's cottage after hugs and promises to return for more visits. Blanche was elated to meet her relative. The faint resemblance to her grandmother might be manufactured in her head, but all the same, Maggie reminded Blanche of Maeve. That same bubbly laugh, the same white hair. *These must be McLoughlin traits.* Blanche thought of herself forty or so years down the road, a white-haired writer on the Santa Maria Island beach, with a little sleuthing on the side. Sister-cousin would probably prefer that Blanche diddle away at the *Island Times* with her news articles and maybe take on writing a book or two. Better to enjoy some peace and quiet rather than continue with this propensity to turn up dead bodies wherever they went. All the same, Blanche couldn't turn away from the intrigue of a good mystery.

Will the murders ever stop?

Now Declan. And the news surrounding William's demise was indeed troubling. Throw in that Declan might have had something to do with it, which was even more troubling. Blanche considered Maggie's advice: *Enjoy yerselves!* But the gossip she'd passed along was difficult to ignore. Tony Costello had been there at the drowning—as well as a number of the local lads—with Declan. More avenues opened, more stumbling blocks, but Blanche was an able sprinter. She'd get around them. Or so she thought.

They biked past green pastures with sheep grazing over the stubble and rocky land. It was fairly treeless out this way. They were not that far from the sea—in fact, the coast was accessible within an hour or so. The sky was startlingly blue against the lush fields. They bumped down a narrow road under a canopy of leaves and came to an abrupt stop when happening upon a herd of cows crossing the road. The herder, with a stick and a ruddy smiling face, waved his cap and apologized and asked after their health.

"Fine, fine! Thank you! And you?" Blanche teetered on the bike.

The herder's reply was faint amid the mooing of his lumbering companions. "Aye, *foin*, and it's a *foin* day, 'tis." Which they always seemed to say even when the rain was coming down.

They set their feet to the pedals. "Well, there would be the butter for yer bread, Haasi," Blanche yelled. The brogue had returned.

"Aye." Haasi waved.

Blanche called out: "Getting mighty thirsty back here. Fancy a beer at the pub?"

"I do. Fancy or not. And I could do with some of that grand 'sossage' and the cows reminded me of cheese."

Blanche laughed. "So Irish of you!"

"The stomach part?"

They parked the bikes in front of Barrett's Pub in Ballycill and entered the dim interior, except for the sun casting weak squares of light onto the rough floor. Late lunch-time workers and locals gathered at the tables, bar stools, and the booths lining one wall under the windows. The place glowed with the business at hand, which smelled of hot food and yeasty beer. Blanche's eye caught mounds of mashed potatoes and shepherd's pie, golden glasses of beer, and the mostly happy, round red faces of the patrons.

They hardly looked up from their glasses and plates and conversation. The lively buzz made Blanche think they might be sharing the news of the day: Declan O'Brian had been found at the castle with a knife in his back. Blanche ducked her head. Then she realized how ridiculous it was to hide her face. No one knew her. Or did they?

Haasi and Blanche perched at the bar.

"And what can I be doin' fer ye, ladies?" The barkeep finished drying the beer glass and put it under the spigot. His smile was welcoming, but clearly he was busy.

"I might have a Guinness," said Blanche, eyeing the dark stout in front of several patrons.

"That's grand." He chuckled. "For some, it's breakfast."

Behind the bar, a poster hung on the wall: "Guinness is good for you." Blanche studied it.

"Ah, if ye'd volunteered a pint of blood this mornin', why, the Guinness would be on me." He chuckled.

"Really?"

"'Tis the custom. Have ye given blood today?"

Blanche hesitated a beat. "No, but…" Haasi poked her in the rib.

The heavy stout was indeed like liquid bread—but not bacon and eggs. Haasi raised an eyebrow. Under her breath, she said, "Don't mention Declan, and don't tell him we had whiskey for breakfast."

Blanche stifled a laugh. "Well, Maggie's scones count as breakfast. Don't they?"

Haasi hunched her shoulders. They watched the thin brown stream of Guinness issue from the brass fitting as he tipped the glass. He stopped to let the foam settle and proceeded again slowly. He stole a glance at Blanche who was leaning on the counter, watching intently.

"It's an art, ye know. Can't hurry the pour. What good would it do to hurry a thing?"

After another settle, he put the glass with a top of creamy foam in front of Blanche and turned to Haasi. "And the same for ye, Miss?"

"Surely." She peered along the bar at the selection, seeming dubious but interested. "I'll try it."

"John Barrett's the name," he said, attending to the pour. "What would bring ye here to me establishment?" He presented Haasi's Guinness with a flourish and a whimsical look on his square, clean-shaven jaw. Blanche figured him for about sixty-ish with bushy gun-metal gray hair and hands the size of pork slabs.

"We're staying at the castle." Blanche blurted this news without thinking.

"Bang. Now you've done it." Haasi murmured from behind her glass. She took a sip of the Guinness, leaving a mustache on her upper lip. "So much for keeping a low profile."

Blanche lowered her head and whispered, hoarsely. "Oh, you know they know. Nothing is secret in this town."

Barrett tipped his head sideways and chuckled. "Ye must be the American lasses then. And how did I know that?"

"That would be us," said Blanche.

"Then ye'd be right in there with that rascal Declan O'Brian." He crossed himself.

"Rascal? You, too?" Blanche sighed.

Barrett didn't miss a beat. "It's a sad state of affairs, but I'd be lyin' to the Queen of Heaven if I said I was surprised."

Blanche and Haasi asked, in unison: "Why?"

He put his hands on his hips and studied them, then demurred. "Now, which of ye lasses is newly part owner of Dunfaedan?"

Word travels. "That would be me," said Blanche. She wasn't sure it was a great idea to fess up, but his sincerity piqued her curiosity. Plus, he seemed to know a thing or two about Declan.

"I'm delighted to make yer acquaintance." He nodded at Blanche and Haasi in turn and looked about the room that had thinned out. He set his ample rear on a stool behind the bar. "I hope ye know what yer gettin' yer fine selves into. The Williams were a grand lot, but, sad to say, that Declan didn't make the castle folk any too beloved about the village."

Blanche tamped down her curiosity. She needed to listen more and shoot off her mouth less. Haasi had no trouble in that department; she was forever on Blanche's case to cool it and keep her ears open and be patient.

Barrett's gaze under those bushy brows shifted across the pub. Blanche followed his line of sight. Like a beam it landed at a table of four workmen. They were all mumbling and grunting away and shoveling in the food, but one of them was staring straight at Blanche. His expression was serious rather than amorous.

"Methinks ye have an admirer, Miss," said Barrett. "Or he's studying ye for other reasons?"

"I know him, or, at least, I met him. He was making a delivery to the castle kitchen. The night before…the murder," she said. "He didn't seem very friendly."

"Tony something." Haasi's attention was fixed on the Harp lager beer sign, her face hard to read.

"Ah, yes. Tony Costello. He does have that route now, doesn't he?" Barrett spoke softly, his tone pensive. "If Declan had been about, Tony'd not be smilin.' He and the O'Brian were not on the friendliest terms."

"And do you know why? As I remember, the tension in that kitchen the night we met was palpable." Blanche sipped her beer as she tried to be cool while she pressed Barrett.

"I'd say there might be multiple reasons but can't say exactly. One might have something to do with the drowning of the lovely William McLoughlin, I believe. But only speculation here. Nobody really knows," he said, quickly, and a bit dolefully.

"Wasn't there an investigation?" she asked, knowing perfectly well there were many.

"Oh, sure, that was done, and gone. Nothing of significance came of it," he said. He turned his head and then came back around. "Now, ye must be a relation to the McLoughlins. How would that be?" The subject of connections seemed to perk him up.

"Very distant. On my maternal grandmother's side—I'm a Murninghan. Limerick, Cork, probably down from Monaghan, too."

"Well, it's lovely to welcome ye 'home,'" he said.

"Home. Why do the Irish call it home no matter where they are?"

"Because 'tis. Home is where the heart is, and Ireland is that."

Blanche could understand the pull, but her heart was on another island some eight hours away. Yet, Ireland was having its way with her. She felt a spiritual connection to the people and the place. Bread and beer, clean air, a warm welcome everywhere. *Céad mille fáilte.* A hundred thousand welcomes. The Irish didn't stint on that; it was bred into them, no matter how poor or crowded or short on time.

Barrett returned to the moment, one less welcoming. "Our Tony might be wanting to keep a distance from ye, should ye develop a hard feeling or two in light of the gossip surrounding the drowning and the agent."

"Hmmm, now why would that be?" Blanche pushed her feigned innocence.

"Declan was tied up with the McLoughlins and the misfortune. He continued in charge of castle affairs and all." He rubbed his chin and slid off the bar stool. "But I can't say. I shouldn't because I don't rightly know. How would I?"

Blanche mulled that one. "Well, I don't know, Mr. Barrett. You tell me? Declan continued on to be agent after the drowning—even with the gossip swirling?"

"Blanche, give it a rest," said Haasi. "The Guinness is great. I think they have something here."

John Barrett's lips twitched in half a smile. He was busy. He went off down the bar to tend another customer. For all his dissimulation, he hadn't said much, but he seemed to know a lot. Everyone did, except Blanche. The death of William the Younger continually spurred hard feelings when brought up. She was inclined to believe the police had done what they could to solve the cause of the drowning. They concluded that foul play was not indicated, but gossip suggested otherwise.

Barrett was back. He picked up the thread. "I suppose the matter's been more or less settled then. Rest in peace, William, and the same must be said for Declan O'Brian. Can't speak ill of the dead." Barrett shook his head, his comments offhand. He tied an apron around his middle. "Will ye be comin' to the wake here?"

Blanche's beer went down the wrong pipe. "*Wake? Here?*"

"Why, sure, and we need to wake the dead agent. It's the custom, ye know. And his directions said it should be in the pub, just as usual."

"In the pub," said Blanche. "You're having a wake here?" She looked around at the rosy-faced patrons, swilling beer, hearty laughs busting out of conversations.

He stopped his polishing and washing and looked at Blanche patiently. "As I said, 'tis the custom. Me pa was once the undertaker as well as pub owner. The beer cellar is a fine place to hold the departed until time for a proper wake. Now, ye come by and see fer yerselves." He nodded to Blanche, then to Haasi, and went off to pour a beer.

"They're going to have a wake? *Here.*" Blanche was incredulous.

"Blanche, we all mourn in different ways. The Irish have their way." Haasi sipped, a twinkle in her eye.

"Yeah, but how are they going to do that? Sprays of lilies and a casket? Served with sausage and beer?" She looked around and shook her head.

"Guess we'll have to see," said Haasi. "It's entirely plausible. I'm looking forward to it."

"Oh, sure."

"I am. I stand on ceremony. Declan is dead, and I want to see how they mark the occasion."

Blanche noted that she didn't say "celebrate" a life, or mourn the deceased, or something like that. She sat back and studied her sister-cousin. "You have a point there, as usual. Yeah, I wonder how they'll mark it." *And who will show up?*

Haasi smiled, but only half a smile. A crooked little twist of her red lips. "We'll see, won't we?"

Barrett was back, leaning over the bar at them. "As for the livin', will I be gettin' ye some of our grand Irish stew? Mary's been simmerin' the lot of it all morning."

He didn't have to ask Haasi twice. Barrett set out bowls of the steaming lamb, potatoes, carrots, and onions in brown gravy with a sprinkle of chopped parsley on top.

"Ah, green. Everywhere. Don't you love it?" Haasi dove into the stew and helped herself to the basket of thick chewy bread. "Ah-yeeee. It's hot!"

Blanche stirred idly. "I'd like to go over there and have a talk with that Tony person. Is he still staring?"

"No, he's not, and don't even think about it," said Haasi, who finally put a spoonful of lamb and carrot into her mouth. "Concentrate on this delicious stuff, Blanche. I've died and gone to Stew Heaven."

Blanche studied John Barrett and called to him. "When is that wake?"

"Would be soon. I expect tomorrow or soon thereafter. Declan won't mind, whatever date and time we choose now, would he?"

Ten

A Lotta Talk, a Lick of Action

"I WANNA TALK TO THAT GUY." Blanche still had Tony Costello on her mind when they finished up at Barrett's and climbed onto their bikes. They decided to take the long way home. The afternoon was nearly gone, and the air was soft with a wash of bright gray light on the pastel storefronts.

"Oh, Blanche. If you wanna, you're gonna. No question about it!" Haasi flipped a braid over her shoulder and pedaled off down the road, Blanche right behind.

Blanche's wheels wobbled. "I just have to figure out how to get to him," she called.

"Oh, that won't be hard. Haven't known you to avoid the direct approach. But let's go easy."

"We may have to set up the meeting, you know, innocuously."

"Oh, right. At the butcher shop? Just walk in and say, let's talk *pig*?"

"Well, why not? There's a lot to learn about pigs. They say they're intelligent...beings."

"Maybe we can ask one: Who killed Declan?"

"Oh, Haas. You're so...so...so."

"Intelligent?"

Blanche's bike took another wobble nearly off the road.

"*Bang!* Be careful!"

It was only a short distance now, past a broad field of hay, a horse barn, and a couple of little white cottages, all of their doors open to the cool early evening. One woman sweeping the stoop waved as they passed.

"The people here are so welcoming!" yelled Haasi.

"*Céad mile fáilte*. A hundred thousand welcomes."

"Except for murder."

"You bet."

Blanche waved back at the sweeping woman, avoiding a lorry full of old chairs that rumbled by. She was not much of a bike rider; she was more of a beach walker, and so, before she returned to her beloved Santa Maria Island, she longed to explore the beach near Ballybunion. But it seemed the agenda kept filling up and getting in the way of that excursion. They'd have to plan the day and stick to it. Put the murder aside, get in the car, eand get on with a tour of Ireland. The clean air was unlike her salty Florida island but light and humid with the promise of water nearby. The gulls wheeled and dipped overhead. It was welcoming and nostalgic; it was "home," as the Irish say.

They pedaled another kilometer or two, and the gleaming stone façade of the grand castle came into view around the bend. It was a stately scene—if Blanche did not take into account the imposing police car parked at the front entrance, its windows darkened. There was no sign of the officials. Just the police car. A sense of foreboding swept Blanche. Memory of the morning's disastrous meeting with local authorities came flooding back and washed away her happy mood.

She skidded to a halt on the drive, fine gravel flying.

Haasi came around next to her. "Oh, boy."

"Yeah, that one. Declan," said Blanche. "How we going to handle *this*?"

"It's probably just more follow-up. You know, looking for clues and such. Nothing to do with *us*." Her tone was tentative.

"Don't I wish. Oh. Right. He was found in my kitchen. *Dead*."

"Duchess, you're getting very proprietary about this castle. The circumstances don't necessarily have anything to do with you."

"That's true. We'll just let the gardai do their talking. Maybe they'll run out of things to say."

Haasi tilted her head. "The police? Since when do they run out of questions? Maybe you should have been a cop, Blanche."

"Yeah, right. I like to help is all."

"I'd say you've already done enough in your short life. The island? Mexico? Vietnam? Wow! There's no rest for the bad guys when you're around."

"That's me." But Blanche felt a chill.

"Don't worry. Let them talk and do their business. It's just going to have to play out, and then we'll be on our merry way."

"Somehow, I feel like that merry way is over a cliff."

"Blanche. We're not lemmings."

"That we aren't. Just wish we'd scheduled our little visit to Ireland, say, about a month from now."

"Well, we didn't. Too late for that, and besides, it wouldn't matter. That guy was going to get his, sooner or later. Too bad we had to witness it." Haasi put a sneaker on the pedal and got back on her seat, ready to ride. "Let's lay low—as much as we can."

"Right. Be cool." She couldn't wait to see what new hell this visit from the police was all about.

They rolled down the drive, around the side of the castle, and pulled up to the bike racks at the back door. It was open. Detective Leary stood in the kitchen, thick-soled feet planted wide apart. He was animated and gesturing while Una stood there, arms folded. His voice rumbled with authority, which made Blanche cringe. She steeled herself and approached. Haasi hummed a tune as she secured their bikes.

"And here ye be now," said Leary. He lowered his tone, gently. "We was just about to go into the village and check around fer ye. In fact, my partner is in the car out front, all set for a look about."

"What can I do for you?" Blanche added a confident note to her voice.

"Aye, we'll see about that now, won't we. It's all busy official business, ye know."

"And what would that business be?" Blanche controlled herself, which was a stretch. She could practically feel Haasi breathing down her neck, and she was grateful. She looked the detective in the eye. She would not be intimidated.

Leary cranked himself up a good foot taller than Blanche. "Miss Murninghan, we need to question you in the death of Declan O'Brian."

Each word, measured and crisp.

The air went out of her. Deflated, she was afraid she'd fall down. She quickly regained her senses. "*What?*"

"I need a bit of your time, Miss." The detective stepped aside and pointed to the settle next to the fireplace. Haasi grabbed Blanche's elbow and steered her off to a seat. Una hadn't said a word, her lips in a tight thin line, her eyes cloudy and unreadable.

"Bang, be cool. Answer his questions and be done with it," Haasi urged, under her breath.

Blanche determined to comply. *Or try.* "I don't know what this is about, but certainly…What can I possibly add to the discussion? I told you all I know." Her voice was strained.

She and Haasi sat down, hands clasped between their knees. Leary sat across from them on a straight-back chair, positioning a clipboard on his lap. Una, now frowning, stood by the door. Her silence spoke volumes about the gravity of the situation.

Does Una know something?

Leary abruptly turned his attention to his paperwork and cleared his throat. "We've done a rush on this." He glanced at his wristwatch. Blanche checked the clock. It was after seven, more than twelve hours since discovering Declan dripping blood onto the kitchen floor. Leary looked at Blanche, his gaze like an arrow. "Miss Murninghan, your fingerprints are on the knife that was found stuck in the torso of Declan O'Brian."

Blanche shot to her feet. "Now, wait."

"Please. Have a seat," he said. "First thing, we compared all the occupants of the castle that morning, and you are the one come up on that knife."

"How did you get my fingerprints?" she blurted.

The detective was grim, or serious. She couldn't tell which; his craggy features let no one in. He glanced at Una. "We had a warrant and access to the castle earlier today. The investigation has been moving at a clip. No question, the fingerprints on that knife belong to one Blanche Murninghan."

"Now just one moment." Blanche was on her feet. "That can be explained."

His expression was stony and at once kindly and patient. "We hope so," he said. "It's a sorry turn of events."

"I was in that kitchen! I picked up a knife!" *What am I saying?*

"Apparently," said Leary.

"I think I need a lawyer," said Blanche.

Haasi gave the detective a hard look and grabbed hold of Blanche. "You haven't done anything," she whispered.

"I know, Haas, but this doesn't look good. It doesn't sound good either. I need help."

"That's wise." He wrote a note on the clipboard. "Consulting with authorities, I mean."

"Should I call Gustaitis?" Blanche felt as if she'd jump out of her skin.

"Think we're gonna have to go local," Haasi said, eyeing Leary.

He'd been all polished and put together, and now he seemed weary. "I am not here to bring formal charges," he said. "It may come to that, but it's not the case now. The Dublin office will be involved further, and the district superintendent is deep into the investigation already. I simply wish to inform you of the preliminary findings. We need to ask questions…"

"Shoot." Blanche winced.

"We must establish the location of the residents of the castle. There seem to be mitigating factors. But you were here in the kitchen—the night before the murder. There's no proof of your *direct* involvement in the murder of Declan O'Brian, except for these fingerprints, of course."

"*Proof of my direct involvement? That I killed him?*" She could feel her face turning beet red, her short fuse fizzling. "Why do you even insinuate that?"

"I'm trying to make it clear. At this stage, we have no conclusions. Nothing that says you had criminal intentions."

"I'll say," said Blanche. "I've only been here two days, hardly time to develop *criminal intentions.*"

"That may be so."

"Yes, it's so. I'll say nothing more. I need legal counsel before I go any further with this." Her forehead felt like it would burst, and her chest was pounding. She'd definitely lost all her cool.

"Let's go, Blanche. Enough's enough," Haasi said into Blanche's ear.

"He can't hold you. We'll talk to a lawyer."

Leary was on his feet, rocking back and forth in those substantial shoes, his hands behind his back. He was a big man, but one who didn't seem to throw his weight around meanly. "I can see how you might say that, Miss Murninghan. But facts are facts. Or should I say fingerprints speak for themselves."

"You do know that we were in the kitchen the night before the murder. And there were many people coming in and out?" Blanche looked up at the policeman.

He spoke softly. "Aye, we've noted that. We'll sort it, Miss. Get it done right." He brightened up as if remembering another detail of his official mission. "May I suggest—no, insist—that ye both not leave Ballycill. That would be *you*, Miss Blanche and Miss Haasi. Ye must remain until we resolve the matter at hand. That's one of the reasons I'm here—to detain ye, in a manner of speaking. That, and of course to inform ye of our findings so far. And, as I said, there'll be more questions." He relaxed some, now that the news was delivered. He was courteous, professional—and what he said was exasperating.

Blanche remembered her manners. "I know. You must have lots of questions. And I'm not going anywhere," she said, leaning toward Haasi. "I want this situation cleared up as much as you do."

He was nodding, thoughtfully, one huge fist thumping the clipboard. "You can see about counsel in the village, should the need arise. Perhaps Una can direct you?"

Una stepped forward. "Peter Flynn might be the one. He has a fine head on him, knows his way around a law book, he does."

Haasi studied Una, clearly sizing up this burst of eagerness. Her gaze shifted to Leary, then Blanche. Cool and calm.

"Do not worry, B," Haasi murmured. "We'll get to the bottom of this mess."

They sat in the drawing room, staring into the last of the embers. Splitting a beer. It had been a day from hell. Blanche wanted to take her head out of this vice of troubles, but there seemed no way out.

"Bang, really, don't worry. They'll note that the fingerprints were put there under Declan's direction."

"But the knife. They think that went into his side—by me."

"Well, it didn't. And that's that." Haasi tossed off the last of the Harp and set the glass down with an emphatic click. "Let's go up. I don't know how we're still *awake*."

"'To sleep, perchance to dream. Aye, there's the rub…'"

"Blanche, don't be so maudlin. You're not Hamlet, and you're not gonna die."

"Oh, all right already. Why do you have to be so damn *right* all the time?"

"I don't know." She laughed, dryly. "'Cause you taught me all I know?"

Next morning, Blanche and Haasi sat in the dining room, surrounded by covered dishes of eggs and rashers of bacon, sausage, breads, grilled tomato, and an assortment of jams and juices. Blanche had little appetite; Haasi needed her "strength." They planned to visit Peter Flynn, the lawyer, to pick up a bit of advice—under duress—after Detective Leary's visit.

"Sleep well, Duchess?"

"Sort of. But I kept waking up, imagining myself in stripes."

Haasi slathered the soda bread with strawberry jam. "Awww, you'd look good in stripes. In *anything*, really. A nice orange jumpsuit?"

"Will you stop?"

"Listen to me." Haasi slapped that bread and jam onto her plate. "They don't have a thing on you, and they're not going to get a thing on you. We're going to figure this out and be done with it. And *him*." She had an edge in her voice that could have sliced through the pile of bacon on her plate.

Blanche only picked at the egg and a blood sausage, which she sampled and pushed aside. She was trying to be Irish and try everything. "I hope you're right. It's only our third day, and I'm off to get a lawyer."

"Under the circumstances, it can't hurt. Just to be safe."

"That's us, all right. Always picking the safe route." She gave Haasi a half smile and poured herself another cup of jitters.

"Eat up. You're gonna need fuel."

Mae appeared in the doorway, wringing her hands. "Miss Blanche, Miss Haasi, I've been informed that the wake is about to commence at Barrett's Pub. That would be the wake of Mr. Declan O'Brian. To be sure." The toes of her sturdy shoes twitched at the hem of her long skirt. "I expect it will go for most of the day, but I was asked to inform ye. If ye don't mind me tellin' ye."

"Thank you, Mae. No, I don't mind at all. I appreciate it," said Blanche, forcing a smile at the thought of "celebrating" Declan O'Brian's life.

"Like I said, eat up," Haasi murmured. "Strength, B."

Eleven

Sweet Bite

"MAYBE WE SHOULD DROP IN at Barrett's and pay our respects?"

"I don't know, Blanche. Don't you think we should steer clear of anything to do with Declan O'Brian? Including his dead body?"

"I suppose. But John Barrett said it's the custom, and I like to go along with custom," Blanche mused. They were finishing coffee, deciding what to do with the day—besides the visit to the lawyer. "Let's just go and make a visit. Keep it short. Keep a low profile, what with gossip around here. He was the castle agent, after all." *And I want to see who shows up at the wake.* Blanche kept the thought to herself, a hedge against Haasi's reluctance to get further involved. Blanche sighed. Haasi was surely thinking the same thing. They could compare notes later— once they "celebrated" the life of Declan O'Brian.

Haasi shrugged. "Sure. Might be interesting to see who shows up."

Blanche grinned.

Barrett's Pub had a modest black banner at the door. Inside, the mood was subdued. Near noon at the "local," business was usually picking up but not today. Declan O'Brian lay on a plain oak table, a huge slab of ice beneath. He was dressed in a black suit, and his face was ghostly white. *Well, he is a ghost.*

Haasi and Blanche hesitated at the door. John Barrett came up beside them. "Good day, ladies. Lovely of ye to take the time." Blanche looked around. It was apparent they were among the very few who had taken the time.

"Hello, Mr. Barrett." Blanche managed a smile, and a quick glance at Declan. She felt queasy. "Is it always the custom to, well, lay out the body in the pub? In this fashion?"

"Tradition. We've carried on many years just so and down life's path and out the door to the *simitary.*"

Blanche looked around. "Beer—and caskets to go?" Haasi nudged Blanche.

Barrett was clearly amused. "The cellar is nice and cool. The mister was after resting there 'til now, and then later it'll be off with him." He cleared his throat. "Once we say goodbye, that is. The Irish have a way of stringing out the good-byes, but in this case, we will get on with it. By the way, it was Mr. O'Brian's express wish that his departure be marked in this way. We like to oblige." His tongue was firmly placed in his cheek as he intoned the last wishes of Declan O'Brian.

"Hmmm. Do you expect anyone, in particular, to show up?" Haasi glanced among the few attendees. Two elderly women stood in a corner whispering, and one old man with a cap in his hand stood near Declan's feet. A middle-aged woman was hidden from full view near a window, half in shadow, her face pasty and without expression.

"No, I do not. But we will proceed with the formalities, just the same."

The door swung open. Boots stomped across the old wood floor to where Declan lay. The visitor was a stocky fellow, wearing a mussed chambray shirt and a tweed cap he didn't remove.

Blanche recognized him, and his sour expression: Tony Costello. He leaned over the body. "Dead, all right, ya bugger." He looked around quickly then as if to take back the words. He jerked away and came across to the bar and John Barrett. "Are ye after a pour, John? A wee whiskey would suit me," Tony said.

Barrett, his lips compressed, walked around the bar and took down a bottle of Paddy whiskey. He didn't look up. He set a glass in front of Tony Costello and poured. Tony downed the whiskey in one gulp. He nodded in the direction of the corpse. "As God is my witness, it's better this way." One of the old women hissed and crossed herself. Costello sneered. He stacked some coins on the bar and clomped out of the pub.

"What was all that about?" Blanche and Haasi stood still as statues during the five minutes or so Tony Costello came to pay his respects.

Barrett shook his head. "No love lost there," he said, tersely. He continued wiping the bar to a near-empty pub.

"I so appreciate you seeing us," Blanche said, her agitation rising. They'd gone from Declan to lawyering, and her brain was spinning. "I hope you can help." Haasi put a cool hand on her arm. The two sat in uncomfortable high-backed chairs with rush seats. They'd dressed in black sweaters (in deference to Declan), slacks, and light jackets. Blanche wore a velvet headband to tame her curls. It did nothing to tame her mood. They smiled across the desk at Peter Flynn, Esquire.

The lawyer folded his hands on his desk. He was a dapper fellow with a puggish face and a sharp white shirt under a tweed jacket. He tilted his large head at Blanche in a manner of intense interest. "I'm happy to help, Miss Murninghan. Please, start at the beginning."

"Where is the beginning?" She took a deep breath. Her stomach was in a knot. "I guess that says something about my frame of mind."

"It's unfortunate. The murder, of course, and your connection to it. We want to clear up the matter as far as you're concerned, and the better your recall, the further we are ahead."

Knowledge makes perfect. Remembering the damn details may save me.

"Blanche, I guess you should start with our arrival—and your impression of Declan," said Haasi. "We didn't exactly get off on the right foot."

Flynn's bushy eyebrows shot up.

"He was a narcissistic wanker, I think you'd say." Blanche delivered this opinion in an even tone.

"I see," said Flynn. "He did have a reputation." He looked down and shuffled some papers, distractedly. He cleared his throat. "I have some details, but I want to hear them from you. I knew Declan O'Brian, and you are quite right. He did make an *impression.*"

Haasi made a sound like air coming out of balloon. Blanche suppressed a need to jump out of her chair and begin pacing.

Flynn picked up a legal pad, his gnarly fingers wrapped around the Paper Mate. Blanche related the story—touching on background with

Sam and Malcolm. The lawyer wrote notes as Blanche went through the arrival at the castle, Declan's argument with Una, the dinner and tour, and the final scene of horror with Declan draped over the sink in a pool of blood.

"How very grim." He rested the pen on his lower lip and frowned. "Go back to the tour. You say he took you through the kitchen the night before the murder. And that he showed you around. And you picked up a knife? Out of the drawer?"

"Yes, at his insistence."

"That's odd."

"He was odd." Haasi chimed in.

Blanche agreed. "And charming but rude. Tell me, how did this man ever get the position as agent at Dunfaedan? There was a cloud over his head, even rumors he was a witness, or had some involvement, in the death of the nephew, William McLoughlin. I don't see how the McLoughlins would ever hire him."

Flynn sat back in his chair with a loud squeak of old leather and creaky wheels. "Now there's a tale for you." He tapped his fingertips together. "In my opinion, O'Brian himself set up the arrangement, and he took his fine time about it. Declan weaseled his way into the picture with the help of his father. Then after all the maneuvering, he courted and supposedly became engaged to the daughter of the banker who was tied up with the executors of the McLoughlin estate. This banker thought it would be a good idea to have his dear Mary financially looked after by Declan O'Brian, and he was after seeing to the final preparations of making O'Brian agent of the castle."

"That's even odder. Declan O'Brian didn't seem like the marrying type," said Blanche.

"You are certainly right on that score. Mary disappeared. Indeed, she went away for some six months or so, and when she came back the romance was all over. By that time, Declan O'Brian was fully ensconced as agent at the castle. And what did he care about the poor girl? Lord knows. Seems he never had intentions to marry the girl."

"A real gentleman." Haasi shifted in her chair and let out a derisive chuckle.

"What happened?"

Flynn stood up and looked out the window. "Six months? Just long enough to head to Dublin, have a baby, and come back here."

"*Declan's child?*" Blanche couldn't believe the twisted history of the agent. It kept getting worse.

Flynn nodded. "Everywhere you looked, he left someone in the lurch, or devastated. I'm surprised he lasted this long." He frowned and paced in front of a large window behind the desk. Beyond was the butcher shop. Its sign, "Comestibles, Beef and Poultry" in chipped blue letters, swung over the doorway.

"I'm sorry," Haasi said.

Blanche followed Flynn's gaze. "Wasn't Tony Costello—the butcher's son—at the scene of the drowning of William McLoughlin?"

Haasi shot Blanche a look. Flynn's eyebrows lifted in surprise. "That would be correct. So the facts state. But we never did get many details from the lads in attendance that day, and the investigation hit a wall."

Blanche jumped from her chair and walked over to the fireplace where the embers gave off some warmth. She paced the lovely old worn Oriental that had probably withstood many an interrogation. "I've got a hunch Tony Costello knows something of Declan's murder. Somehow, he's privy to it. Don't you think?"

"Blanche, where is this coming from?" Haasi murmured.

"From my brain?"

"Oh brother."

"I don't know, Miss Blanche. Tony Costello is not the point here. You're leaping about the moment at hand when we need to clear you of the Declan situation. Eliminate you from the list of suspects. If they question you further, you must call me at once, and I'll pop over. I suspect that team of detectives will swoop in and most likely an inspector from Dublin will, too." He handed Blanche a card with his name and phone number.

"Blanche had nothing to do with the murder of this guy. We'd only been in Ireland a day. Why would Blanche kill him?" Now Haasi was shaking her head.

"I totally agree with that assessment. You make sense, but often murders make no sense. There may be passion involved. Often there is planning among the crafty. The situation with that knife is that your fingerprints are all over it. That's a fact."

His words hit Blanche like cold water. "I was in that kitchen! Declan gave us a tour. You need to put it on the record, Mr. Flynn. Get hold of the gardai and set it straight."

"It's open, but not shut. The situation, so noted."

"By the way, what's Mary's last name? Is she around? I'd like to talk to her."

Haasi visibly stiffened. "OMG."

Flynn didn't seem to notice Haasi's dismay at Blanche's interest in Mary. "Why, yes. It's Mary Fogarty, she'd be. Mary lives in the village," he said. "A part-time secretary to the local priest at St. Columba's. A lovely lass, she is, and sorely treated by the likes of Declan O'Brian— and the gossiping wags of Ballycill."

"I appreciate the information, Mr. Flynn. I would definitely take care in approaching her," said Blanche.

Haasi let out a sigh.

Flynn laughed. "You two are quite the anomaly. Who's the caretaker?"

"Me." They both stated the obvious together.

"Well, it's clear you care a great deal for each other. But may I remind you. This is a murder investigation, and you need to let the authorities handle it. Step lightly here. I am quite certain you will be cleared of any wrongdoing, Miss Blanche, but you must be patient."

Blanche tried to absorb his advice and failed miserably.

Flynn smiled. His large, merry eyes and friendly face meant to lighten the mood. "Now, it's not so bad after all."

"And Mary?" Blanche asked.

"Incorrigible." Haasi shot Blanche a look. "What can I say?"

Flynn hesitated, then pointed out the window. "You can see the church from here, you can." He swung the windowpane wide open. The steeple beyond poked the blue sky. "She never married and lives in the small yellow cottage next to the church. Does a bit of bidding for the local priest and has a little business set up there. Knitting, crocheting, sewing lessons and such for a few ladies of the village. But, thinkin' upon it now, it's not likely she'd have tea and a biscuit with you. She's quite soured on life, poor girl, no thanks to the unfaithfully departed Declan O'Brian."

They left Flynn's office and started off toward the heart of Ballycill. It was a bright day, and they'd planned to walk about and explore the shops during the rest of the afternoon. Stroll to the markets and visit the pubs. At least, that had been the plan prior to meeting Peter Flynn. Now Blanche clearly had her eye on the church—and her thoughts on Mary Fogarty. "Come on, Haas. Let's go."

"Where you off to in such a hurry?"

"Church?"

"Since when did you get so religious?" Haasi tapped Blanche on the shoulder. "Why, Blanche? Can't we let the girl be? Didn't you hear what Flynn said? After her experience with Declan, she probably wouldn't be too happy talking about him, or meeting anyone who's had anything to do with him. Including murdering him."

"What's that supposed to mean? We—I mean, I—didn't have anything to do with his murder."

"Except you found him dead in your kitchen."

"Haas!"

"Bang! Now, don't get all mad. I'm just trying to make some sense of this."

"I don't want to make sense of it. I want to find out what the hell happened." Blanche stopped walking and scratched her head. "Mary might be able to help. We might persuade her. I have an idea she'll give us insight into this Declan, and that's what we need. Insight."

"And Tony can't do that? Thought you wanted to talk to him."

"I do. Mary and Tony."

"Well, not at the same time, I hope," Haasi grumbled.

They walked up an incline and around the tidy little square in the center of town. Blanche stopped and pulled Haasi to a bench under a cascade of pink and white flowers next to a fountain. "Look, let's keep it positive. Maybe bring her some fruit tarts or something."

"Again. Why, Blanche?"

"Because, for one thing, the more I know about this guy, the more I may be able to distance myself from this murder. Besides, I think he had something to do with William's drowning, and I can't let that one pass." She stood up and strode across the street.

Haasi was right in step. "A two-fer?"

"You're such a good sport. To put up with my endless meddling."

"How can I not?" She sighed. "I have to admit, you keep it interesting."

A row of small businesses lined the village street. At one, a glass expanse showed off woolens, lace, and linen, next to a tool shop and a small grocery. A short, stout woman clucked at two beautiful, pale children with red hair and dirty faces, a dog ran between Haasi and Blanche. Haasi's eyes grew round at the sight of Lafferty's Confections.

"Looks good, right?" Blanche grinned. "How about we pick up some treats for teatime."

"I'm sure Una has that covered."

"For Mary?"

"Are you serious?" But Haasi knew the answer to that question.

Blanche peered into the window of the bake shop. They headed inside, and a bell tinkled over the door. They were immediately enveloped in the lovely, sugary, floury scent of bread and cookies and cake. Haasi smiled as she approached the display cases packed with sugar-dusted cookies and custard-filled tarts.

"G'day to ye." The clerk was as plump as a goose and cheerful as a toddler with a new toy. "What can I get for ye?"

"Hello! We're going to have tea with a friend and would like to pick up something appropriate … for teatime?" Blanche mulled the array of treats. "It all looks so good."

"I'll say. How about some of those sugary thingies with the fruit on top," said Haasi.

"Our specialty. The Linzer pastry with raspberry! Delightful. How many?"

"A dozen?" Haasi turned to Blanche. "I'll have to try one and see if it's the right choice." Blanche rolled her eyes.

They left the shop with a box of the pastry, minus the one Haasi was devouring, a dab of raspberry on her lip. "Oh, yes, these will do nicely!" she said.

They ambled down the sidewalk. "Blanche, we're going *now*?"

"Why not?"

"Don't you think we should go back to the castle and call first? Or ask around? Or *something*?"

"These Linzer *thingies* will do the talking. Right? If we call, she'll probably hang up on us. I believe in the direct approach," she said, her sandals clapping the sidewalk.

"Bang. Of course, you do. Why do I even ask?" Haasi grumbled. They walked past the shops, Haasi chomping pastry, Blanche heading straight for the church. It loomed into full view at the bottom of the hill near the river. The late spring day was surprisingly warm, and promising.

"What are you going to say when we get there?" Haasi smacked her lips at the last of the Linzer.

"I don't know. What should we say? Let's start with hello."

Twelve

All He Wrote

"HELLO, MY NAME'S BLANCHE Murninghan and this is my cousin—"

The door slammed in their faces. The woman who'd answered the door, most likely Mary Fogarty, had only opened it a crack. Her hair was severely pulled back from her forehead, her skin white and not of a kindly hue. She wore a baggy black sweater.

"Not exactly a warm welcome," Blanche whispered to Haasi behind her hand. She was not daunted by Mary's greeting, such as it was.

"Maybe we should have called first, Blanche. *Like I suggested.*"

"What? And have those delicious Linzers get all stale?"

"Blanche, we just bought them."

"You know what I mean."

Haasi wore a doubtful expression.

"We'll just give her a minute to cool down, or whatever."

"What. Ever." Haasi stepped back from the stoop and studied the landscape of rose bushes under the dark windows.

If there was one thing Blanche had learned from being a journalist, it was this: *Persistence pays off.* And curiosity. She had both in abundance. These tendencies had landed her more than one story, and a whole lot of trouble. On occasion, she'd had to dig her way out and thank the Lord she was still alive. Haasi knew this—all too well. She was the most patient sister-cousin. She was also good with a knife, a rope, and a menu.

Blanche balanced the box of treats on one arm and knocked softly.

"Miss Fogarty? We've brought you this lovely surprise from Lafferty's. Won't you talk with us?" Blanche practically sang the words, her mellifluous tone sliding up and down the scale. Haasi was in full eye roll now.

Blanche sensed the presence of Mary Fogarty on the other side of the door. She could almost hear her breathing. A cat meowed softly.

"What is it you want?" Came the harsh demand.

Blanche looked to Haasi for an answer, but she hunched her shoulders. Blanche returned to the door, her mouth almost pressed against it. "We just want to have a bit of a chat."

The door opened. "About?"

Blanche squared her shoulders. "Hello!" She smiled, her best and brightest. "We're just visiting. From Florida?"

Mary started to retreat, again, when Blanche put her foot on the threshold. "Now, what if we had some church business? You're the secretary, are you not?"

"Yes, I am." The door swung open. The cat slinked out of the house and twirled itself around Blanche's leg, meowing like crazy.

"Kitty must like Linzers. What a sweetie." Blanche leaned down and tickled the calico behind its ears. It rubbed her leg furiously. Mary's expression broke into the hint of a smile.

"She usually doesn't like people."

"Well, I'm people. And this is my cousin, Haasi Hakla." Blanche thrust the box at Mary. "We'd love to have a short visit with you. That is, if you have a minute." Haasi seemed to be doing her best to be in pleasant agreement, but barely.

Mary huffed, her deep-blue expression drifting from Blanche to Haasi. She finally stepped aside and extended her arm in a half-hearted welcome. She looked down at the cat. "Come on, Dolly. Let the ladies pass."

Blanche and Haasi followed Mary and Dolly into the dim entry that opened onto a surprisingly bright sitting room. The peat fire glowed—Blanche was getting used to that earthy, comforting scent—and a small sofa and chairs covered in crocheted shawls snuggled around the hearth.

"Please." Mary pointed to the seating arrangement. A woman of few words, and slow gestures. She took the box from Blanche. "Thank ye. I'll just bring us some tea now and put this on a plate. 'Twas kind of ye."

Dolly sat on her haunches in front of the fire. The cat lazily scanned the visitors and the room, and then she went over and curled down into a puddle of reddish fur at Blanche's feet.

"What are you now, Blanche? The cat whisperer?" Haasi gave her a wry look.

"I guess. Whatever works. Maybe she likes my soap?" She patted Dolly on the head, and she meowed in appreciation.

Haasi shifted about on the over-stuffed chair. She spoke through her teeth, only her lips moving. "Blanche, what are we doing here?"

"Trust me."

"Right."

Mary shuffled into the parlor with the tea tray, her face a grim sight. Blanche thought quickly about her next move. "Here. Mary, let me help."

"'Tis fine," she said, brushing past Blanche and setting the tray on the table with a clatter. She'd arranged the pastry on a china plate. "And thank ye again fer the Linzers. Actually, a favorite of mine." Dolly circled the table legs.

"Guess Dolly likes them, too." Haasi could be adept at thawing a conversation—when she chose to do so. Blanche silently thanked her sister-cousin.

They each settled back with cup and saucer, Mary with a sigh, all of them looking blankly at the fire. Her eyes were not those of a happy person. Blanche felt sorry for her. "Mary," she said quietly. "Really appreciate you letting us visit."

"Well, what is it I can do fer ye? I'm sure it's not church business like ye said."

"You're right. I need to talk with you."

Mary raised her eyebrows. "And I just bet ye do."

"It's about Declan."

"I heard." Mary's lips quivered at the mention of his name. Something closed off behind her eyes.

Blanche sipped and took a bite of the pastry. Dry to her taste, it sat like a lump at the back of her throat. *This is not going well.*

"Look." Blanche swallowed. She bent and picked up the cat and began pacing the room. "I'm sorry to invade your privacy. But this Declan has more or less invaded *ours*."

"And how is that? Why, you've hardly been in Ballycill but a short time—and Declan's dead!"

"How did you know all that?" Blanche blurted.

"This is a very small place, Ballycill. You know that much. Declan was murdered, in the kitchen of the castle—*yer* castle."

"It's your castle, too. The McLoughlins meant for the village to benefit from the running of it."

"They were a fine people, they were. It's sad what happened to the young William."

"But not to Declan."

Mary looked at Blanche sharply. "I didn't wish him dead though I can say I'm in the minority." Dolly, oblivious, purred loudly in Blanche's arms.

"I'll get to the point. I want to be honest with you." Blanche lowered her voice and stopped pacing. The cat leapt from her arms and climbed into Mary's lap. "I heard something of your past, and that's why I'm here. I think you might be able to help."

"Duchess," Haasi murmured.

"I know, Haas. But I gotta get on with it." Blanche resumed her seat and leaned toward Mary who crossed her arms, tightly. "Please, Mary. I know Declan was not good to you. And in death, he's doing a number on *me*."

Mary had seemed patient. Up to a point. Now she looked surprised. "What do you mean?"

Blanche clenched her fingers in her lap. "I'm under suspicion. In Ireland little more than a day, and the gardai have me on the list of suspects!"

"*Why would you kill Declan O'Brian?*"

"Precisely. Makes no sense at all." Blanche felt obligated to divulge. "Except that my fingerprints were on the knife … the one in his back."

Mary's eyebrows shot up.

"He'd given us a kitchen tour, and I'd handled the knife—and it somehow got stuck in him!"

"Strange, the gardai would go after you," Mary said. "You are the least of those who would have motive. There are plenty in this village who hated him. It's a long list. But I'm not on it. Let me tell you, I was no fan of Declan O'Brian, but I had my reasons."

"Reasons? For wanting him dead? Or wanting him alive?"

"Alive is always better than dead, now, isn't it, Miss Blanche?" Her tone had a wry twist.

"Well, I don't know. Consider the circumstances. It seems to me the village is better off without him and his toxic influence. He had a way of stirring people's temper. I could tell that, and I only knew him a day."

"He did have a temper," Haasi added, between bites.

"But, Mary, you do regret his … demise?" Blanche asked.

"Yes, reluctantly," said Mary. "Like I said, everyone has reasons. For everything. And I had mine."

Blanche backed off for now. She'd come around later. She was intrigued at the assortment of motives and sentiments among the villagers of Ballycill. She was desperate to sort them out. Declan was reviled—and somewhat held in weird esteem, perhaps managing to hold a place of respectable authority among some. And Mary had *reasons.* Blanche could only imagine the demands and emotions the deceased castle agent had stirred up.

Haasi dropped four lumps of sugar in her tea. "Mary, we need more on him. Like Blanche says, there's this cloud of suspicion hanging about. Is there anything you can tell us that would be useful in clearing Blanche? Seems he was not good to you, but we can't let this rest. And I'm sorry to bug you, but we need to get to the bottom of this. Altogether."

"The cad. Alive, or dead. It just doesn't stop." Mary stood up and went to the window, her back to Blanche and Haasi. They waited, their teacups suspended.

Blanche would have loved something stronger than tea, but this would do. The afternoon custom was so *civilized,* and she wondered at the Celts who held hospitality in high esteem but could slay hundreds at a turn—or just one at a time in the kitchen of a castle. She looked around the room. A single, framed photo of an old-fashioned couple, stacks of assorted books, a brass candlestick. Her home was spare and neat but somehow cheerless. At least, there was not a clue here that even hinted Declan had haunted Mary's life.

She was still turned toward the window. Her shoulders began working up and down, and then she was shaking, her head bent. Blanche shot Haasi a look. "Uh-oh."

Blanche went over and lightly touched Mary's shoulder. "I've opened it up now. I'm sorry, Mary."

"It's always open. It never heals. Never goes away." She put her face in her hands.

"Mary, I saw you at Declan's wake." Blanche had suspected it was Mary, and now she was sure. She was the woman in the shadow near the window, expressionless and still, just watching.

"Ye did. Something about that man. I couldn't let him go, not in life or in death. He's stuck with me. I had to see him dead that day at Barrett's. To put him to rest. Finally. But it'll never work that he's truly gone."

"Again, I'm really sorry." Blanche frowned. What could she say that would take away even a bit of Mary's pain? Nothing. She'd been carrying it so long it had become a part of her.

"He said he was sorry, too. Everyone is sorry." That bitter tone again. She pulled a handkerchief out of her pocket and blew her nose. Now that she was animated, Blanche could see the younger Mary, a woman with a fine oval face and passion in her dark eyes, once formerly in love and now doused of all those warm feelings.

Haasi came over and spoke in a whisper. "He's dead, Mary. He treated you badly. And others, too. But we have to move on, together. Will you help us? Please?" Haasi had a way about her, soft yet insistent; Blanche had to control a tendency to sound demanding instead of coaxing.

Mary let out a sigh. She raised her hands, deflated. "What could I possibly say or do that would make a difference? What do you want?"

"Want? Or *need*?" Haasi's question hung in the air. She took Mary's arm and led her back to the chair in front of the fireplace. Haasi poured her a cup of tea and then went to stoke the embers in the grate. It still felt cold in that room.

"Are you chilly, Mary?" Haasi took a shawl from another chair and put it across Mary's knees. At that gesture, the look on her face—again, one of surprise—spoke volumes and begged the question: *How many people have been kind to her?*

Blanche held her tongue. The minutes passed; the cat purred. The three bonded around the comfort of tea, and contemplation, and the fire that burst to life.

"I met him through my father." Mary began, her fingers twisting the crocheted shawl. "Declan was young, a rugby player, the most handsome man I'd ever seen. The blue eyes—and that black hair. Always unruly. Just like him. I loved to run my fingers through it, thick and black and shiny …" Her throat seemed to catch, then she scoffed. "I was in school, a child, barely seventeen. High school, I think the Yanks call it. I don't know why he looked at me. A book worm, a quiet person. I was really quite unpopular, if I do say so myself." A lost look crossed her face. "I never came out of myself, is all. Until I met him. He had a way about him. He made me think I was … beautiful. It's the oldest, stupidest story, and I fell right into it." She sounded bitter at the harsh memory.

Blanche hoped that wasn't the last word. She caught Mary's gaze and held it. The hearth crackled, Dolly mewed and circled, the air was close and redolent of spice from the teapot.

Mary looked away, but a kind of vitality still sparked her expression. "I got pregnant, of course. Everyone knows that, and Declan's dad would have none of *that* in the village. A blot on that son of his. Despite his little plan—originally—to have Declan marry the banker's daughter. *Me.* Declan wasn't about to marry me. I know that now. He never intended to. His father made arrangements to send me away to a home in Dublin to have the child, and I had little choice. No choice, at all. I'd planned to stay in the city and raise my child though I can't know what I was thinking. A single mother with no connections and no prospects? My father was disappointed, and I was ashamed…

"It was an easy pregnancy, an easy birth, and I had hope for a new life, with or without Declan. But when I awoke from the birth—they drugged me, ye know, it was desperate. The baby was gone. They wouldn't tell me a *thing*, not even the gender. It was as if everything inside me, ever, was ripped away, and I wanted to die. Finally, I came to wonder if Declan and his father had something to do with taking the child. They wouldn't say."

"Oh, Mary," said Blanche.

"Ye have no idea what it feels like. A door closing like that, forever." Her words were hard, hopeless. Then she let down, her shoulders drooped. Blanche let this sorry moment sink in. *Shared grief is grief by half?* Again, her grandmother's words came to her.

Mary reached for the tea and looked from Haasi to Blanche. "Yer so kind, I see that, and I know ye mean well."

Blanche sat back. "We do. At least, we mean to, Mary."

"How can I help?" Her voice was small, resigned.

"Well, you're helping clear up some of the mystery around Declan. He and his father seem like they were completely out for themselves. Even to the exclusion of the little one." Blanche began to feel more anger than sympathy. "How did you come to live here? At St. Columba's? Did Declan or his father have something to do with that?"

"No. My father made the new living arrangements. We'd fallen out, but he relented and helped me," Mary said. "The priest here, Father Joe, was generous and welcoming. I needed the help, and I couldn't stay in Dublin, not with all the sadness. I had a cousin here, so I came back, and eventually started working—and staying to myself, mostly. It hasn't been all that bad. Except that it's a small village, and Declan was always in it. *Somewhere.*" She forced a defiant little smile.

"Do you feel better talking about it, Mary?" Blanche chose her words.

Haasi smiled. She hadn't taken her eyes off Mary. "Bet ya do."

Mary picked up Dolly and combed her fingers over the cat's furry head, a bit aggressively. The cat squirmed. Mary nodded. "Declan's dead, and so is his father. What's done is done, I suppose." She turned to Blanche. "I need to deal with the living. Now. Tell me. Surely my past with Declan has nothing to do with you finding him stabbed dead in yer kitchen in the wee hours of the mornin'. I'm after tellin' ye now, my story doesn't have a thing to do with it."

"Wow, you know all *that*. Word does travel around here."

"Like I says to ye. It's a small place. Secrets and gossip and details fly about, they do." Mary said. "And the truth, sometimes. Though it's hard to separate all of it."

"What can you tell us about *him*? His habits? Quirks? How did he spend his time?"

"The talky vine says he worked hard, or made it look like he did. His athletic background drove him to exercise and keep a schedule. Don't believe he knew *shite* about managing estate affairs, but his father got him the job as agent at the castle, as ye know. He put up a fine front, Declan O'Brian did."

"Does seem strange, but then, the father's bank was tied to the McLoughlins, and Declan's father was looking to place him in a good job. That part seems to fit. But how could that job happen after the rumors that Declan had something to do with the drowning of William the nephew? I can't think the estate would have anything to do with him after that story went around."

"The rumor was quashed. Real good." Mary gave Blanche a quizzical look. "But, to tell the truth, I always wondered. A lot of the people did—and do. What was Declan doing that day on the river?"

"Yeah, I wonder, too," said Haasi. "And the banker and the money? Seems that was at the center of it. Follow the money, and the power."

"Indeed," said Mary. "That makes sense and so little does. But how to follow up? Especially at this point. The father and son are dead, and so are the McLoughlins."

"Why don't we back up. Declan got the job. How the heck could he keep it after what he did to you, Mary?" Blanche chose her words, steering back to Declan's position.

"Ha! Just the look of him! I tell ye, he had a way. He was fully ensconced as agent by the time I got back. The McLoughlins were gone, and his father was practically running that board at the company that oversaw the castle affairs. Where were they going to get someone else? Over the heads of all those types?"

"I suppose," said Blanche. "Seems like a tight-knit bunch."

"You said it."

"Anything else about Declan? Besides his scheduling, and exercise? Maybe—habits? Did he have any hobbies?" Blanche clung to the idea there was more.

"Pfffft," she said, bitterly. "Hobbies? He did like to dress up, so dandified, and buy them fine wines, so they say in the shops that orders it from France. And anything with a skirt! There he was, dancing around with his sweet talk."

"Wining and dining the ladies. I get the idea." Blanche leaned forward; the teacup precariously balanced on her knee. "Anything more?"

Mary gazed into the embers. "He did fancy himself a writer, there is that. Even at a young age he compared himself to Bernard Shaw and Jonathan Swift. *What a joke!* Always writing in his journals, his stories and essays. Tried to get himself published, he did. But he was rejected out of hand from what I could tell. He painted another picture, of course, but one time, a long time ago, I saw the pile of letters. And once or twice I peeked in his journals. A regular *gobshite*, he was."

"Well, now, isn't that interesting. Declan, the *gobshite* writer," said Blanche. "What sort of writer is that?"

"Vulgar? For *shite*?"

"Made for him," said Haasi, cryptically.

Blanche was already thinking about what she could do with Mary's revelation. She imagined the narcissistic Declan O'Brian jotting down the inner-most thoughts of his exploits and desires. Writers always got back to that—their *innards*. Blanche, the writer, knew a thing or two about that activity. She knew what a deep dive writing could produce into thoughts and feelings because she'd been there and done lots of that.

Declan, the keeper of journals and diaries, stories and essays? Hmmmmm.

Blanche glanced at Haasi. Her expression was flat; she was being her particularly unreadable self. But Blanche could read that face. They needed to compare notes.

Blanche was itching for a *tete-a-tete*. The spark of an idea was about to burst into flame, and even though she anticipated Haasi's reluctance, there was no way around it. She couldn't let it go. She'd definitely need Haasi on board for this one. Blanche could just hear it now: *Oh, Duchess.*

Thirteen

Rumor Has It

BLANCHE'S NEWLY HATCHED IDEA stayed with her, but it would have to wait. Haasi was still wrapped around the meeting with Mary, who had hugged them goodbye, thanked them for coming, and promised to visit the castle soon.

"Blanche," said Haasi. "That was bad. I feel so awful for Mary." The two walked along the narrow sidewalk through Ballycill toward the castle. The strings of "… there's whiskey in the jar …" poured out of Barrett's pub, and the aroma of bread and soup wafted from Nora's cafe across the street. The Irish hurried to drink and dinner.

"I know. She's had a rough patch of it," said Blanche, distractedly. "We should follow up with her, you know, about Declan and his hobbies and stuff."

"Well, I'm not so sure she'd appreciate it too soon. We really stirred it up in there."

"She came around, and I think she was even relieved to talk about it."

"Probably. There must have been something cathartic in it for her."

"I love Dolly, the cat! I think I'd like to get a cat, Haas." Blanche picked up her step.

"Blanche! It'd be out there chasing the gulls and scratching in the sand and you'd be sneezing your head off. You have allergies, don't you?"

"Maybe. But Dolly is sweet, and she certainly knows how to

introduce guests. If it hadn't been for the cat, don't know if we'd gotten in the door."

"The Linzers helped. Yum. Better than the cat. Now I'm getting hungry."

"Oh, Haas. But we do need to see Mary again."

"B. Why can't you let this go? I don't see how disturbing her peace will help."

"The girl's in the pits. And I think we have a little something in common."

"Oh, Duchess."

They were walking fast. They'd promised Una they'd be back for a late dinner, but now Blanche slowed her step and put her hand on Haasi's arm. "Doncha' think that was insightful? The stuff she told us about Declan? We could do something with that."

"We could? It was good background, but I don't see how any of it's going to get you out of this mess. Once and for all."

Blanche looked at Haasi sideways. They were walking along a long stucco wall near the center of the village. She drew Haasi over, and they sat together. "Just look at how everything grows here. Kinda like Florida but not really."

"OK, Blanche, I'm sure you don't want to talk about ivy and petunias. What's up?"

"I have an idea."

"Just what we need." Haasi gave Blanche a gentle poke.

"Declan was a writer. From the way Mary described it, I think 'writer' is a relative term. But he wrote."

"Uh-huh. So what? You write, too. Excellent articles for the paper, and that book you're always working on. What's Declan's writing got to do with it?"

"Journals, Haas. Mary said he kept journals. What do you suppose you put on those kinds of pages?"

"Your inner most thoughts and dreams and plans—and deeds?"

"Ta-da."

"You do not want to be in the brain of Declan O'Brian. From what I've heard, it was a cesspool in there."

"I don't want to *stay* there. I just want to have a peek around."

"Peek and run. 'Fraid that train has left the station."

Blanche popped up. The wall was near the roadway. Haasi pulled Blanche back onto her seat before a Honda flattened her sister-cousin. "Bang! Will you be careful?"

"I know. I will. When we go over to Declan's house and have a look in his apartment, or house. Or wherever it is he holed up." Blanche's words ran together in a stream, or more like a tidal wave.

"*What* are you talking about? We are not going to Declan's house. I'm sure the police are all over that place."

"There are few police here. Quiet, sleepy little Ballycill. From what I can tell, there must be only a few for the whole townland. They've got things to do—other than hang out at a dead man's house."

"Blanche. They have a team of investigators from district working on this. It would only take one walking in on us. And then we'd both be in the clink." Haasi sulked. She always did when she was losing ground with Blanche.

"Listen. We'll be quick about it. Just look around, see if we can find anything. If we're lucky, bet we'd find things that would be *extremely* helpful. Like journals, notes. Don't you think? I get excited just thinking about it."

"Bet you do. Declan would be happy to know he got you excited," said Haasi. "But *think,* Bang. We'd be lucky if we didn't get arrested, or shot." Haasi sat back and crossed her arms. "You want to break into Declan's house. You are crazy."

"Hmmm."

They continued their walk back to the castle from downtown Ballycill and their meeting with Mary. There was plenty of time between steps for Haasi to talk Blanche out of her nutty plan, but nothing happened in that department. Blanche stole a glance at Haasi. She was deep in thought. And Blanche wouldn't budge. She stayed cool, and positive. Haasi could understand *positive.* "Just a peek and run, Haas."

Blanche was itching to get the goods on Declan, one way or the other, and his writings were just sitting there. *Somewhere.* It was a huge temptation, one that Blanche could not tamp down.

"Blanche, I really don't think it's a good idea. Breaking and entering."

"Why do you have to put such a fine point on things?"

"'Cause I do. It's bad enough that we might get caught. We need to avoid *that*. At all costs. But if I join you, and you have another charge—on top of murder ..."

"Haas, stop making sense again."

"Well, someone has to."

Blanche walked fast and talked even faster. Haasi, gently, pulled at her arm. "Why don't we just let the gardai figure it all out? We could drop the thing in their laps. Just tell them Declan was a writer of sorts. We don't have to give them a lot of details about how we came up with the info. Let them pursue that angle. They can check it out for themselves."

"Maybe. But listen, Haas. I got reasons."

"Oh. Sigh. You always have reasons!"

"I don't like this dark cloud hanging out there over my head. Besides, did you ever consider? Whoever did Declan in is still on the loose. Who's to say? What if the killer strikes again? And then, on top of it all, this business about William still nags me. They say they closed the case years ago, but I don't know. It doesn't sit well."

"Bang. Look at it this way: If Leary and Nobegly and his crew had found something, they would have acted on it. And if the investigators really had something on you, besides fingerprints that were obviously placed in full view—and at Declan's invitation—don't you think he would have taken you in? Just relax."

Blanche's brain cells were clicking like mad. A dog sat near a cottage gate and barked at her. She looked at the dog: "Yeah, I agree. It's something to bark about."

Haasi kept walking, then turned around. "Now what?"

Blanche was at a dead stop, hands on hips. "You just said something."

"I said a lot of stuff. *What* did I say?"

"... *at Declan's invitation* ..."

"So?"

"Why did he 'invite' me to pick up that knife? Why was he so insistent? He really wanted my fingerprints on the thing. I thought it odd at the time but didn't give it much thought. Not until *now*."

"Well, maybe he just wanted you to get the heft of this fine kitchen tool. I don't know. Come on."

Blanche strode ahead in step with Haasi. "The guy was one manipulative SOB. Has to be more to it than *heft*. He knew I wasn't going to chop carrots, or something. We gotta talk to Una."

"You sure are the talky person. Mary, Una—and you said you wanted to talk to that Tony, too."

"It can't hurt. It's what I do."

"Yup."

Una met them in their favorite part of the castle, a small drawing room with a fireplace, walls of books and art objects, and a view of a garden through the French doors. The brilliant green against the gray mist was a fervent contrast to the jungle green and blue sky at home in Florida on Santa Maria Island. But Ireland had its soothing charms, and Blanche needed some of that. She opened the door to the garden and breathed in the clean, soft air.

"Dinner will be at eight, Miss Blanche?" Una set down a tray of appetizers, sherry, and small stemmed glasses on the low table in front of the fireplace. "Mae and Nancy have the kitchen in order now. She's after preparin' steak and *pomme frites*. I believe that's a favorite of Americans—steak and fried potatoes? And a lovely salad of bib and radish from the garden."

"Oh, that's great," said Blanche, heading for the sofa. Haasi was warming herself at the low peat fire. After their walk, the afternoon had turned chilly.

"Thank you, Una. You think of everything!" Blanche grinned at the array of salmon, fresh bread, cream, and chopped chives. She picked up a small round of bread. "Can you stay and chat?"

"Oh, certainly. It's me pleasure."

"I think the pleasure is ours." Haasi smiled. "You take such good care, Una."

"I wish I had been a wee bit better at it," she said, sitting on the edge of a chintz-covered armchair. Her gaze drifted. Blanche offered the tray, but she declined. She took a glass of sherry.

"How so?" Haasi selected a slice of salmon and deposited it on a small china plate.

"I feel partly responsible for your involvement in this Declan situation."

"Really?" Haasi and Blanche responded in unison.

"I should have put off that detective." She huffed, dismissively. "Oh, he's a persnickety one."

"I guess he's just doing his job. Can't be avoided with the murder." There was no conviction in Blanche's tone. "I get so worked up, and I shouldn't. Declan was found in our kitchen, after all. And that knife …" She took a large sip of sherry, a lovely dry sip that warmed her mood. "This is so very nice."

"Oh, we Irish have a way with the drink. So they say." A rare chuckle lifted Una's thin cheeks. The small glass seemed lost in her large grip. "It's been quite a time of it for ye, now, hasn't it."

"It has. And this business with Declan is a dark cloud."

"That would be Declan O'Brian in a word." Una took a sip of the sherry.

"Una." Blanche scooted forward, her knees touching the glass edge of the coffee table. "Tell me, please. Do you think Declan had anything to do with William's drowning?"

Una sat back and exhaled sharply. "They couldn't prove a thing, the gardai. They tried though, first with Declan, of course. They went through the townland, one by one, they did. Had an investigator from Dublin turn it all inside out! Then, as suddenly as the awful thing happened, the business went away. That's how it often is with tragedy. It just goes away, and there's not a thing one can do about it. People don't want to be reminded." A look of sadness crossed her expression. "It was a long time ago."

"I heard the argument you were having with Declan." Blanche spoke softly, earnestly. "I couldn't help but hear. That afternoon, late, after we got in. You said you had something on him."

She scoffed. "I couldn't prove anything about the misdeeds of that Declan O'Brian. But I live with my suspicions, I do." She tossed her head, a bitter tone creeping into her words.

"Did the argument have something to do with William?"

"Everything has to do with William. He was a grand boy, doncha' know."

"You took care of him? As a young one?"

"Like he was my own. Aye, he was a darlin'. And the colonel, a fine man."

"How so. Tell me, please."

"The colonel died in 1954 at the age of eighty-six," she said, wistfully. "He'd been born late in his father's life as was often the custom with many Irish bachelors who marry into their fifties and sixties. William the nephew was barely a toddler when the colonel died, but he grew up hearing of how the British came to Ireland, cut down what little trees there were, and took over the farms."

"They lived with that history," Blanche murmured. "Endured it." Again, she tried to imagine her own family heritage, but she felt as far removed as the moon.

"The hills are watered with tears," said Una, her eyes glistening with age and memory. "But we're used to it. The invasions. The grand one with the Normans in the twelfth century. The colonel grew up in chaos at the turn of the century when Ireland was achieving independence from the Crown. It was a time of great upset, and he was right there in the middle."

"And he joined the British army? That seems so strange," said Blanche. Haasi nodded, her eye on Una, the salmon forgotten.

"He did, indeed, and not so strange. It was a common path for those with land and education. It's an irony, isn't it? But he was staunchly Irish, descended from invaders and Irish chieftains. The McLoughlins were more 'Irish than the Irish' in their love for the Republic." Una smiled, suddenly contemplative at this outpouring of history. "We Irish are a strange personality, don't you think?"

Blanche smiled. "I'd say you have that right, Miss Una. Sometimes you never know which side will turn up."

Haasi nudged Blanche. "I'll say."

"What do you mean?" Blanche feigned shock.

"I'm saying you have more sides than a Rubik's Cube." Haasi grinned. "And I wouldn't have it any other way."

"*Sláinte!*" said Una, raising her glass. "To the McLoughlins, and the

Murninghans. Beyond the pale, so to speak."

"Beyond the pale?"

"It's an expression, probably British in origin. Beyond the pale was the place beyond the sphere of Dublin, or the 'black pool,' as the city was named by the conquering Vikings in the eleventh century. The colonel's reach was beyond his village and castle; he loved his country and traveled often, representing Ireland. In France, he met and married the French Caroline Marintette, a distant cousin of Henry of Navarre. They came back to Ireland and rebuilt Dunfaedan. He made it his business to stay in the service and work within the system, provide employment here and give back to the village.

"The colonel's father fed many families during the famine of the 1840s and after. Years later, no one questioned the colonel who continued to donate from the military stores. He had close friends all the way up the chain of command, even to the throne itself. It was said he had stories on them; others said he was simply a good man who hated the subjugation, humiliation, and theft of the Irish people." Una sat back, her shoulders hunched in that same gray cardigan. "A gracious man, and so was his nephew."

"And William the nephew?"

"A happy soul, he was. Much lighter in manner and speech than the colonel. And how he loved the horses. And the ladies loved him, but he never settled down. Worked about the estate and traveled. Oh, it was such a tragic day, he drowned in that damnable river." She took a sip and shook her head. "A sad day. Young and handsome, in his early twenties, he was. More than twenty-five years ago, and I mourn it like it was yesterday."

"And Declan." Blanche pressed on. "What about those rumors he had something to do with the drowning?"

"He was on the banks that day. And several of the lads were witness to it but no one would talk about it, or they couldn't. They'd been playin' about—some say they'd had a jar or two. But that's all I know." She sat back, wrapping her sweater around her tightly.

"It just doesn't seem right someone didn't see something and give the police a straight answer."

"Aye, Miss Blanche," she said, a bit sharply. "It didn't happen, and what good would it do now? It does no good to raise the dead, does it?" She crossed herself, then twined her fingers in her lap.

Blanche picked up her sherry. She went over to the fireplace, sipping thoughtfully. Haasi busily picked at the tray. She appeared to ignore the conversation, but Blanche knew otherwise.

"Una," said Blanche, turning abruptly. "Again. That argument I overhead between you and Declan—right after we arrived. He wasn't happy when you suggested he might be replaced here as agent."

Surprise played across Una's face. *Feigned?* She smiled, nervously, and looked away. "So, you heard all that, did you? The man was a darkness. I can tell you now."

"But you did have something on him?"

"I had no proof, just this Irish intuition of mine and me old ears to the ground and many a rumor running around in Ballycill." She looked up at Blanche. "There's that then—I do believe he meant to do me in."

"*What?*" Blanche sat down next to Una, and Haasi stopped chewing.

"I do. I believe it." Una tossed her head. "He warn't the kind to brook patience, ya know. He wanted me gone as much as I wanted him gone."

"Una, did he try anything?"

She seemed distracted. "In all those days, not that I know of. But I feared it, deep down, I feared him."

"Where did Declan live?" Blanche spoke coolly, insistently. Haasi popped a cheese cube and studied Una.

"Well, yer not gonna go visiting ghosts now, are ye? Wouldn't do ye a bit of good."

"If I never see Declan again it will be a good thing," said Blanche. "Dead or alive."

Una's bushy eyebrows shot up, her eyes open and clear. "Now, that would be something."

Blanche stole a glance at Haasi, who was busy with salmon and chives. "It would be nice to take a drive out that way, don't you think? I'd love to see more of the area. So would Haasi."

"'Tis a pretty drive and a lovely place for ye to visit, in any case. Declan's house is near Ballybunion with the beach a short distance away. I know how ye love the beach. He had a cottage here on the castle grounds but hardly spent time in it—loved the sea air, he'd say, and 'tis a grand spot. Ye can't miss the house of Declan O'Brian just beyond the hill near the crossing of the pub and the church down toward the shore. Ye can ask about it if ye get lost. They all know the house of the scoundrel, Declan O'Brian."

Fourteen

Cellblock Blues

THE POUNDING WAS STEADY, and not unlike the sound of boots on a wooden floor. But it wasn't boots; it was the front door, and the noise echoed through the castle. Blanche awoke out of a perfectly lovely dream of waves crashing onto the shore under a brilliant pre-hurricane sky—one of her very favorite weather events on Santa Maria Island. The sun always shone before the big hit, calm and lovely—and deceptive. But she was a long way from Florida, she realized, waking up and looking out the window at the misty Irish morning.

She threw the covers aside and stood on the plushy rug next to the bed. Another day at the castle, another loud wake-up call. *What is it this time? And it's only Day Four?* She was beginning to think the Irish had a particularly abrupt approach to mornings. A good shock to the system seemed in order, along with the caffeine.

She grabbed her robe and went out into the hall. Voices rose from the entry way. The rumble of authority grew louder from below, unpleasant and familiar. Detective Leary was back, and from the sound of it, he'd brought trouble with him. His singsong demands overtook Una's low, calm tone.

Haasi hurried down the hallway toward Blanche and stopped at the head of the stairs. She was dressed in black slacks and a white T-shirt, her hair wrapped in a crown of braids. She shrugged at Blanche. The two of them made their way down the steps.

"Can't wait to see what this is about," grumbled Haasi.

"Don't like the sound of it."

Una and Leary stood eyeing each other in the entry. The door was wide open, letting in gusts of cool air. Una looked up at Blanche with a dour expression and a nod, and Leary studied the rug, shifting his boots and jiggling a pair of handcuffs nervously.

"Really!" Una drew herself up several inches and stared at the handcuffs. "Do you need those things? Can't we discuss this over a cup of tea?"

"No need to discuss the matter, Miss Una. Me visit is a matter of form."

"Well then, do you think the hardware is necessary?"

Blanche and Haasi froze at the foot of the stairs.

Leary frowned. "Maybe not. Force of habit," he said. He folded the cuffs and put them in the pocket of his rumpled raincoat. It wasn't raining; Blanche assumed the raincoat had to be standard issue.

He looked straight at Blanche, then blurted: "Good morning."

"Good morning to you," she said stiffly.

"Ahem. Miss, I need to take you to district, if you don't mind. For questioning."

"Questioning? *Why?*" Blanche was barely awake, but anger and surprise gave her a rush. Mostly, she was furious.

"The business at hand. We have more areas of concern regarding the murder of Declan O'Brian, and you might be quite helpful in the investigation. No time to spare."

"That's crazy. Why would I know anything about his murder? I hardly knew him."

"You found him dead in the kitchen."

"So? We've been over that. So did several other people find him there." She was becoming heated the more they talked.

"Further, you may have been privy to his manner of running things about here, given prior research and information. And, further, and most importantly, your fingerprints are on the knife." He exhaled sharply, relieved of the burden of carrying this knowledge by himself.

"We know the circumstances surrounding the knife business. I picked one up in the kitchen—*at Declan O'Brian's invitation.*"

"Ah, yes, and that is all well and good and under review," he said. "But there is another matter come to light."

"Pray tell." She put her hands on her hips. Haasi, close at her side, was steamed, but she listened quietly.

"It seems Mr. Tony Costello overheard you arguing with Mr. O'Brian in the kitchen during the evening before the murder. Mr. Costello was making a delivery at the time. He said the words between you and Declan O'Brian were of an angry nature."

"You bet my words were of an angry nature."

Haasi put her hand on Blanche's shoulder. "Wait. Blanche. Just talk to him."

Blanche immediately deflated. She swallowed her seething remark and yanked the cord on her robe so tight she nearly cut off her breathing. "All right. Let's get this over with." She spit the words. "I'll get dressed and go down there with you. But I'm telling you, this is a bunch of *cow shite*."

Una looked grim, rolling her eyes toward the ceiling. She settled her hands over her middle.

Detective Leary worked hard on his composure. He was polished, but seemingly, he was dealing with an unusual circumstance. Murder was an uncommon occurrence. Ballycill was hardly the crime capital of Ireland. "I'm afraid it *is* necessary, and a matter of protocol." He rocked back on those large black boots. "These crime scenes grow cold fast. We need to be on top of things."

Haasi's hand was still on Blanche's arm. She'd cooled off as suddenly as she'd blown up. Leary was being patient, almost kind. He was just doing his job. Blanche determined to cut him some slack. "Detective Leary, I'll cooperate, and I hope I can help. But I doubt it."

He tucked his thumbs in his waistband. "If you'll just be puttin' some clothes on …" He blushed. "We can get on with it and be done and you can be back here to your fine castle."

Haasi pulled Blanche aside. "Just go with him," she said, a biting edge to her tone. "In the meantime, I'll see about getting Peter Flynn on it. Don't say a word until you see Flynn. I'll tell him you're on the way to district headquarters. I'm sure he knows where that is."

Leary's ears perked. He nodded. "That would be advisable, Miss. You certainly don't want to muddy the waters without some advice. Muddy enough already, it is."

112

Haasi turned her back and whispered to Blanche. "This is—what do they call it?—*cow shite*. We'll get you out of hot water. Just hold on."

"Please."

Blanche sat in a small room at district headquarters. The ride out to the Limerick office was pleasant enough if she closed her eyes and didn't think about sitting in a police wagon. Detective Leary apologized a hundred times for the inconvenience, but he said the questioning was for "administrative purposes" and every stone needed to be turned over, et cetera, et cetera. Blanche was not mollified though the investigators, and Peter Flynn, had been professional and kindly. It was an unusual situation—for all of them. She just wished they'd hurry up and spring her. She wanted to talk with Flynn. He'd gone off to Cork City and wasn't due back in the area until the afternoon.

In the meantime, Blanche slumped on the hard metal chair in the tiny gray room and tried to keep her anger from spiking. All she could see were Declan O'Brian's flirty lying eyes floating in her head, and all she could think about were the dirty tricks he'd played on Mary—and, most likely, on her own departed relative William McLoughlin. *And on me*. It drove her to drink, which she couldn't do, except for the tepid offering in a cracked pitcher on a tray. The place definitely had an odor, a mix of mildew and old food. She caught a peek into an adjoining room. A cot with a nasty rough blanket in the corner completed the amenities.

Detective Leary clomped into the room. "Miss Blanche, the investigator and Mr. Flynn are on the way. Once we have concluded our questioning and they have cleared it with the superintendent, you should be free to go." He seemed glum, and skittish, which made him just a little bit adorable. "For now. Free, I mean."

Blanche stood up. "Why can't I be free now?" she coaxed. Then, too late, it crossed her mind to shut her mouth, but that was not "Bang" Murninghan's way. "I don't think you can hold me. I didn't do anything, officer, and I really have nothing further to say about Declan O'Brian."

"It's a murder investigation. We're just following the preliminaries, the leads. Just." He shifted from one foot to the other. He cleared his throat, avoiding her eyes. "Can I get you a bit of tea while you wait? Shouldn't be but a wee moment. Or two."

"*I don't want any damn tea.*" She pounded the table and hurt her fist. She shook her hand. "Will you find out what's keeping the investigator?"

Stop, Blanche.

His demeanor changed to overly patient, and possibly tone-deaf. Blanche figured he was used to an Irish temper. "Now, Miss Blanche. Settle down. By and by, they'll be here, and in the meantime, we'll accommodate you best we can and you can be on your way. And, again, I'm sorry for the, er, arrangement." He looked around the room at the dismal set-up and backed away gradually and was gone.

Blanche flopped back onto the chair. She cast a wary eye at the cot with Irish fleas and lice that possibly nested there and might leap at her. "Can I at least have a newspaper or something?" she shouted.

Nothing. The heavy door at the end of the hall was shut tighter than the lid on a sewer. This was like being in a sewer, sunk in a deep, dark hole. *How do people survive in the system? For days? Years?* The thought of it made her shiver. She hoped she didn't have to find out the answer to that question. She was cured forever of becoming a criminal—for real.

Fifteen

She's Back

THE LAWYER, THE POLICE, AND BLANCHE sat in the small square room at district headquarters. It was time for questioning. Blanche was in no mood for it, but it had to be done, and she was anxious to get it over with. She'd spent the morning in a quandary, waiting for the attorney and the detective to show up, drinking bad tea—and fuming. Yet, she reminded herself to be grateful for the kindnesses the Irish had shown her and Haasi in the short time they'd been in Ireland. Blanche was *home* in the motherland, and she'd take it to heart. It was a difficult situation—with suspicion of murder hanging over her head—but she needed to put things in perspective. *This too shall pass. Thanks, Gran.*

Blanche shivered. She knew what else her grandmother would say: *Be sensible, Blanche. Count to ten, and don't tell all ya know.*

Detective Inspector Myles Flannigan of Dublin clenched his hands on the tabletop. He was a trim little man with a pencil mustache and slicked-back hair and a twitchy eyelid. "Seems there's been some new light shed upon the matter at hand."

All eyes were on the inspector from the murder squad. Blanche's fingers twisted the bottom of her shirt into a knot. Up to this point, the investigation had been tucked into the caseload of a team in Limerick. Now the four sat opposite each other on chairs securely fastened to the concrete; it was a rigid, uncomfortable meeting. Blanche tried to adjust her seating, to no avail. *What do they think I'm going to do? Throw this chair? What a good idea.* She pulled her thin jacket close. She was cold and clammy, and sweating the outcome. Didn't they know she was innocent? She coughed loudly. She had to get out of here.

Flannigan repeated himself over the burst of throat clearing and paper shuffling. He seemed as anxious as Blanche to get on with it. "*New light*," he said.

"Well, yes. I should hope so," said Flynn, imperiously. He didn't look the least bit imperious in his thick tweed jacket, hair like a bush, and green eyes that could not hide an inner merriment and kindness. In an aside, he said to Blanche, "I am sorry for the delay, Miss Blanche. I was held up in Cork City."

"Well, I'm so glad you're here. I hope you can *do something*." She choked out the words, quietly. Flynn raised his eyebrows.

"No problem, Mr. Flynn," said Leary.

"*No problem?*" Blanche bit her tongue, remembering her need for patience and her need *to try*. Leary gave her a level, unreadable look. Sometimes she was her own worst enemy with that mouth of hers. She shrank down in her seat, grateful that he seemed only mildly annoyed from the outburst, or maybe he was used to it from *criminals*. This was so frustrating. It was all a misunderstanding. They should adjourn now and go to lunch at the pub. Blanche looked around at these downturned faces. That was not happening.

Flannigan waved a folder and flapped it onto the table. "We have some new information. Just." He riffled through the paperwork and peered over it. "According to the coroner's preliminary report—which turned up today—Mr. O'Brian was killed at approximately two o'clock in the morning—give or take an hour. The temperature in the room may affect the exact timing of the murder itself."

Blanche sat up in the chair and thrust her arms onto the table. "What was Declan O'Brian doing in the kitchen at that hour?"

"We were hoping you might be able to tell *us*, Miss Murninghan. You had dinner with the deceased, and you were present in the castle at that hour," said Inspector Flannigan. He had just enough of a smirk to stir Blanche's anger. He tapped a fist on the table.

"I was sound asleep at that hour." She gritted her teeth.

Flannigan leaned forward. "Ah, but you heard something in the night. So it says in the notes."

"Well, briefly. Sounds. For maybe a few minutes. I went right back to sleep. Tony Costello had told us earlier there were deliveries 'round the clock' at the castle."

"So 'tis."

"I have no idea who or what was making the noise outside my window. I volunteered the information on the morning of the murder." She tried to keep the peevishness out of her voice and failed. "And I have no idea what Declan was doing in the kitchen."

"You didn't see him after dinner? Say, for a cozy drink or two? Some chat, say, in your … boudoir? I understand he suggested a nightcap."

Blanche could feel the color rising in her cheeks. "Yes, he suggested it and I declined. So did Haasi. We were tired after a day of travel and wanted to go to bed."

"And did you? Did he?"

Blanche shot up. She was furious. "What are you talking about?"

"Please, sit down." The detective's long index finger pointed to the chair. She sat.

"Where did you hear about our conversation with Declan?"

"What does that matter? We spoke with everyone in the castle, and we understand delivery people came up to the kitchen. The staff were aware of the evening plans and the comings and goings." His smarmy—oily?—tone lingered. Blanche wanted a shower.

"You must know then that Haasi and I left Declan well before midnight."

"On the surface of things, it seems so." Flannigan gathered the papers and tapped them into order. "Miss Blanche, now, what about the sound you heard outside your window during the night."

"Yes. It was dark, and late … I don't know."

"Hmmm." The detectives compared notes, mumbling back and forth. Flannigan consulted his notebook, flipped through it, and nodded his head. Leary crossed his arms on his chest.

"See here," said Attorney Flynn. "Miss Murninghan was in her room at that hour. And staff will attest to that."

"You may be right," said Flannigan. "Nancy Culpepper, the staff on hand at the castle, admitted to being awake, and she said that you, Miss Blanche, and Miss Haasi, were indeed in your quarters *around* the time of the murder. All of this is approximate, at the moment."

"It's unlikely we were the perpetrators."

"The matter will remain under investigation," he said, curtly.

"I do hope you settle it soon, because I had nothing to do with Declan's murder." Blanche leaned forward, her fingers splayed on the tabletop.

"So you say," said Flannigan.

"That'll be enough," said Flynn. "You need to follow up on all your other leads, detective. I think my client has heard quite enough now. You have nothing to hold her here. In fact, the staff can tell you all you need to know about the evening's events."

"The staff?" Blanche was puzzled. Actually, how much did they know? The castle was a wonderland of peace and calm and beauty, but there was something creepy about it, too. Ghosts lurked in the shadows, creaking and whistling, slamming a window here and there, rising across the lawn in shifting white clouds. Secrets. She couldn't shake the feeling that much of what she saw about the place covered some bad history.

"We questioned the staff and matched our findings with the time of death. Nancy says O'Brian lingered in one of the drawing rooms by the fire and had a drink or two, but we don't have an exact timeline. We need to question her further. And the others."

Blanche exhaled sharply. "Wait a minute. The staff were up and about? *No one heard anything more? Specifically?* That sounds awfully odd to me."

"Odd is the operative word." Peter Flynn interjected, quickly. "But it *is* a castle. The walls are quite thick, you know."

"Yes, it is quiet there. But sound travels, especially at that hour." said Blanche. *Sound travels and people have a tendency to keep their mouths shut. Not get involved.*

"This is all we have." Flannigan stood up abruptly and looked at his watch. "For now, with what we do have, including the time of death established, Miss Blanche, you are free to go."

"*Free?*"

"You are not *completely* cleared of involvement. You must remain on the premises. In Ireland. The case is far from closed," Flannigan added, hastily. He picked up his hat and twirled it. "T's to cross, et cetera. We are reviewing all the statements, and frankly, we have more to gather. There are details to comb through. But you can go. For now." He strode to the door and turned. "I must get back to Dublin. You will hear from us. Good luck to you."

It was late by the time Detective Leary returned Blanche to the castle. She sat uncomfortably silent during the ride back. The detective, with a quick glance or two in the rearview mirror at his passenger, white-knuckled the wheel of the police car. "I'm sorry for yer troubles, Miss Murninghan. But, believe me, we'll have this sorted out. We've got a crack team on it."

"I'm sure you're doing your best, but you know I had nothing to do with this."

"I am inclined to agree. But, ye see—"

"Yes. The formalities."

"Aye. Especially when there's a murder." He swerved around a bush hanging over the narrow road. Blanche saw the castle come into view. The day became brighter with the promise of beautiful food and a warm welcome from Haasi and Una—and freedom.

Blanche sat up. "I'm sorry. I've been curt, and disappointed. You're just doing your job. *But I didn't do this, and now I'm going to get out there and find out who did.*"

Leary jerked his head back. "*We* will do our best. Ye relax in yer fine castle and let us do our job." They climbed out of the police car, and Blanche lingered before walking off.

"May I ask you something?" She certainly hoped so.

"Why, of course." He seemed so eager to please, even when he couldn't.

"You must know about the death of my relative, William McLoughlin. Do you have any information about it? Any way I could find out more? How he drowned in that river?"

He took off his hat and scratched his head. "Aye, it was before my time, I'm afraid. I was just a wee lad when it occurred. But, I have to say, the tragic drowning spurred my interest in safety and law enforcement."

"How so?"

"Always wondered if more could have been done to investigate the circumstances, and prevent it in the first place. But the case was closed. Quite rapidly. Dublin got involved, and they put their stamp on that file. It was all sealed and done up tidy."

"And you don't have any ideas yourself? About the drowning?"

"Sadly, I don't." He put his hat on, nodded, and moved toward his car. "Now ye have a good evenin', Miss Blanche. Seems yer due."

"Sure. Right. Thanks."

Una answered the door to the castle. Her usually serious expression changed to a wreath of smiles as the heady scent wafted from the kitchen into the entry way. An aroma of something delicious mixed with the profusion of lilies on the hall table. "So good to see ye, Miss," said Una, her eyes avoiding scrutiny of Blanche's miserable expression and state of dress. "We'll be having the dinner for ye shortly. Now ye just have a rest and a nice wash."

"Oh, thank you, Una. Is Haasi about?"

"Oh, that she is." They looked up to the top of the stairs and there was Haasi's beaming face. Una laughed and padded back to the kitchen.

Blanche let out a sigh of relief as Haasi flew down the stairs and grabbed her in a hug.

"Am I ever glad to see you. How was it?" She held Blanche by the shoulders and shook her gently.

"Fine."

The short answer seemed to appease Haasi. "I hope you're hungry. Una's got these beautiful little potatoes and lamb shanks."

"Always thinking about that tiny stomach of yours." Blanche laughed. "And me." She was so glad to be "home," and back with her sister-cousin. "I'm hungry, all right. And thirsty."

"Jameson's neat." They went directly to the drawing room, their favorite among the fifteen or so rooms, and poured themselves a couple of whiskeys. They clinked glasses and silently sipped in front of the window, looking out at the trees and white benches, the trimmed hedge, and gravel path. *The gravel path. That sound in the night. I can't get it out of my head.*

"Gee, it's beautiful," said Haasi, wistfully.

"But it certainly has its dark side," said Blanche.

"Well, you know, the murder, the secrets. Seems we've turned up that dark side. Let's look on the bright side."

"Yes." Blanche sipped.

"We didn't do any of it. This mess was already here. Too bad we have to deal with it." Haasi sighed. "You did your duty over there. Now let's just get on with our visit." They both stared out at the quiet evening descending in shades of orange and pink.

"Did you ever see such … tiny gravel?" Blanche pointed through the French doors at the last of the path curling neatly around the back of the castle.

"Huh? Where did that come from?"

"I'm thinking about that night."

"Try not to, Blanche. It's lovely gravel, but don't obsess about it. It's not as nice as sand. Wow, I miss our sand."

Una appeared in the doorway. "If you like, I'll serve in the dining room about eight then," she said, smiling.

"Thanks, Una." Blanche drained the glass. Suddenly, she felt light-headed. She sat. "About twenty minutes then?"

Una nodded, and Blanche turned to Haasi. "We gotta talk."

"No kidding."

"First, I have to decompress and refresh." She poured half an inch more and downed it. "I've decided I'd make a terrible jailbird."

"I'll bet. No cold beer and no sand under your feet." Haasi sat in a large chintz-covered armchair, smiling. Obviously, she was glad to have her sidekick sprung.

Blanche shook her head. Haasi lifted her glass.

"Listen, Haas, I know this trip is turning into a nightmare. We'd talked about nice drives and lots of pubs, and I'm so sorry for all that's happened. Let's start all over."

"I just hope you can be clear of it, and we can get back to being tourists, not suspects in murder. Go clean up. I'm starved."

"That sounds normal."

Blanche found her suite in pristine order, looking like she'd never occupied the room. It gave her a tug of regret; how easily she'd been erased from the scene in such a short time. *That's kinda sad. But what the heck am I doing here?* Suddenly, she wanted to be back in her musty cabin on the beach, the gulls making a ruckus in the late afternoon, Liza, Jack, and Cap yapping at her over crab claws and key lime pie. And Emilio? She'd talked with him before she left, and she missed him. Maybe he'd be coming up from Mexico soon … to his murder-suspect girlfriend.

She was a fish out of water here. In Ireland. Yet, her grandmother had referred to this place as "home." *The Irish always do. The auld sod is "home."* Blanche was having a hard time getting the feel of that, especially under the circumstances. If it hadn't been for Maggie, and the welcoming nature of the pub owners and the staff at the castle. Even Mary and the detectives and Garda Handley and Declan O'Brian had their moments. They had been kind, and warm. *It's always the people that make or break a place. And I need to be patient.* She repeated it ten times.

She sighed and flopped on the bed. She needed to shower and change. Wash away the stench of suspicion. Get the whole experience out of her head. She did not want to go to prison.

Blanche was in and out of the sprayer in less than ten minutes and dressed in a light wool shift and flats. The hair was something else; she'd about given up on the curls and simply brushed and crimped the whole mess with her fingers. She walked back down to the drawing room. Haasi was still standing at the French doors looking out.

"What do you see, Haas?"

"I see brilliant, grand days ahead."

"Girl, what would I do without you."

The two went into the dining room and poured one more whiskey from the crystal decanter on the sideboard.

Blanche swirled her glass under her nose. She loved the smell of it almost as much as she loved the feel of it. But she needed to be careful. *In the middle stands virtue. Wow, I never seem to end up in that middle of anything except a murder.*

They wandered over to the window to look out over the demesne. The River Shannon sparkled in the distance and the rhododendron flourished along the drive. Mauve clouds hung over the landscape. The sight made Blanche catch her breath. It gave her a wave of appreciation despite the unknown. *You were right, Gran, about the magical beauty of this place. Now, help me, please …*

"B. I've been checking out some of the places we can visit." Haasi wore an emerald green dress belted with a thin leather strap and boots. "Maybe we'll get to it soon."

"Yes, let's. We're getting so Irish," said Blanche.

"I'll say." She raised her glass.

They stood in the window watching a raven dip into the trees. Blanche was reminded of the "cocktail hour" of gulls on the beach on Santa Maria, their frenzy before the sun went down. She sighed.

"Una says the demesne is covered with daffodils in the spring," Haasi said.

"You mean the lawn? The hill? The yard?"

"Yup, that stretch of green you see out there, and on it, daffodils as far as the eye can see. I can't imagine—I've never seen anything like *that*."

"Nope, we got lizards and hibiscus as far as the eye can see."

It could have been the alcohol, or it had to do with where she was from. Lately, she'd thought about where she was *really* from. She was Irish. This was her "home," as Gran called it, and, yet, it seemed so unfamiliar—and pretty sinister—despite the warm welcome.

"What's the matter with you, Blanche?"

"I feel so out of place. And old. Hundreds of years old."

"Blanche, you're barely thirty-four."

"I know, but there's something about Ireland. It's in my blood and heritage and all, but I feel like I have a fever of sorts."

"I hope you recover." Haasi tilted her head at Blanche and smiled. They both understood "blood" had surprising implications; they both had the same great grandmother, who'd had a fling with a Miccosukee Indian chief. Haasi was also Irish on her mother's side, but Native American Irish. To Blanche, that seemed *very* Irish for an island people who had assimilated visitors and conquerors from all over the world.

"Haas, does this place seem as foreign to you as the moon? Sometimes it does me."

"How would you know? Have you been to the moon?"

"Only what I see over the Gulf of Mexico."

"Yeah, foreign all right. But the people here are warm, the food is good, the sky and land are pure and fresh. I like it all right. And besides, it's ours, in a way, so I gotta love it."

"Oh, Haas."

"We need to finish this business and get back to the island. *Our island.* This one's nice and all but I prefer Santa Maria."

"Yup," said Blanche. "I hear you. The Gulf. The pines whispering, the waves crashing or just …"

"Now you're getting all nostalgic," said Haasi. She poured herself half an inch of whiskey and topped off Blanche's glass. "Remember the day we 'ran' into each other?"

"Hardly call that running. You were sitting cross-legged in a copse of Australian pines on the beach, chanting Miccosukee at the water. What? Three years ago?"

"Nearly four. Does seem faraway, doesn't it, with all we've done, all the places we've gone, and here we are on yet another adventure." Haasi turned to her. "What would life be without an adventure, or two?"

"I wouldn't know." They burst out laughing.

"Let's have some fun and get out of here." On cue, a flock of blackbirds flew out of the bush and over the river, disappearing into the mauve and cobalt sky.

"I'll say." Blanche sipped, pensive once again, her thoughts returning to their circumstances. "I can't help thinking. Why didn't the staff say something earlier to the police about our whereabouts that night? We weren't anywhere near Declan."

"So we say. The staff tried, but there's *protocol.* Leary said Dublin got involved, and they had to get together and go over every speck of detail. You know how that is, B."

"I do. I just don't understand the reluctance of the staff."

"I think Mae and Nancy were shocked and scared out of their wits. They needed a little prodding to speak up."

"Haasi? The great prodder?"

"Could be. And Una."

"What did you do?"

"Got hold of Garda Handley, and he contacted Leary. He had the staff fill in some more—about where we were at that hour. I wanted them to be sure to note how Declan wanted us on that tour, and you with that knife."

"I'm glad Una said something. She seemed so taciturn and dour and quiet!"

"Actually, she was super pissed they carted you off to the station like that. So rude, she said. But you know me. Piss me off once, not so good. Piss me off twice, well, things don't go well. Actually, I think I passed my threshold with that Declan. And, jeez, Blanche, you didn't kill him. I had to do something."

They clinked glasses. "Cheers, and thanks. Again." She smiled ruefully.

"Don't mention it, and don't even think of killing someone because then I don't know what I'd do."

"Haas!"

"Whiskey talking."

Blanche stared out at the dusky sky, the black outline of treetops. The window was open. The birds and cows communed in the early evening. "The questioning was not fun. That detective from Dublin insinuated stuff…"

"The business of heated words with Tony Costello didn't help any."

"Yup."

"They'll clear it up, B. They have to. And then we'll get out of here and look back and *laugh*."

"Ha. Ha." It was a dispirited attempt.

Una shuffled into the dining room and set a silver chafing dish on the sideboard. "Would ye like me to serve ye ladies?"

"No, no, Una. Thank you!" said Blanche. It was well after eight o'clock, and it had been a long, hard day. "Rest up!"

"Enjoy. It's grand you're back, Miss Blanche. This lovely lamb will settle yer stomach, and the police will settle their business soon. No doubt."

"Una, I know you talked to the police. About me. Thanks for that."

She smiled, less with contentment and more with resolve. "Police business. Sometimes they don't see the whole picture. Too tangled up in all their … tape, so they are." She shook her head and walked back to the kitchen.

Blanche looked after her, musing. "Now what do you suppose she meant by that?"

"By what?" Haasi was wandering up and down the buffet, salivating.

"The whole picture."

"Oh, glory, Blanche." Haasi eyed the glistening slice of lamb with its sprinkling of some sort of green garnish. Murder was clearly off her radar. "Only Una knows. Let's eat."

Once seated, they attacked the lamb, the sauteed peas, the brown bread. The wine poured, Haasi's eyes glowed as she mopped gravy with the bread. "How do they do it?"

"They know how to cook? Better them than me. I have trouble boiling an egg."

"Oh, I know. But one of the things I love about our adventures is the eating—while we stumble upon a dead body or two. Remember the *barbacoa* in Mexico City?"

"Remember eating hot dogs on Tuna Street?"

"Not to mention the tuna salad."

Blanche put her fork down with a determined click. She took a sip of the excellent Argentinian Malbec and swirled it around, deep in thought. She pushed her plate away.

"Uh-oh. Now what." Haasi poised the fork and knife on the edge of the gold-rimmed china. "You're off again. You've got that look. No more din-din for Blanche?"

"No more din-din. Will you just listen?"

"How can I not? I'm captive."

"Just a little bitty drive out Ballybunion way? In and out, so to speak? Just a peek around."

"Oh, all right, Blanche." Just a hint of exasperation peppered her tone. "Enough already. Like I said, I'm captive—to the charming way you suggest we get arrested and thrown in jail for trespassing on a dead person's property."

"You know that's not going to happen."

"With you, anything can happen."

Sixteen

Crazy Blood

THE NEXT MORNING, Haasi and Blanche finished their coffee—Haasi steeling herself for the trip out to Declan's, and Blanche raring to go.

Haasi said, "You mind if I take a turn around the block on the bike? I need to get the cobwebs out of my head before we attempt the drive out to Ballybunion. Too much whiskey last night. You're such a bad influence."

"I've been accused of worse. Of course. Go for it. I've got some notes to go over, and the menus for the rest of the week. And I want that recipe for homemade mayo."

"Glory. You'd do anything to get this Declan business out of your head." Haasi laughed, put her napkin on the chair, and waved. "I might take an hour then. See ya la-ta."

She wasn't gone five minutes when a commotion started up in the kitchen. Keys jangled. Una was crowing—with delight? Another female voice rose above the door shutting, feet moving, as the chatter worked its way toward the dining room. Blanche sat with coffee cup suspended. Haasi was right about the cobwebs; too much whiskey last night, and now this?

A loud female voice exclaimed: "Oh, my dear! What has happened? What a particular piece of *devilment!*"

Blanche shot up. Maggie Fitzpatrick McLoughlin bustled toward her, an outlandish red fuzzy cape flying about her shoulders. She carried a cake box. Una was right behind her, rattling her keys, and

127

speaking insistently. "Now, Miss Maggie, you must understand …"

"Oh, it's fine, Una." Blanche opened her arms for a hug. "Maggie! How great to see you!"

"The least I can do is pay my little cousin a visit." She swept around imperiously to Una.

"I'm sorry, Miss Blanche," said Una. "It's early and all. I wasn't expecting visitors."

"It's *fine*! Really."

Una smiled and huffed at Maggie and turned on her heel.

Maggie and Blanche couldn't help hiding a laugh. "She takes good care of ye, I can see," said Maggie. "Oh, it's giving me an attack of the perplexies, all this business with Declan and such. Can't imagine how yer holding up, dearie."

"I'm OK, come on. Sit."

Maggie flipped the cape and sailed toward the table, muttering and shaking her head. "Well, I certainly hope so. They better be quick about sorting it all out and leaving ye out of it. Enough already!"

"I agree. Have some coffee. Or tea?" Blanche pulled out a chair. "They promised they'd handle it swiftly. Some of this investigation happened so fast—the fingerprints and timeline. Other stuff, like the persons surrounding the whole thing, well, that's taking longer."

"I pray to the heavens then." Her agitation increased, the longer she fussed. The box tipped and quivered in her grip. She set it on the table and swept the cape off her shoulders. She softened her tone then. "Oh, I know the gardai are doing their duty, but it must be terrible fer ye."

"It's a mess, that's for sure." Blanche sighed. She just didn't want to think about it. She took a cup and saucer and the coffee pot from the sideboard and placed it in front of Maggie. "Cream and sugar?"

"Oh, a wee bit, to sweeten me up, doncha' know."

"And you'll have some of this fantastic cake that Nancy baked." She brought a silver tray with a dense, dark frosted ring of cinnamon, raisin, and nuts.

"Aye, now yer after makin' me little gift look like a dead rabbit." She chuckled and took a glorious mound of white frosted goodness out of the box and deposited it in front of Blanche.

"Haasi will have a heart attack of delight when she sees this. Maybe

I'll have a small one right now." She took a seat and beamed at Maggie.

Blanche didn't have any desire for food, but the cake looked scrumptious. "I'm so glad to see you, Maggie."

She took tiny sips and bites, arranged the folds of her voluminous skirt and perched on the edge of the chair. "The very idea ye had anything to do with that scoundrel's demise! Of all the things on this green earth! Crikey!"

Blanche held the coffee cup in two hands and was suddenly glum. "Tony Costello seems to think I was angry enough to kill Declan! I need to talk to Tony."

"Tony Costello doesn't know one end of the stick from 'tuther."

"Why would he say such a thing? That I was angry and such."

"Because he was asked? Did ye have a cross word with Declan?"

"Well, sort of ... But it wasn't anything of a murderous nature."

Maggie huffed. "Could hardly been enough of a row for ye—fresh off the plane—to stick a knife in him."

"I'm glad I have your support." Blanche gave in and pecked at a slice of cinnamon cake and just a taste of the lovely vanilla confection Maggie brought. "Yum, delicious!"

"Ye needed it now," said Maggie. She nibbled and savored, her thoughts drifting toward the open window between the heavy draperies. "'Tis such a lovely place, our townland and thereabouts. I hope ye get to enjoy it some before ye take off for Flar-da."

Blanche thought of their impending trip to Declan's for a peek around. She had enough sense to keep that to herself. "Oh, we will. We're planning a ride over to Ballybunion to the beach. When Haasi gets back. She's out taking a spin on the bike. Sorry you're missing her."

"She's a lovely sister-cousin, that one. So happy ye found each other." Maggie had a twinkle in her eye. "Good thing that great grandmother had the sense to fall in love. With the chief, was it? Ah, ain't love grand."

"Well, yes, it can be."

"Now I'm blathering on like the old bitty that I be. Me visit has more prongs than a fork. Was wanting to see ye, but I also come to tell ye a few things. I've had a chat or two at Barrett's and around the center. Seems Declan's murder has stirred up all sorts of memories—and ghosts."

"Ghosts?"

"The young and handsome William McLoughlin, for one. Rumors are flying."

"How? What? *Why?*"

"I don't know. Word is Tony had a pint too many and opened up about the events surrounding the awful day of the drowning."

"Really? What did he say?"

"Not clear on that. But seems he dwelled on it, remorsefully. He didn't say much about Blanche Murninghan's anger at Declan, or the murder, despite what the gardai say."

"And?"

"Seems that after all the Smithwick's, he babbled on about the *senselessness* of the drowning."

"We can all agree there."

"And how William could have been saved, if only …"

Blanche lurched to her feet. "*If only?*"

"It is a wee tidbit. We never knew it. That maybe something could have been done to prevent it."

"Tony Costello was there that day. You told me about the lads and their jars. The bunch of them together. Someone has to have seen something, knows something about the drowning, and he, whoever saw it, doesn't want to say. Maggie, there has to be a connection among Declan, Tony, and William."

"Well, now, the lads did know each other. They had been known to kick the ball about and visit the local and such."

"The local?"

"The pub, dear. 'Tis the center of community, so to speak."

Blanche stood up and began pacing, an index finger tapping her lip frantically.

Maggie chattered on. "There are plenty of people around these parts who would have liked to be done with that O'Brian. Tony may be one of them. I don't think Blanche Murninghan is among the guilty."

Blanche sat down and took a large bite of cake. "How inconclusive. Ugh."

Maggie patted her hand. "Now. Don't ye worry none. Like I says to ye, it's bad business, and it's all done and in the past."

"I can't let it go. I want to know what happened to William—and Declan."

"I know ye do, but ye must take care of yerself. The Flynn will be gettin' ye off the hook. And ye and the dear sister-cousin should have a nice ride out to the sea for a bit of fresh air." She sat up straight and tossed her head. "Ye certainly could use some after this. What a welcome *home!*"

"You give me hope. So nice of you to come by. I have to get out there and find out what the hell is going on. Get to the bottom of this gossip. Talk to Tony, to start."

"You will, dearie, ye will, but be careful. And look to yer bright future." She shook her head and studied Blanche, who crossed her arms, a cold determination in her bones. Maggie reached over and nudged her. "Now then, buck up some, a fine lovely Irish girl like ye. Descended from the Celtic queens."

Blanche laughed. "Haasi calls me 'duchess.' And I'd say this is one royal mess."

"Now, now. My girl, you stand on *heritage*. Let me tell ye. Ye cannot understand Celtic history without understanding the place of women in it. We have considerable status, freedom and rights, and ye must remember that and carry on.

"Why, Plutarch wrote that from the fourth century B.C. Celtic women intervened in war negotiations. Women ambassadors negotiated with Hannibal. When the Romans came to Britain, they met Celtic queens with land and political power—and status." Here Maggie sat up straight and clasped her hands. "I'm not just talkin' about the ladies of thousands of years ago. No, I'm not, for sure. Why, our dear Mary Robinson—a seven-term senator and the most popular president we've ever elected—served through the nineties until just a couple of years ago. And then, wouldn't you know, our eighth Irish president— at present—is the highly competent Mary McAleese, an author and academic with a doctorate in canon law. So, there. It's a grand history, it is, a fine tradition down life's path."

"Maggie, you skipped a few years."

"I did, did I? In the interests of getting to the heart of it. Quite." She gave a curt nod and sighed. "I should tell you there were hard times between the Celtic queens and our fine Mary's. Why, when I was young, a woman could not be on a jury. That right belonged mostly to the men who were property owners. And, Lord, we couldn't step into a pub without a man vouching for us.

"Marriage was full of potholes. Many women lost their jobs upon marriage, especially the civil servants. If the mister was violent, she was stuck. She couldn't collect from the state without himself agreeing to it. And back then, in my time, she didn't even think about divorce.

"Then along came Mary Robinson and the women's movement, among them journalists such as yourself. They pushed for their rights in *The Irish Press* and *The Irish Times*. It weren't easy, but change did come. Gradually. But it did come."

"That's lovely. Wonder what they'd do if they found themselves in a jail cell?"

"You *know* that happened more than once. But mostly, they wouldn't brook it. They'd *rise above it*, as me mam used to say."

"Your mam said that? So did my gran, Maeve Murninghan. It was one of her favorite expressions." The thought of it distracted Blanche and drew her to the beam of sunlight bravely lighting a spot on the table.

"Ah, Maeve." Maggie sighed, dramatically. "Now there's a story for you—Queen Maeve—Queen Medb, she'd be in Gaelic. And your dear Gran, descended, no doubt, from one of the greatest Queens of Ireland, Maeve of the Connacht."

Blanche imagined her grandmother laughing her head off at that notion. But Blanche was intrigued with Irish history, and, of course, adored her own "Queen Maeve." She leaned forward, eager for a story and more time with her lively, funny, wise, new-found relative. "Do you know Queen Maeve's history?"

"That I do. She's woven into the very fabric of our myth and legend, but she's quite the real person, ye know, and a grand one. High and mighty, they've called her, and might I add, I don't think history has treated her fairly. A bit hard-hearted and hard-headed maybe—but what would you call a gent of the very same nature? Why, you'd say he was a leader and strong, brave and shining like the sun. Well, let me tell ye, Queen Maeve was all that. Shining like the sun. Bright as the gold eagles that adorned her raiment. A fair-haired beauty, she was."

Blanche leaned on the table, a fist stuck under her chin, so delighted to learn about Maeve. "Tell me!"

"I shall. The legend of Queen Maeve. She was a great one, strong and wise, fearless and beautiful. The daughter of a king with many sisters, she commanded armies of men. In fact, it was the army she sent off to secure a prize bull that set her story in stone. She was a proud queen and would not be bested. In some ways, the mission was a foolhardy errand, and in other ways, it illustrated the power she had over Ireland two thousand years ago and the reach of her wealth. She was formidable.

"An amusing story of sorts, and sad, because it brings into focus a story of war. Men wage war; women do, too. It's the history of the world, and Maeve is a grand part of it.

"It's said that the disaster started with pillow talk. Now picture it. Maeve and her husband, Ailil, reigned over most of Northwest Ireland. Their lovely round house of polished redwood with a thatch roof was much like the regal palaces of the day. It was elevated on carved wooden pillars, light and airy, like some modern retreat, with the bedroom and royal hall at the center. They decorated with copper screens and silver bars and gold birds with eyes of jewels. So it was written in ancient manuscripts.

"Maeve and Ailil lounged about on furs and soft pillows, and believe it or not, we have details of their conversation from writings in the great Irish epic, the *Tain,* an ancient tale about the adventures of kings and queens, their battles and conquests. Mostly battles and fighting, I'm afraid.

"In this connubial exchange, things started heating up. Ailil made a comment about how fortunate Maeve was to be married to him, a man of vast worth and wealth. She took exception to that. He was a fine fellow, but she was certainly wealthy and powerful in her own right, and his boasting didn't sit well with her. She pointed out her armies of thousands and bonds maids, extensive lands, and animals. Ailil persisted, and so the husband and wife began to compare holdings. In the accounting, Maeve discovered that she was short one prize bull. Ailil outnumbered her. He laughed at his triumph, but she wouldn't have it. She challenged him and sent a messenger off to 'borrow' a prize bull from a distant chieftain.

"The messenger arrived at the chieftain's hall to procure the bull, and he proceeded to party and get drunk. He bragged that Maeve would have taken the bull by force if she were denied the loan of it. The chieftain became furious when he heard this, and out of spite, he refused to send the bull to Maeve.

"I'd say the Irish temper is quite evident in the telling of this story: Maeve flew into a rage, and what ensued was an awful battle—shot through with pride and ill will—and hundreds of men were killed. The quest for the bull led to the famous Battle of Cooley, all told in the *Tain*. It was written some years after the event, but all the same it bears close resemblance to the facts on the ground."

"Whew! Did she get her ... bull?" Blanche asked.

"Who knows? In all that fighting, they probably forgot about it." Maggie clearly enjoyed embellishing the story. "But there she was. A star of the *Tain*. Maeve in battle was a fair woman with soft features, she wore gold birds on her shoulders and a purple cloak with gold on her back, according to the wounded soldier, Cethern. She carried a stinging, sharp-edged lance and held an iron sword over her head."

"Wish I had some of that right now." Blanche clasped her hands between her knees. "Maggie, thanks for the story. You've taken me right out of my head full of troubles."

Maggie laughed. "It's a grand story. Shows the fierce humanity of our queen and her brashness and greatness. She'd not have a man talk her down, now, and get the best of her. She was a 'massive figure,' so the epic goes, and singularly tough. Some say, strong with a heart of stone. When her son was killed in battle, she dismissed the news, saying 'Leave him to the gods,' and she went about her business."

"That's sad. Wonder if she and Ailil lived happily ever after," Blanche said.

"Supposedly. But he was one of several paramours, which was not uncommon in those days. She was lusty like the rest. Before Ailil, Maeve's first husband did not measure up to her code: the absence of 'meanness' (the opposite of generosity)—and the absence of jealousy and fear. So, she moved on. Life was shorter then. They didn't waste time." Maggie gave Blanche a sideways glance and rolled her eyes. "The Celts invited each other to bed with no hesitation and were quite frankly enamored of each other's physical traits, especially strength. Maeve was known to offer her own 'friendly thighs' in a bargain."

Blanche laughed. "Maggie, I don't see a lot of similarity between this Maeve and my beloved grandmother. But they both sure had a strong set of wills. The queen sounds like a wild woman."

"Ha! The Celts were a hearty, practical folk! And do ye know? The warriors ran naked into battle wearing only sandals and a torc—a twisted gold piece about the neck. Possessed in spasms of fury, they were. Their enemies were terrified of the Celts."

"Wow." *Some crazy blood there.* "When was this?"

"The Celts came to Ireland beginning in the fourth century B.C. From all over the European continent and from as far away as Egypt." Delight seemed to strike her. She smiled, impishly. "Who knows, maybe Maeve and Cleopatra were soul sisters of sorts."

"Or distant sister-cousins."

Seventeen

Funny Business

MAGGIE WAS ON HER WAY BACK to her cottage. Blanche hadn't gotten to her to-do list, but she couldn't concentrate. It had been a *grand* chat with Maggie, and she felt better for it. Bucked up with Maggie's support—and stories. Their talk had touched on a lot of history, but the news about Tony Costello's drunken talk in the pub needled her. Maggie had left Blanche with more questions. *How to get to Costello?* It couldn't be all that hard. They both lived in the same village.

She was mulling it over when Haasi walked into the dining room after her bike ride. Blanche was ready. "Should we go?"

"Go where?" Haasi pretended ignorance.

Blanche laughed. "You know where. Come on."

"Oh, all right." Haasi was on board. With strings. She agreed to take a drive out to the former digs of Declan O'Brian near Ballybunion for a brief recon. Mary had given Blanche the idea to look for Declan's writings—and Una had given her directions to his house. Haasi's idea was to try not to get arrested and end up in jail. Both of them, for trespassing and for meddling if there were such a law.

Blanche maneuvered the car down the narrow road. Less than a week in Ireland, she felt like they'd packed years into their short time. So much had happened. So many people—and a murder, no less. She sighed. Time was whipping by, leaving joy and horror in its wake faster than she'd ever imagined; their peaceful idyll was turning inside out. But today, it was dewy and bright. She focused on that. A herd of cows happily chewed grass, and the clouds in a startlingly blue sky touched the black hills in the distance. *Life goes on and not all of it's crazy.*

"We're just going to get in and get out. Fast. Right, Blanche?" Haasi brought her back to reality, and the mission. She fidgeted in the passenger's seat, holding a map. Once again, she reminded Blanche of their agreement. "No funny business."

"No *funny business*? That's real funny. I'd say this whole trip falls into that category. Don't worry. I want what you want. Check out his place, see if there's anything important, and get the hell out of there."

"Breaking and entering and finding something will hardly be admissible as evidence. I've seen enough cop shows to know that. Ireland or wherever."

"Maybe. But if we find something, we can plant the idea of what to look for with those detectives. Tell them what Mary said about his journal writing, and they can go from there."

"I hope you're right. Let's just get this over with and get back. They already want to kick us out or lock us up."

"So far, you've escaped the clutches of law and order in Ballycill, Haas. Let's keep it that way."

"I don't know, Blanche. What's yours is mine."

"Aw, Haas."

"Blanche, what exactly do you expect to find at Declan's?"

"Who knows. Sometimes it's fun to be surprised."

"As if we haven't seen enough of that."

"Look. Once a writer, always a writer, even if it is that dweeb, Declan. Bet he has all kinds of jottings and gibberish in that crib of his. I can't wait to have a look."

"I betcha can't."

They sped along the narrow road toward the coast, a good hour from Ballycill. The land seemed to turn almost sub-tropical. Conifers and ferns, bamboo and blue gum grew along the low hills; it was a green paradise of lush growth. A monument to Mother Nature on the edge of the Atlantic. They were approaching the far west of Ireland, and the sky changed to gray and white, a shelf of white clouds hovering, threatening.

Blanche eased the car toward the wide-open spaces, looking left and right. "Reminds me of walking down the beach on Santa Maria to the point. I always feel like I'm falling off the end of the world there." Both hands clutching the wheel, Blanche breathed the salt air.

"Yeah," said Haasi, staring straight ahead. "Free. At the meeting of water and sky. And let's keep it that way. No jail time."

"Oh, Haas."

"This looks like the way Una described. Past that signpost, around the curve at the large white farmhouse."

Blanche was driving too fast. Haasi gave her a signal. But she was anxious to get there and find something and nail that coffin. Tight.

"There. The corner with a sign to the ferry that Una mentioned, and that road ahead," said Haasi.

Blanche steered the car down the road. It became narrower and bumpier and finally turned into deep ruts and weeds. At the far end of a long length of stone fence, a house came into view, a white-washed, austere square design with four dark windows and a blue door. Not a sound could be heard about the place. No people, no animals—no police tape. Just a house, lonely, and, Blanche hoped, empty.

The property was neatly kept with flowerpots of greenery on either side of the door. A winding path of stones led up the front. Blanche slowly pulled the car around to the back. She checked the rearview. Desolate fields and roads, all around. The car would be nicely hidden behind the house. Buckets and gardening equipment were piled at a back stoop. A scraggly pot of herbs in need of care and a broom stood next to the door.

"I mean it. Let's be quick," Haasi whispered.

"You don't have to whisper. Who's gonna hear? The bird on that stone over there?"

"I don't know. Just feels like there are ears everywhere."

"Bird ears. OK. I hear ya." The undulating stillness, the never-ending green, filled Blanche with an emptiness and a certain amount of anxiety to find *something*. To make things right. She banged on the back door.

"*What the hell are you doing?*" Haasi's gaze darted over the field—a stretch of green and brown peat and rock, treeless and flat.

"They call me 'Bang'?" She grinned.

"Glad you don't carry a gun."

Blanche glanced around. "If someone's in there, I sure as heck don't want to walk in on them. Being loud sometimes has its advantages."

"And being quiet has more," Haasi grumbled, drew her shoulders in, and peered at their bleak surroundings. "Almost too quiet around here, if you ask me."

The land was silent except for the intermittent wind that reminded Blanche of ghosts and faeries. She hadn't heard a good thing about either in Maggie's storytelling, and it gave her new urgency to get on with it and get out of there. She rattled the door handle. It was locked.

Haasi grabbed a bucket and placed it under the back window. She gave the frame a shove. The pane slid up easily. She turned with a grin at her triumph: "Milady, Duchess of Dunfaedan, here you be."

It was an easy hop over the sill into a large, dim space. A soot-covered fireplace opened like a large dark mouth on one side of the room with a table for ten and ladderback chairs in front of it. Blanche eyed a basket of shriveled apples in a brass bowl. An old oriental rug. Seating for two in stuffed chairs in front of a bay window. A large desk opposite the fireplace. The room was meant to be cozy, but it failed; something cold and dusty and dry pervaded the air. Thoughts of Declan O'Brian did nothing to warm it.

Blanche made a bee line for the desk. A couple of ledgers were stacked on the shelf above the blotter with a calendar and a cup of pens in an old china mug. She flipped through the pages of one ledger. The neat lines of script revealed nothing extraordinary: columns for supplies, equipment, repairs, payroll for staff.

Blanche went back over the list, and her mind wandered; these items seemed to fit the running of an estate. *I guess. How would I know?* The headings were the pedestrian labels for operation of a castle. What she knew about that she could have put on a single sheet of paper.

She had no idea if the payroll was fair, but the payments were regular, probably translating to at least a couple hundred dollars a week for each person—at least fifteen thousand American dollars a year. Probably more for Una as a household manager. It didn't seem like much. That said, the country's economy was far different than that of the US. This was something she wanted to check to ensure the pay was equitable. After all, Gustaitis had asked her to be *responsible.* Una had not complained, but she may not have been in a position to do so. The staff were provided room and board off the proceeds of running the "company" of the estate. She didn't find any payment for Declan.

Blanche shoved the ledgers aside. Haasi was busy skirting the edges of the room, looking over the reading material. "Haas, what you got?"

"Not too interesting. A bunch of catalogues for farm equipment, one old Agatha Christie, and a map of Dublin."

"Well, at least he's got good taste in mysteries. Gotta love Agatha."

"You'd say that, wouldn't you. Sometimes I feel like we're in the middle of one. What do you have?"

"Not much so far."

"Maybe we should go?" Haasi went to the bay window and peered out at nothing.

"Not so fast. I feel like I'm on to something, getting warm over here." She didn't feel the least bit warm but believed in the power of positive thinking.

"Oh, I bet." Haasi shot her a look. "Hurry the hell up. Please."

Blanche pulled the chair away from the desk and reached for the last ledger. *Let's just have one more look ...*

Then she saw it. Under the desk, up against the wall, a wooden chest. It nearly blended into the paneling. She tossed the ledger up on the blotter and burrowed under the desk. She tried the brass handle on the lid. It was locked. "Where there is lock, there is key," she said out loud.

"Blanche! Where are you?!" Haasi turned from the window. "What are you doing under there, and what are you mumbling about?"

"There's a locked chest under here."

"Oh great. As I recall, you're pretty good with that sort of thing." Such a discovery had been key during one of their previous capers.

Blanche's voice was muffled, but strong. "Yes, I am." She felt all around the chest for a way in. Nothing. She returned to the top of the desk and furiously, carefully, turned everything over, looking for a key. She attacked the small drawers, the blotter, the back covers of the ledgers. Inside out. In frustration, she pulled one of the small drawers loose and tossed it upside down.

"Abracadabra," said Blanche.

"You better get that magic going. I'm about to drag you out of here."

Taped to the bottom of the drawer was a key. Blanche pried it away from the underside. She hunched back down under the desk. The key fit the lock, and the lid creaked open. Inside were more ledgers. She pulled out an old green fabric-covered volume and fanned through the pages. In the back was scrawled: "Extra-curricular" and a long column of regular payments in pounds. Pages of payments. Switching to euros in 2002. She did a quick calculation. This "extra-curricular" recipient was getting regular installments of nearly five hundred dollars a month. For years and years. *For what?*

Haasi peered over Blanche's shoulder. She turned the pages, underlining with her finger. "Wonder where all this is going? Extra-curricular? Probably not art class or music lessons."

"Blanche, I don't know. That really doesn't tell you much. We should go." She darted back to the window and looked out.

"Why? It's quieter than a gnat's picnic around here. Haas, what are you doing?"

"I'm on watch. Don't exactly want to have a meet up. Under the circumstances. Besides, what if the gardai decide to show up?"

"Unlikely. Think we're safe. Seems there aren't even a half dozen gardai for this whole area. They've got better things to do. Besides, they've already been here." Blanche paged through the ledgers. She drew a notebook out of her pocket and jotted some figures.

"How do you know?"

"Garda Handley mentioned it, and they're waiting on Dublin for word on the investigation."

"It'd be just our luck …"

"Come back here and look at this!" Blanche thrust the ledger at Haasi and pointed to a row of payments.

"Odd." Haasi picked up another ledger and opened it. More unnamed recipients for payments. "And these dates are irregular. Some here, some there."

"Somebody gettin' somethin' for a whole lot of nothin', I bet."

"Now, why do you say that?"

"'Cause these payments don't fall into any of the categories for running the estate, which Mr. Declan O'Brian has meticulously listed in the other ledgers. What do you think of that, Haas? There's a board of accountants and bankers involved so he probably had to be pretty careful about expenses." Blanche busily returned the ledgers to the chest and the key to the hiding place.

Haasi paced from window to window. "Blanche, I don't know what to think, but somebody is going to have to get into all those numbers and figure it out, and it's not going to be you or me."

A loud crack broke the silence. It came from behind the house. They hurried to the back and peered out at a shed behind the house. A large tree branch had fallen onto a wheelbarrow and scattered stones and peat across the patch of yard.

"The devil," whispered Blanche.

"Declan? He probably doesn't want us snooping around."

"Or the faeries."

"Faeries? I thought they liked us."

"They don't like to be disturbed. You know, from dancing the hornpipe and such."

"Blanche. Enough already. Let's get out of here. I'm starting to get the willies."

The morning had turned grayer still, the wind picked up and seemed to lift the eaves of the house. The window they'd used to access the house slammed shut with an exclamation. They both jumped.

Eighteen
Dunk

"I MEAN IT, BLANCHE. Let's go. *Now*," said Haasi. "We're just asking for it."

Blanche hesitated. "It wouldn't be the first time." She checked her watch. "Haas, we haven't even been here fifteen minutes. Give it a rest. I promise …"

Haasi stamped her foot.

"Haas, did you actually stamp your foot?" They both burst out laughing.

"Ten minutes, tops," said Haasi.

"I hear ye." Blanche looked around the dim parlor of Declan O'Brian, hands on hips. "Where to start." She was not satisfied with the discovery in the ledgers in the desk. *There has to be more.* She eyed the stairs and pointed in that direction. "Just one more peek. Up there." Blanche already had her foot on the first step. Haasi was getting grumpier, but she followed.

"Blanche, be reasonable. What are we going to find upstairs, going through his underwear drawer, or whatever?" She coaxed, without success, crossed her arms tightly, and shivered.

Blanche took one creaky tread at a time. She peered down at her sister-cousin. "Haas. *One more minute. Or two.* I swear."

Haasi sighed. "Sure could use that drive to the beach. I need air."

They huddled on the landing at the top of the stairs. A large room opened to either side of where they stood. They walked into what apparently served as the master bedroom. It was spare and luxurious,

143

including a pair of brass and crystal lamps, fur, and heavy mahogany furniture. The four-poster bed was outfitted with a red damask duvet and white pillows edged in scarlet trim. Red velvet curtains shut out the world. Lots of red.

"Happy Valentine's," said Haasi.

"Looks like our Lothario had himself a nice little setup here. Wonder how many local ladies he seduced in this place. *Really* gives me the willies." Blanche stepped around the room, taking it all in, careful not to disturb dust motes and ghosts.

"Smells funny, like vanilla and … cotton candy? Ugh," said Haasi. "OK, I've seen enough."

Blanche looked under the bed, opened a closet door, checked a bureau laden with candles and … *toys*? "More ugh over here. Seems to be something for everyone."

"Don't play with those, unless you want your fingers to fall off." Haasi peered out the window at the drive up to the house. "Hurry up, Blanche."

"Well, lookee here. More journals or ledgers or *something*. He certainly was a prolific one." She emerged from the closet with a box and pulled several bound volumes from it. Haasi joined her on a large fur rug.

"Doesn't look like *Little House on the Prairie*," said Haasi. "What are those? Diaries?"

"Yup. Found them in the way back, behind those boots."

Blanche opened one of the journals. Scrawled haphazardly, with vulgar sketching to match:

… dedicated to the ones I've loved,
To those so close and those far flung,
The pretty girls with faces smooth,
Hair so black and skin like silk;
To the girls so young, the ones so dumb,
To the ones I took and the ones I've stung.

"Oh, please. Yeats he's not." Haasi picked up another book and flipped the pages. Her cheeks grew red.

"*What?*"

Blanche opened a journal. "OMG, what this guy did with olive oil and mirrors—and marshmallows? Do they have marshmallows in Ireland?"

"I guess. For certain things. In this case, he skipped the s'mores recipe. What a guy." Haasi threw her book back in the box. "Well, that's our porn lesson for the day. Are you happy now?"

Blanche fumbled around and came up with a date: October 19, 1978. "Hey, that's around the time William drowned. Listen to this:

> "He was there on the banks, saw the whole thing happen. What the hell, the stupid bloke. He came at me, accusing me. Got to take care of this. Convince him that WM slipped on the mud, carried himself off downstream. And I know how to be convincing, all right.
>
> I don't have an obligation over here to save the world, especially WM, with his charm, what a pain in the arse. Everything he touched turned to gold. The whole town licking his boots. Glad he's gone, and for my part, couldn't be happier he's gone. Now the way is clear ..."

She thumbed through the pages frantically, but the sentence remained unfinished. "What's this supposed to mean? Clear for what?" Blanche held up the book and shook it.

"Blanche, you're not going to shake any sense out of this. The guy was demented."

"But who is *he*? Who's Declan talking about? *He* was on the banks."

"I don't know. But that part about WM sort of backs up the rumor that Declan was there at the drowning. Do you think he may have had something to do with it?"

"Is the pope Catholic? Does the bear ..."

"All right already." Blanche was convinced of the obvious. "This last bit about the way being clear. To do what? He didn't finish the thought."

"Can't be good, whatever it is."

"We should have another little chat with Mary. Let her in on this."

"I don't know, Blanche. She's pretty touchy about the whole Declan business. How's she supposed to know who Declan's referring to here?"

Blanche paged through the diary. "I don't know, but it may jog her memory." She picked up another journal. "Haas. Have a look. See if any names are mentioned. I don't see any except a reference to WM. Obviously William."

"Nothing." Haasi tossed the last of the diaries back in the box. She leaned over, scooting the volumes aside. "Hey, what's this?" A small, enameled case was tucked in a corner of the box. Haasi picked it up and turned it over. "This looks interesting." She handed it to Blanche.

"Great. Now our fingerprints are all over this stuff. Hope that doesn't become an issue."

"What isn't." Haasi sighed.

"Aren't you curious?" Blanche studied the case for a latch. It sprang open. Inside was a silver Celtic cross nestled on a long, coiled chain. She lifted the cross slowly from the satin liner.

"Now, that looks familiar." Haasi reached for it and held it up to the dull light from the parted curtains. The cross was exquisitely carved with runes and Celtic vines and knots. On one side, a series of careful lines, like notches, were inscribed at the base.

"I'll say. I do believe I've seen that before. We need to chat with Maggie—and Mary, for sure. Seems Declan O'Brian was the keeper of the cross. Do you think this belonged to him? Or somebody else?"

They restored the cross to its case and all the volumes to their hiding places. Plumped the furry rug, returned the chairs and doors to their original positions. They wiped fingerprints from all surfaces, as best they could. Blanche checked once more for any traces they may have left. She felt sure they didn't leave a mark. But she did leave with plenty of questions and the sense that Declan had been involved in the drowning. She also wondered about that odd score of payments. And the girls he'd "stung"? Were the payments involved with them? And why so much and so many, and what was up with "extra-curricular?"

So many questions, such a patchy, dark timeline.

They went out the same way they entered, Haasi creeping over the sill in one sinewy leap, and Blanche, bumbling, hitting her head on the window frame.

"Jeez, Blanche. Will you be careful?" Haasi frowned. They both glanced at the house before climbing into the car. The windows stared back like vacant eyes; the wind blew the grasses flat and iridescent in the misty air.

Blanche turned the engine over and rubbed the bump on her head. "Careful? Me? Sometimes I feel like I'm crashing through life headlong."

Haasi chuckled, ruefully. "That's Bang Murninghan, for sure."

Blanche engaged the gear shift and sped away from the house in a shot of gravel, eager to put distance between them and Declan.

"Are you all right with dropping back at Maggie's place, Haas? I want to tell her about that cross we found. We can see Mary, too. I'd love to talk to her about that diary." But she was also thinking about Tony. He kept popping into her mind.

"Now? Let's go to the beach."

Blanche clutched the wheel and looked west. "Yeah, beach is always a good idea." She steered the car onto the main road and picked up speed.

"I do come up with one occasionally," said Haasi. "And as for your idea to talk to Maggie and Mary, do you think we should tell them we broke into Declan's?"

"I don't think they'd turn us in, if that's what you mean. But I would like a little input for all my questions. For one, why would Declan have that Celtic cross?"

"Blanche. We're in Ireland. Remember? There are lots of Celtic crosses here."

"True. But the one we found was antique silver, very finely wrought. It looked exactly like William's. You know, in that picture at Maggie's." She turned to Haasi to get her reaction. "I think the police should have a look over there."

"Hey, how about slowing down!"

Blanche grinned and let up on the pedal. Her mind was spinning, and she didn't know where it would end. Their discoveries should settle in. Maybe cook for a bit.

"Yes, the beach is a very good idea. We're close."

"I think we just head west. There should be a car park down that way."

"Perfect. What could go wrong?"

Haasi pondered that observation. "Not a thing. Nice clean air. After being in Declan's bedroom."

Blanche laughed. "Lucky he never tangled with you. Might have ended up missing some parts."

"Duchess."

The thick hedgerow flapped at the windshield as they drove down the narrow road toward the sea. It was afternoon; they'd spent an hour snooping at Declan's—way over Blanche's time limit but Haasi had been grudgingly accommodating.

No one else was on the road. The tourist season of summer was far off, and Blanche had the feeling they were tucked out of the way of throngs, no matter the time of year. Ireland was small, only a hundred fifty miles across at its broadest, but large swaths of it felt desolate. Beautiful, but empty. And so green. The Irish sure were right about the wearing of the green: the shamrock, the hills and fields rolling endlessly under the blue sky. They passed little civilization, though a quiet farmhouse occasionally appeared beyond a stone fence. Cows and horses lolled about lazily, chomping grass.

They dipped over a hill and the sea beyond rose up gray and flat, the shoreline dotted with tall spindly conifers and boulders.

"Wow, end of the world."

"Yup."

"B! Watch where you're going"

Blanche shifted to a lower gear and swung around a corner. Haasi stiffened. Out in front of them, a top-heavy truck with furniture sticking out of its load tipped side to side. It came straight at their car. To the right was a stone fence, to the left a field.

"Uh-oh." Blanche held the wheel steady. The truck's horn bleated, its headlights and grill like an ugly face. It didn't budge. Blanche sucked in her breath, and Haasi's fingers flattened on the dashboard as the truck veered around them. Blanche caught the back of it in the rearview mirror, trundling off along the ruts in the road.

"Damn!" The car swerved on the uneven surface. She held on, but it was no use. Before she knew it, the wheels hit a cleft at the edge of the road, and they careened into a shallow ditch. Fishtailing and skidding, they bumped to a stop. The truck was long gone. Its loud revving of gears and honking disappeared into the misty silence, the driver apparently unaware of causing this major inconvenience.

Haasi was still braced tautly on the dashboard. "Well, that's just great. Out in the middle of God knows where."

"I'm sorry, Haas. Should have kept my eye on the road."

"Well, it's hardly your fault." She looked around at the flat open field. "And there's *no one* out here."

Blanche spun the wheels to the distressing sound of rubber meeting mud. The car was definitely stuck. "Maybe if we lay something flat under the wheels. Any cardboard back there?"

"Oh, yeah, just happens to be several nice pieces of cardboard in the back seat." Haasi's rueful expression said otherwise.

Blanche opened the door. "Looks like we're going to have to get out and push."

"And pull."

"But first, Mother Nature calls. I'll just go over there …" She got out and took a few steps on the spongy ground. *Squishy ground.* It was remarkably flat and devoid of bushes and trees, and the earth gave off a humid vegetable odor. Not unpleasant. But *weird.*

"Bang! Wait! I think this is what they call …"

Blanche let out a shriek. Her feet disappeared into the muck. Now she was stuck. She lifted each foot gingerly, and the more she backtracked, the more she tried to wiggle out of it, the worse it got. She was not only stuck; she was sinking, fast. It was all too familiar— the feeling of getting stuck; she'd done that many times before. But this was a physical sinking. Visceral and real. She looked around at the soft ground pulling her down.

"Don't move!" yelled Haasi. "It's the bog!"

Blanche looked back at Haasi, terror in her eyes. When Haasi had that look about her, things definitely were on the downslope. Blanche sank a bit more. "Don't worry," her voice tinny and stretched tight as a wire. "I'm not going anywhere!"

Nineteen

An Auld Sinking Feeling

"BLANCHE! OH MY GOD!"

"Good idea! I need some almighty help over here!"

Haasi flattened herself on the ground and crawled toward Blanche. "Give me your hand."

Haasi couldn't quite reach her. Blanche flailed about, which only made it worse.

Haasi's command was deadly calm. "Bang. Be still, the more you yank about, the faster you're going down."

Blanche had never felt so helpless in all her life—well, almost. She fixed her eye on Haasi who resembled a large lizard, all arms and legs "swimming" along the surface of the mushy ground. Blanche didn't move a muscle. Haasi was within inches …

"Slowly. Stretch toward me. Lean back," said Haasi. "Extend your arm."

Blanche leaned, but the auld sod had a hold on her. The bottom half of her was completely immobile like she was in a plaster cast. She squinched her eyes shut and imagined she was a tree. *Grow, dammit, just an inch more.* She grabbed hold of Haasi's hand.

"I'm not letting you go!" Haasi held on, two-fisted, and wiggled closer to Blanche who was up to her waist now. Haasi took a deep breath and lowered her head.

Blanche inched deeper into the boggy ground. "Don't go to sleep now! We got work to do! At least you're on this side of the ground."

"OK, I'm thinking."

"Well, think fast," said Blanche. "What the hell is this stuff, Haas?" She choked with fear and confusion, and a splash or two of muck. They were both pretty much covered in it.

"Decaying vegetation and seepage underground. The bog. Been like this for ten thousand years."

"Why is this the year I find one?"

"I don't know, Blanche. But you did, now *don't move*. I'm going to get us out of here."

"*Us?* You could pretty much walk away. Or slither. You look like a large lizard, Haas."

At that, they broke down, laughing, and it relieved the tension in Blanche's throat. She could breathe again, but for how long?

"Oh, I swear, Blanche, when you said you inherited a castle, I didn't think bog-sinking was part of it."

"I like to keep things interesting."

"That." Haasi's tone was weary, and just the least bit wavery. She was now covered in mud. She shook her fingers of the slime and resumed her hold on Blanche. "Can you take your shoes off?"

"*What?*"

"Make yourself light as possible. Like the little feather that you are. Now keep leaning back. Like I said. Not forward." Her casual tone returned. Haas was a cool one, even in the worst of times.

"How do you know that's gonna work, Haas?"

"I know all kinds of stuff. Like bog bodies don't decompose, and their hair turns red because of the acidic nature of the water underground."

"Thanks for the history lesson. What am I going to *do*?" Blanche stood still and leaned back slightly. She couldn't move an inch to get rid of the shoes. "By the way, I'd look terrible as a redhead."

"So would I. But we're not going there now. We're not going *anywhere*." Haasi spoke in a low, deliberate tone. "No sharp movements, I mean it. I've got to try to pull you out. You need to relax."

"Relaxing in the bog. What better way to spend a vacation." Blanche looked up at the gray sky. She could smell the sea from her deeply disturbing position. "Jeez, I hope it doesn't rain. Just what we don't need. More mush. I'm soaked."

"Shit, B." Haasi gripped Blanche's hand and pulled slowly. "I think this is the stuff they told us to steer clear of. Like, stay on the path and don't go off exploring. That sort of thing."

"Now you tell me. Too late for that. Should have looked before I sunk."

"You didn't know. That truck did not do us any favors." Haasi spoke laconically and glanced around. Not a sound of human or animal broke the silence. They were indeed *stuck* for finding help.

"Haas, thanks. You're so *chill*." Blanche held on, her brain going a mile a minute in never-ending circles to nowhere.

"Yup. It's getting cold out here, the breeze is picking up." Her confidence, and coolness, somehow remained intact. She grabbed the back of Blanche's jacket and tugged, gently and insistently.

Blanche took a deep breath. "Go back, please, Haas. Crawl back. I'll try … Maybe you could get help." Blanche leaned over at the waist and clawed the ground. The blades of grass and rocks came off in her hands, the bending and grabbing for hold on the earth a useless effort.

"*Don't lean forward. You could drown.* I'm not going anywhere, and I'm not letting go of you. Just hold on. *Stay still.* I'll pull. Slowly. And keep your arms up!"

"It's not happening, Haas." She could feel her body inching down into the muck. There was no bottom, no end to this. Except *The End.* "Get back! Go see if there's something in the car … a shovel, a crowbar …"

"What? Pry you out of the ground?" Haasi spoke firmly. "Listen, I'm telling you to not move. Let's just relax for a minute. Breathe."

"I guess. While I can." The heat rose up Blanche's neck. She looked down at the earth sucking her in, now well past her waist. "What the hell are we going to do? I'm seeing my life flash before me. I'm so sorry I got into this mess, but worse, I got *you* into this mess. What's wrong with me?"

"Nothing's wrong with you. Nothing that a good bath couldn't fix. That, and a shot of Jameson's." Steadily, Haasi pulled. Blanche could feel movement in her leg. She leaned back.

Moooooooooo.

"Blanche, did you hear that? Cows!"

"Yeah, so what? What good's a cow? Now. *How now brown cow.*"

"Where there is cow, there is person. Maybe. *Somewhere.*" Haasi rolled over onto her side, not letting go of Blanche. Around the front of their stuck car, beyond the ditch, she saw him: a herder, a lumpy little guy with a flat tweed cap, baggy trousers, and high, sturdy boots. A donkey clomped along behind him.

Blanche had never seen such a beautiful apparition.

"*Help!*" Haasi and Blanche yelled in unison. The bow-legged little man hurried down the road toward them. He stood on the edge of the shallow ditch, one hand on a hip. His expression was one of amusement rather than alarm. He was whistling something eerie that blended with the wind.

"Aye. What have ye done to yerselves?" He had the ruddiest face and the liveliest smile. Had St. Patrick or some other saint landed from heaven to save them? She could only pray, and she hadn't done that in some time. She considered, fleetingly, of starting now.

Blanche waved frantically, and precariously, for it made her sink an inch faster. "Hello there! You must know something about bogs, sir! Being local, and all," she yelled. The mud splashed up to her neck, cold, irritating, and itchy. Haasi was covered in it from rolling and stretching. She grabbed Blanche's arm.

"Aye, that I do," he called back. "Yer quite right about that, Missy. Now hold on. Looks like a bit of trouble is upon ye, but we'll all be on our way for sure. Likely." Her savior took a tentative step toward them and stopped. "Don't be strugglin' now or the ghosts below will grab ye by yer toes and pull ye under." He cocked his head and *laughed*.

"That's so damn reassuring!" grumbled Blanche. "HELP!"

"Sir, we need help. *Now!*" Haasi grit her teeth, her tone insistent, almost menacing. She lay on her side, her braids coated with mud, her jacket, formerly light blue denim, now a greenish brown. She clutched Blanche's arm. "Any good ideas?"

He tipped his hat like they were meeting at a cocktail party. Eyes twinkling. "Kevin O'Riley here." He turned back toward the small, sturdy donkey standing patiently on the road. "Meet Blitsy." O'Riley fiddled with a long length of rope secured to the donkey's hinders.

Blitsy chewed and lolled her head from side to side, obviously bored with the whole situation. O'Riley whistled while he patted the furry ears. He turned. "She's been down this road a time or two. Pulled Margaret Brown's calf out of the bog not too long ago."

"How would she do with a dazed and confused one-hundred-pound American woman?" Blanche was on the verge of giddiness and desperation. But she was overcome with happiness at the sight of Kevin O'Riley and his rope and donkey.

"I'd say ye have a lot in common." He blessed them with a merry expression. "Why in all the saints in heaven would ye get yerself into a mess like this?"

"We didn't ask for it!" Confirmation came from Haasi and Blanche at once.

"Now, can you get us out of here? *Please?*" yelled Blanche.

Haasi tugged. "He's gotta be one of those saints in heaven come to earth."

"Well, our prayer is not answered. Yet."

O'Riley busied himself with the harness and the rope, all the while mumbling—and singing—about St. Patrick and crazy women. He seemed to be taking his time with the preparation. It was then Blanche saw the stick, actually, a long staff typical of herders. *Aha! Salvation is near!*

"Will you hurry, Mr. O'Riley? Please? I'm going fast," yelled Blanche. "I see that staff there. Maybe that…"

"Aye, dearie, for sure, it's part of the plan. Kevin O'Riley will not be letting ye go to yer heavenly reward in this fashion. Do be patient." He gave Blitsy another pat on the head and turned to the disaster unfolding. "And ye, young lady, up to your whatsits, I'll be sayin' it once again, try not to move!"

O'Riley looped the rope onto Blitsy's harness and stepped carefully over the edge of the road. "Easy does it. Now, Missy, the wee one, flat on the ground, ye need to put the end of this around yer middle." He thrust the long end of the rope toward Haasi who did as instructed. A sailor of sorts, the girl was always good with a knot. She tied the rope securely over her jacket and locked arms with Blanche.

"Now, hold on tight," said O'Riley. "And don't let go, for the love of St. Pete."

Saint Pete? What about Saint Patrick?

In a bit of a ballet, O'Riley threw an apple onto the road in front of Blitsy and tapped her flank with the stick. The donkey didn't hesitate. She came to life and ambled toward the treat. It was just enough of a steady pull, along with the encouragement of the stick, to pull Haasi along the slimy surface and extricate most of Blanche from the bog. Haasi tightened her grip on Blanche.

"Almost there." O'Riley put his hands on his hips and surveyed his handiwork.

"Good Blissy," yelled Blanche.

"*Blitsy*. She's sensitive, ye know." O'Riley shook a finger at Blanche. He reached in his pocket for a handful of sugar cubes and threw them expertly beyond the donkey's nose. Blitsy took a few more unhurried steps again. Blanche and Haasi found themselves flat on the soggy ground, panting and huffing with relief.

"OMG, born again." Blanche swiped at the mess on her front.

"Is that what you call it?" Haasi looked to the sky. "Thanks to this little old saint walking around on earth."

O'Riley retreated back up onto the road, took off his cap, and scratched his head. The donkey chomped away. Blanche and Haasi crawled and rolled back to the other side of the ditch to join their saviors. They stood up, with difficulty. "Blanche, you look like you've been dipped at the chocolate factory," Haasi said.

"Some chocolate. Ugh." Blanche flicked a mud-encrusted curl off her forehead and shook her fingers free of bog slime. "I need a bath. Are you OK, Haas?"

"I couldn't be happier." She grinned at O'Riley who stood twirling his cap and smiling. "You're a lifesaver. Thank you, sir."

"The thanks is mine to give," he said with a slight bow. "Yer pretty good with a rope there, me lassie."

"I try to be."

The donkey pawed the ground impatiently, now that the action was over, and the treats were gone. "If ye don't mind me askin'. What are ye fine ladies doing out in this beautiful corner of God's country? All of it beauteous, except for that part …" He lifted his chin in the direction of the bog pit.

Blanche shivered and reached into the back seat of the car for a small throw. She took a step toward O'Riley and began rubbing the bog off her hair and clothes. "Well, as you can see, we didn't stop for the sights. We were sort of run off the road by a large truck. Then the car got stuck, and I got stuck."

"Awfully grateful you came along," said Haasi. "Don't know what we would have done if you hadn't." Her voice trailed off.

"I'd say ye'd be dancin' the jig at the pearly gates by now. But only God in heaven can say."

Haasi and Blanche exchanged glances and exhaled sharply. "Dodged that one," said Haasi. She was remarkably clean as compared to Blanche, having only wallowed on top of the bog. She wore a mud-speckled sweatshirt under the jacket and tight jeans and stomped back and forth on the road to free herself of flakes of grime.

"Now then, the car," he said.

"Yeah, now what do we do? Can't exactly call AAA," said Blanche.

"Not sure what that would be, but me thinks Blitsy can help with the car, too. Car and bodies and cows. She'd be the one to call. Just happen to have another apple on me person. Hee-hee."

"What can I do to help?" Blanche patted Blitsy's ears.

"She's after doin' the rest now." O'Riley maneuvered the donkey into position. "Ye get into your carriage, Miss, and turn it over. Blitsy and the O'Riley, we'll get ye righted, all right."

Blanche did as directed. *Oh, the rental company is going to love me. But at least I'm alive. Maybe I'll get a discount for that.*

With a spinning of wheels and a sideways swipe toward the bog, which sent additional shivers through Blanche, she managed to drive the car back up onto the road and avoid running over the donkey, O'Riley, and Haasi. Blitsy eyed the prodding staff and chomped the last of the apple. The car sat, running, and Blanche got out.

"Now, if ye please," said O'Riley. "If ye don't mind. Ye was about to tell me what the blazes ye be doin' in these parts?"

"We were visiting a Mr. Declan O'Brian's establishment," Blanche blurted.

"Bang. Duchess." Haasi rolled her eyes. "We were going to visit, but it seems the gentleman is deceased. So we were just going to drive around. Then, maybe, have a look at the beach."

"The tour director." Blanche nodded, furiously, pointing to Haasi. "That's about right. You don't happen to know Mr. O'Brian, do you?"

"Of course, I do. Did. Only knew of him, not personally. It's a small place, ye know."

"How well did you know him?"

"Like I says, didn't know much. He was here and about, in the pub and whatnot. The gardai was passin' along here, and we got the news of his untimely death."

"Other than that, what did you hear about him?"

"Won't speak ill of the dead, mind ye. He had visitors. Some ladies, so it's told. And, lately, a fellow from up where ye be comin' from."

"Visitors? Pray tell."

"Now ye be prayin', all right. Well, and it's a good thing." His cloudy blue eyes looked off to the distant hills. His thoughts seemed to wander.

Blanche could practically see the gears going round in his head. Her curiosity spiked. "What about those visitors? What sort of fella was that who went to see Declan?"

"A stocky one, he was. Don't know his name. But he must have had business with the O'Brian, so they say. He weren't too friendly."

"How do you mean?"

"We don't have much traffic down this way, but we do have our pub. Our Talligan's, a wee bit of a fine place near here. This heavy-set fella would come by. I seen him a time or two. He weren't a happy soul, and ye could tell by the talk on him, he weren't too high on Declan O'Brian."

"You never caught a name?"

"Nope, didn't want to. But might be the pub owner, Jack Bantry, knows. Then, again, that might not help neither. Fella kept to himself."

Haasi tugged at Blanche's muddy arm. "Come on, girl. Enough already."

"Haas, just a sec."

Haasi shrugged. "Thank you, again, Mr. O'Riley. I hope we can repay you down the road for saving our lives, though I don't know how." And she climbed into the car with a backward warning glance at Blanche.

"Yes, please call at Dunfaedan if you ever need help," said Blanche.

"Ah, Blitsy and me are fine, but thank ye for the offer. 'Tis been a pleasure, well, in a manner of speakin'." Mr. O'Riley took off his cap and scratched his brow. "Dunfaedan. That's where the O'Brian had a seat. Now that I think on it. He had a cup or two one night and he was braggin' on the ladies and that domain of his, like he was lord of all. He warn't no lord, that I can tell ye."

"Did you ever speak with O'Brian?" asked Blanche.

"Never had the displeasure." He crossed himself. Blitsy eyed him.

Blanche shivered, wrapped the jacket tighter. That seemed to put the capper on it. He wasn't going to speak further because he probably didn't know any more about Declan O'Brian, and if he did, Blanche would be pushing into territory that was private and mythically Irish. Secrets thrived, and everyone knew more than each was willing to tell.

"Can't thank you enough." Blanche stepped toward him as if to give him a hug.

His eyes crinkled with wry amusement. He looked her up and down. "Ye better get yerself to a good bath now. Been more than pleased to meet ye and yer lovely friend. May one day we meet again either here or in the beyond. Now, stay out of the wee bog, if ye don't mind me tellin' ye. Or call Kevin O'Riley if ye a mind to get stuck again. Hee-hee." And he turned on the bowlegs, dug the stick into the rutty road, and hobbled off. Blitsy followed. Blanche caught up to him for just one more question.

Twenty

A Cold Air

THEY FOUND TALLIGAN'S PUB with little difficulty, thanks to Kevin O'Riley. Blanche had leaned on their savior for directions: "It's just over that hillock there with the sheep and the large rock to yer right and then straight on 'til ye see a white cross on the roadside and a large paddock with black horses to yer left and then yer on the right path. Straightaway."

"Blanche, how are we going to go to a pub looking like this?" Haasi was reasonably tidy, but she always managed to look put together, her straight little body in simple clothes, her smooth skin, and shining black braids. They'd gone through a box of tissues and half a jug of water cleaning up.

Blanche shrugged. "I got most of it off, and so did you. Glad I had the extra sweats in the back. You don't look half bad." She grinned and checked herself in the rearview mirror. "Now the face and hair are a problem, to be sure. I'll just give it a dunk when we hit a restroom."

"You look like you have a tan. A mud tan. Here." Haasi handed her another tissue and a comb. "Maybe these will help though we both probably smell like vegetable smoothies."

"Yeah, we're smooth, all right."

"Why do we have to go to this pub, Blanche? We've got a perfectly good one in Ballycill. Or that nice little drawing room in the castle."

"The castle is pretty nice. I'm getting used to it."

"Except for murder."

"Oh, Haas." Blanche took care at the wheel, glancing briefly at her sister-cousin with a half-smile. "We'll just stop in and see what they have to say about this regular visitor to Declan's, according to O'Riley."

"Oh, brother."

"That Tony fellow. I wonder about him. Sounds like O'Riley was talking about him."

Haasi considered this. "There are a lot of stocky, taciturn Irish men around here. But few who might have visited Declan. What do we know? Anyway, this Tony keeps entering the picture, one way or the other. You keep saying you want to talk to him. Bet he's not the Linzer pastry type. Maybe the whiskey type."

"Whiskey it will be." Blanche felt like bursting into song, she was so glad to be free of the bog. She drove with one hand on the wheel. *"The hills are alive …"*

"All right. We're alive. Good. Now watch the road."

"We won't take long at Talligan's. Didn't spend much time at Declan's. Like I promised."

"Almost an hour? I'm going to count our side trip into the bog as part of that visit. Jeez, Blanche."

"Haas. Just a quick snort at Talligan's, and a question or two." Blanche grinned, and Haasi grumbled. Blanche decided to leave it alone, for now. Haasi had that longing for home written all over her face. Blanche couldn't blame her. This trip had turned into one disaster after another. She wanted to finish up and get back to the island, and peace.

They parked on a small dirt pad outside Talligan's and went in and cleaned up some more in the restroom. The mud had dried and flaked off. Blanche regarded herself in the mirror. "Sort of like one of those fancy mud treatments. You know, Haas? Though I don't recommend that particular *spa*."

"Oh, Duchess."

The interior of the pub was dark and nearly empty of patrons. A long, polished bar and about a dozen high-backed stools took up most of the space. Several shallow drums hung on the wall and the spigots for draft beer gleamed. A short, thin man behind the bar looked up and smiled when they emerged from the restroom. He had a ruddy face, like red leather, and the whitest teeth. Blanche had heard that the

Irish had problems with their teeth, in general, but some people were blessed. She thanked Maeve's genes for her own healthy chompers.

"G'day to ye, ladies. What can I pour for ye?" He looked them over. "Been out playing in the mud, have ye?"

Blanche looked down. She'd missed some spots. "Sort of. But not playing," she said. "I'd say it was more like praying. I got stuck in the bog down the road. Up to my waist." She climbed onto the stool and smiled at the man. "Sure could use a beer."

"Ah, the mean faeries got to ye." He flashed another smile and went for the glasses. "Ye musn't fool with the faeries, nor disturb their mounds and such."

"Why do I feel like you're pulling my leg?"

He looked ready to break into a good laugh. "I'm sure it's a foin leg, but why would I be doin' that now."

Haasi said, dryly, "Will you make that two beers? Harp, if you would."

"Right-o." He poured the beers and set them on the bar with a flourish. "Stuck, were ye. Ah, 'tis a bad turn when that happens. Didn't ye know of Kerrigan's Bog?"

"No, wish I had." Blanche took a large sip of foam and lager and melted.

"Famous 'round these parts. Many a cow and sheep and, perhaps, a lass or farmer or two been lost to the bog." He winked. Blanche shivered. He busied himself polishing the bar. "So glad to see ye upright and in the best pub in Ireland."

"Really? This is the best pub in Ireland?" Haasi sipped. She twisted the corner of her mouth as she recounted in her head. "Wow. Heard there's almost eight hundred pubs in Ireland."

"Sure, and it's always the best pub—whichever one ye have the fortune to be standin' in."

"I have to agree," said Haasi. "Feels like a winner."

"Mr. Bantry, is it?" Blanche leaned forward on the bar, both hands on her glass.

"Ye be lookin' at himself." Jack Bantry polished the same spot on the bar, round and round, while he studied Blanche. "What can I do for ye?"

"Kevin O'Riley said we might find you here." Blanche tapped the glass on the bar. She relaxed as she felt her limbs return to her. "Mr. O'Riley and his friend, Blitsy, rescued us from that bog, and we got to chatting."

"He did, did he." Suddenly, he seemed guarded. Blanche was struck once again at how personalities could change in a blink, from frolicking to serious.

"Yes, he did. It's important. He said you might be able to tell us the name of a man who customarily visited one Declan O'Brian up the road."

Haasi did a quick take, covered her lips with the rim of her glass, and stared at the row of bottles behind the bar.

Bantry stopped all the busy work and slapped the towel against his thigh. "They be good for nothin', ye ask me. That Tony, he's a sour one, and Declan, thought his own business didn't have a stink on it … Pardon, Miss. I made a vow to me sainted mother. If I can't say something good about someone, well, then I won't say a *ting*."

Blanche eyed him steadily.

Haasi finished her beer. "Well, I guess that about wraps it up. Thank you, Mr. Bantry. What do you say we head out, B?"

"Tony, you say? Tony Costello, perhaps?" Blanche stayed planted on that stool and managed a cool expression.

"Don't rightly know for sure, but that sounds about right." Bantry averted his face and began loudly rearranging a row of liquor bottles. The man at the end of the bar glanced at Blanche and Haasi and then looked away quickly.

It was time to leave. Bantry knew more than he wanted to admit; everyone knew everybody around the townlands, first and last names, and all their business. The place hummed with secrets and gossip.

"Thank you, Mr. Bantry." Blanche wanted to ask more, but she'd let this little meet-up settle in her brain and plan to see Tony soon. She put the money on the bar and headed for the door. Her legs were shaky, her gait wobbly, and she was shivering again. She was glad to be alive. The chill bog had soaked through her clothes, the cold wet invaded her bones, and the beer had only made her slightly relaxed, not elated. Fortunately, they had less than an hour back to the castle.

Haasi stood at the door, a hand out to Blanche. "Come on, Duchess, time to re-establish your reign. You can start with a bath."

Una met them in the entry of the castle. "Goodness gracious! What has befallen the two of ye."

"We fell into Kerrigan's Bog on the way to Ballybunion," said Blanche, stamping her feet on the mat outside the door and removing her sneakers. "Wish I'd known about that one."

Una's hands shot up to her cheeks. "The saints preserve us all! Ye made it out!"

"Thanks to a sweet herder and his donkey," said Haasi, now standing barefoot in the entry hall, a soiled jacket looped over her arm.

"We Irish! Bound to help the traveler in dire straits," said Una, rubbing her hands. Blanche noticed again the ropy sinews, the strong fingers. For a woman getting on, she appeared to be quite … strong.

"Didn't think such a pit was a common thing in those parts," said Haasi.

"It isn't. How you managed to find this one is a particularly bad piece of luck."

"We seem to be falling into more than one pit lately," Haasi murmured. She was already trudging up the stairs.

"We'll look after ye," said Una. "I'll have Mae draw baths for ye, just go ahead upstairs, Miss Blanche, and we'll get after the muddy clothing. I'll be gettin' something nice and hot for the both of ye to drink."

"Nice and hot and alcoholic," added Blanche with a grin. "You're the best, Una." She headed up the stairs behind Haasi.

"I second that," said Haasi from the landing. "Thanks, Una."

Una turned toward the kitchen, then did a quick reversal. "Miss Blanche." She paused midway up the stairs. "That inspector dropped by. Said he was just down from Dublin and needed a return visit to Ballycill. He read the report and wants to speak with you again."

One grimy hand clutched the rail as she stared down at Una. "Did he say when?"

"No, he didn't, Miss. But he'll be back. Nothin' better to do than disturb the peace, it seems."

Blanche froze. Haasi had already disappeared into her room. "I'll see about it, Una. Thank you." She dragged herself up the steps, suddenly feeling the weight of less than a week in Ireland. *I need to get to the bottom of this murder! And get myself out from under it! One bog at a time.*

But first, the bath. The rising cloud of steam, redolent of lavender, was the headiest and best thing that had ever hit her. Much more pleasant than the news that the inspector was still tracking her. Not knowing what he wanted was surely worse than what he wanted. *Right?* She couldn't sort it out right now. She was too tired. And she was too afraid, if she were honest about it.

This too shall pass. Gran's words came back to her like a warm hug; she could certainly use one.

For now, the tub would do just fine. She lolled in the bubbles, staring at the rectangular patch of blue sky in the window, her head resting on a small pillow at the back of the enormous claw-footed tub. She did not want to get out. Ever. She wanted to soak and luxuriate and float away from all the madness her new "ownership" had created. *Oh, Gran, if you only knew.*

But she would get out of this tub, and get out of this mess, eventually. She would. Her head was swimming with the events of the past week. The arrival, the people they'd met—dozens of Irish—the murder, the suspicions. The unanswered questions:

Who killed Declan O'Brian?

What exactly happened to her long-lost cousin, William McLoughlin?

Those were the big questions, and the answers flew about like broken pieces of a thing that begged fixing. How would she put it together? She would not be connected in any way to the murder of that scoundrel, Declan O'Brian. Plus, she felt duty-bound to find out more about William McLoughlin's death—especially after reading O'Brian's assertion in the diary.

He was glad that William was dead?

Who are the likely suspects in O'Brian's demise?

Tony Costello's name kept emerging, for one reason or another. He'd been in the kitchen the night before the murder. Later, he'd stared down Blanche at Barrett's pub. Now, pub owner, Jack Bantry, said he'd spied "Tony" visiting Declan. Mary Fogarty loved and hated Declan's guts. She had motivation to be done with the sight of his face all over town and the memories. Would she be able to sneak in and thrust a knife into the torso of her former lover? Maybe. Oddly enough, she'd made a point of saying she didn't want him dead. Though, truthfully, it sounded like she could take him dead, or alive.

Maggie didn't care for him. No love lost there. Would she have avenged William? She was spry and strong, no doubt. But she possessed a flare for live-and-let-live. Blanche did not think she was capable, nor inclined, to murder the agent.

Then there was the staff ... Nancy, Mae ... and Una. None of them cared for Declan. He'd been accused of pestering the women, and Blanche believed the rumors about his philandering to be true. His designs on Una had to do mostly with control of castle affairs, and probably money. *Did she hold some secret over him?* It seemed that was the case, according to their argument. Blanche had heard the words and threats. Yes, Una, of the large hands and strong mind and body. She'd said "he had it in" for her, didn't she? But an elderly, devoted castle staffer, a tutor and former nurse? *A murderer?*

Oh, this is so confusing.

Maybe one of them did it, maybe more than one—maybe all of them, like in that Agatha Christie mystery. But this was not a novel; it was the real thing, and the shroud of suspicion hung heavily on Blanche's back.

She dipped below the surface of the soapy, perfumed bath water and rubbed her head vigorously, more to shake up the brain cells than get rid of bog slime. She'd already showered most of it off, but she couldn't shake that vegetable-soup feeling. She popped up and rubbed her face. She climbed out of the tub, weak with fatigue—and relief that she hadn't been sucked into the bog and smothered to death. That outcome might have been unlikely, given Kevin O'Riley's gleeful tack on the whole proceedings. *I guess I'll never know and good riddance to that.*

She wrapped herself in terry cloth and shuffled off to the bed and the yummy pillow and duvet, too tired to check back downstairs for food and drink. She was asleep before she could count to one ... donkey.

Twenty-One

Calling at the Castle

BLANCHE SLEPT THE SLEEP OF THE DEAD, but instead of dying she dreamed she was slowly disappearing into an undulating green plain. Someone was pulling at her feet from underground. She sank and flailed about and was angry as hell. She woke up in a sweat, the only constraint a tangle of bedding.

It was early. Outside her window, the gold and gray light gilded the tops of the dark shapes of trees, and the air was lush and fresh off the ocean. The heaving, vast Atlantic, not the salty, sunny Gulf of Mexico she called home. She loved it, it was all water to her, each with its own sunlight and moonlight and beachy smell. She dropped the cover and stretched, shoved her feet into slippers, and stood up. She went to the window.

A cow had escaped from its pen and stood mooing under her window. "Good morning," she murmured. "You are not free to roam, and neither am I."

She sighed, put on her robe, and started for the door in search of coffee. She grabbed the James Lee Burke novel she hadn't finished on the plane, or in the week she'd been in Ireland. *In the land of writers and readers, I'm not doing so well.* She'd also planned to take some notes for a story in the island newspaper. Clint Wilkinson, her editor and boss, had emphasized a theme of *travel*: "No murders this time, Blanche. Only nice little stories about pubs, great beer, and castles. Yours, in particular."

He'd be dismayed at the outcome so far, especially since a previous assignment to Mexico City for purposes of travel writing had ended up in murder, art thievery, and near death for both Blanche and Haasi. She'd have a story about this trip for Clint, all right. He'd bluster and sputter, and Blanche would have to do that same old dance with him to come to some sort of compromise. But he was an old sweetie, sort of like a grandfather she never had. She had an urge to call him; no, she would not call him. Clint would be no help at all now, and she didn't want him to be. And she wouldn't call the rest of her extended family—cousin Jack, or Cappy, or Liza. She had to get herself out of this and not end up on the pages of the Irish press as an American visitor and suspect in a murder of one of their own.

She was glad it was early. The castle was quiet as a tomb. Haasi was no doubt still asleep, and Blanche did not want to disturb her. Sister-cousin needed to recover from their latest disaster in the bog pit.

Blanche headed downstairs and wandered into the dining room. A steamy carafe and bread and jam were already placed on the sideboard, a chafing dish sent off a faint odor of fuel as it awaited its pan of eggs or whatever Una was cooking up. The fireplace sent out reassuring warmth from the whistling low flame.

She carried her coffee cup to the tall narrow window, the heavy silk draperies parting grandly to let in the bright, gray morning against the brilliant green—an extraordinary juxtaposition of light. *Gray was bright. Go figure. Ireland.* The mist hovered above the rolling lawn like a flank of ghosts.

"Good mornin' to ye, Miss," said Mac. She held the silver chafing dish with its ebony handle in front of her with linen towels and turned to place it carefully over the low flame. "I hope you'll be enjoyin' the sossage and rasher, and how will ye be takin' yer eggs?" She waited, hands clasped, head tilted, lovely and long-haired, the red tresses bound in a black ribbon. She had a sprinkle of freckles on her nose.

"Good morning, Mae! I'll have whatever egg you have a mind to throw in the pan."

"Ah, ye Americans! So lively … and relaxed. Sure, and it's a pleasure."

"I could say the same." It was a pleasure. The people were hospitable, the countryside a joy to behold, and the beer flowed. She just wished things could be *perfect*. "I just wish we could finish this business with

Declan and enjoy the rest of our visit. Know what I mean, Mae?"

"Oh, I do, miss. 'Tis a desperate situation."

Una appeared in the doorway. "Thank ye, girl. Ye can fetch the eggs now."

Mae jumped at the sound of Una's voice. "I'll just go then. Will there be anythin' else, Miss?"

Blanche poured herself another splash of coffee and smiled. "No, I'm good. If I don't finish this beautiful breakfast, I know Haasi will eat everything in sight."

Una stood just inside the dining room. "Sure, and it's a blessing the two of ye love to eat and drink and laugh a bit. It's been quiet for so long here, ye could hear the grass growin'."

"That's pretty quiet. Some of that would be nice," said Blanche with a grin. "We came here on a vacation and look how that turned out."

"Ah, it'll settle down, no doubt, and ye can get on with it. We'll have the bad things done up soon enough, I hope."

"Did the inspector say when he'd come by?"

"No, I think the team of investigators has the matter under control. I wouldn't worry," she said, quickly. "Will Miss Haasi be joining ye fer breakfast soon?"

"I'm sure she will. Haven't known her to miss a meal. Right now, she's catching up on sleep."

Mae hurried through the door with a basket of buns and a plate of eggs. "I'm sorry, Miss, to disturb ye so early. But Mary Fogarty, from St. Columba's, ye know, is at the kitchen door. She wants to have a word with ye, Miss Blanche."

"How irregular," said Una, a trace of haughtiness in her tone.

Blanche looked from Una to Mae. "Oh, how delightful! Please tell her to come in." Blanche moved past Una's reaction. "Mae, will you keep those eggs warm? I'll take that basket over here, and will you ask her to join me? Maybe she'll have some coffee and breakfast." It was hard to ignore the twin expressions of surprise on Una and Mae's faces, their lips shut in a thin line. Blanche decided to look on the positive side. *Good will.* And this visit saved a trip to Mary's—and the possible awkwardness of dropping in. Blanche had Declan on her mind, and this could help further her pursuit of answers.

Una nodded. "As you say, Miss." They turned on cue, back toward the kitchen.

Blanche sighed. Maybe she didn't have her "duchess" hat on straight. After all, it was all right to invite Mary to coffee, wasn't it? She just didn't care to second guess the invitation. She stared down the length of the dining table with its seating for thirty, and she felt ridiculous. *I could invite most of the shop owners on Main Street for breakfast, and they'd fit here.* Then it occurred to her, she wasn't exactly dressed for the occasion. She pulled the robe tighter and patted down her curls.

Mary came to the door, her shoulders squared. She was neatly put together in a long-ish skirt and a short, tight little jacket with lapels. There was something stylish about her, something entirely and distinctly *Mary*. Blanche rose, smiling, and offered her hand. "What a surprise!"

"I'm sorry to barge in. 'Tis irregular, to be visitin' the big house with no invitation and the like. Hope it's all right with ye that I'm comin' by fer a short visit." *Shart.* Blanche was still trying to get her ear fixed to the Irish pronunciation; she loved it, and sometimes it drew her up *shart.*

"It's perfectly all right. It's not like there's no room at the table." Blanche grinned and looked down the polished oak surface with silver candelabra. "Please, sit."

"Oh, Declan O'Brian would frown upon it, deeply. The townspeople do not visit here. Just. They say it wouldn't be proper."

"Well, I'm glad you're here. It was a good visit we had the other day, and I was telling Haasi, I wanted to see you again."

Blanche had noticed the basket looped over her arm, and her glance darted there. Mary held it tighter. Blanche pulled out a chair. "Nothing improper, or irregular. Except for the way I'm dressed. Please excuse me," she said. "Just your average day here, trying to solve this Declan situation. And recover from the bog pit."

"Oh, that's terrible about the Kerrigan fix. No one told ye about it then? Now, why would they?" Her voice drifted, distractedly.

Blanche poured a cup of coffee for Mary, but she hardly glanced at it, sitting on the edge of her chair. She seemed nervous but smiled, her gaze landing on the gold-framed McLoughlins, the heavy gold brocade draperies, the sideboard of gleaming covered dishes. She patted her shining hair, tied back with a navy ribbon. She still clutched the basket.

"We had no business out there," said Blanche. "What a dumbbell I am. Haasi knew about bogs, but it was too late to warn me, and she certainly didn't know about that one. Fortunately, one Kevin O'Riley and his little Blitsy happened along …"

A mewing sound came from the basket on Mary's arm. She colored to the hue of a tomato.

"Those aren't buns you have in there." Blanche laughed and reached for the plaid linen covering the basket. A tiny, furry orange head popped up, its bright beady little eyes darting about its surroundings. It tried to jump out of the basket, but Mary had a hold of it.

"Oh, glory be to the Lord! Misty, get down in there!" Mary half petted, half scolded the clueless kitten who persisted in climbing out of the basket.

"How adorable! Misty? Probably should call it Pumpkin." Blanche came around the side of the chair and peeked at the kitten. "May I?"

"Of course. I heard the ladies were complaining about mice, and Dolly had a litter of kittens. You'd a met 'em the other day, but Dolly was particular about where she dropped them, and I let her be—in the storage out back of the kitchen. Dolly took such a liking to you. I wasn't sure about this, but I thought this one could use a new, lovely home."

Blanche held Misty Pumpkin in the crook of her arm and paced the dining room, bouncing the kitten up and down like a newborn baby.

"Well, now, I think the little one has taken to ye, too, like her dear ma." Mary smiled, crossing her arms. "I didn't mean to spring her on ye, over breakfast and all. She was sleeping so, cuddled down in there on them rags, but that's a kitten for ye. Up and about like a baby, or a toddler…" Her voice ran down thin and poorly.

"It's all right, Mary," Blanche said quickly. "Of course, we'd love to have her. Thank you!" Blanche resumed rocking the kitten, singing, "Too-Ra-Loo-Ra-Loo-Ra …"

"Ye know the song then?"

"My Gran used to sing it to me. It's an Irish lullaby." She sat at the table, and the kitten snuggled into a ball in her lap. "I'm sorry. My manners. Will you have something to eat? Eggs? A bun? Please help yourself to whatever is there on the sideboard. Please."

Haasi bounded into the dining room. She was dressed for hiking, in sneakers, denim blue jacket, and jeans. Her hair was tightly braided into two long shiny plaits. "Hi, Mary! Good to see you. And what's all this? Company?" She laughed as she reached down and pet the kitten. "And new friend!"

"Good morning!" Blanche and Mary, in unison.

"And to you, a fine one, I see." Haasi went right to the plate and sausage and bacon. "Yum. Gonna load up and I'll join you. Mary, get something to eat—and maybe some bacon for the little one?"

Mary sat, hands folded in her lap, eyeing Blanche. Haasi dug in. Blanche was busy chatting up the kitten.

"Blanche speaks kitten." Haasi grinned. "But I'll bet that cat doesn't speak Florida. Blanche, don't get too attached."

"I'm in love."

"I don't mean to be a pest, foisting a cat on ye. She can go back to her ma, but I think she's old enough for a job," said Mary, brightly. "Head mouse chaser of Dunfaedan."

"And a sweetie pie," said Blanche. "I'm glad you didn't just drop off this little darling and go. I really want to chat."

Haasi shot Blanche a look. "Duchess."

"Oh my, are ye a duchess now? With the inheritance and all?" Mary seemed genuinely puzzled on the topic of royal succession.

Haasi burst out laughing. "No, not really. It's just our little … nickname, a *pet* name, if you will."

Blanche gave Haasi a wry look. "Yes, we communicate—and keep each other out of trouble sometimes. But not often enough."

She doesn't want me to tell about our little visit to Declan's, but I have to … eventually.

"Uh-huh." Haasi resumed devouring the pile of food, which now included grilled tomatoes and a hunk of brown bread the size of a small brick. "I love this bread. How about you, Mary?"

Mary smiled. She hadn't moved from the edge of her seat. Her long fingers clutched the coffee cup, but it didn't reach her lips. She glanced toward the door to the hall and kitchen. "Of course, we're raised on it, and it's no secret. Lots of good flour and water and a bit of kneading.

We surely have the knack of it, after all these years."

Blanche looked up from petting the kitten and leveled her gaze at their visitor. "Anything else on your mind, Mary?" Blanche asked gently. "Besides Misty Pumpkin—and a bread recipe." She grinned at Haasi. "Seems like you have something you want to say. I'd love to hear."

"It's about Declan."

"Oh, great." Haasi took a large swig of the orange juice. "I hope it's good news. We sure could use some."

"I don't know if it's news. But there are things I want to tell you. I feel like I was evasive with you on your visit. You were so kind, and I believe genuinely interested … in making things right." Her speech pattern drifted between hard English and a soft brogue.

"Well, thank you, and, yes, we do want to make things right," said Blanche, eagerly.

Haasi nodded. "I couldn't agree more. All we can do is help, and if you have something to add to clear up some of this mystery—for the gardai—that would be great!"

"They have to figure it out. But it's wrong you should have a cloud over yer head," said Mary. "Declan is dead and yet he's still causing problems."

"That's it. I'd like to know more about Declan, if you're willing to share. The more I know, the easier it will be to make some sense of this mess."

Haasi gave Blanche a tight smile, this time, on the sly from the sideboard where she was helping herself to seconds.

"I don't mean to pry in your business, but anything you say may help," said Blanche. "You told us about his writing. Is there anything else you can think of? It'll all stay private, of course. I promise." She looked over at Haasi again, but her sister-cousin was concentrating on dissecting a slice of tomato.

"All right." Mary hadn't touched her coffee or made a move toward so much as a bun. She held the cup like a prop. "I don't know what you did with what I gave you. But I think the gardai will find his records and books and have a good look around. I know they've been out there to his house. Haven't heard a word of follow-up. Seems the district had a team of investigators working on it."

Blanche swallowed a large gulp of coffee. It burned, and so did the realization that they could have run into the murder squad during their little expedition. "I'm sure. I'm going to ask the authorities what they've found out there, not that they'd tell me. But you did mention he liked to write, keep journals and such. I imagine there could definitely be something in those journals."

Mary looked at her sharply. "Journals? How do you know he kept journals?"

"Lucky guess? Luck of the Irish?"

Haasi's smile was now at the point of cracking. "Oh, definitely, journals. What else would he write besides the essays you mentioned? The gardai will know what to do. Most assuredly. Let them at it. Yes. Great."

"All right," said Blanche, firmly.

Mary looked from one to the other in mild confusion and shrugged. "They're sure to find the payments."

"The *payments*? You are referring to payments Declan made as part of his job? He was the castle agent, after all."

"That's what I'm coming to tell ye. I'm not only here on a mission to catch mice. You were right, Blanche. This face can't hide a thing. There're records of payments, aside from running the castle."

Blanche's brain flashed back to the secret volumes under the desk in the locked chest. The mystery payments. The "extra-curricular." She put her chin in her hands, and let Mary go at it.

"Money that had nothing to do with the upkeep of Dunfaedan. He was paying me. I'm sorry I took a single pound, or euro, from him. But he sweet-talked me. Said he had a reputation to repair and maintain. He didn't want me to do any more damage to his *name*. As if I wanted to talk about him or have anything to do with him ever again." Her tone turned bitter and hard. "He never said anything about the damage to *my name*."

"Oh." Blanche listened with radar focus.

Can this get any more freaking complicated?

She spoke softly. "Mary, giving you money is not a crime. I'm not sure how that has much to do with the murder."

"It probably doesn't. Directly," she said, hastily. "But I wanted you to know in case it comes up, and it will. He did send me money. I told him not to come over and give it to me. He made deposits to my bank account. To help, he said. To shut me up, more like."

"The police have a lot to sort out," said Haasi. "They'll find the records, and his writings, and the payments are sure to come up. Bet they'll learn a lot about Declan O'Brian."

"They're going to wonder about those payments. And dig into them, for sure," said Mary. "I just bet they have ye in the dark, and I wanted some light on the subject. It might help, it might not. It does help for ye to know what Declan O'Brian was up to. Shuttin' me up."

"It does sort of clear up, I mean, say something about Declan. Not sure what…" Blanche gave Mary a sideways glance.

"Ye have to believe I would have no incentive to kill him and end the payments. I want to set that straight." Mary twisted the napkin in her lap, the food and coffee forgotten. "I never told anyone about any of this, but now it will come out. It just feels better to say it, to lighten the weight of Declan O'Brian on me soul."

Blanche checked the doorway. They were alone. She touched Mary's arm lightly. "Did you have anything to do with his murder, Mary? Or know anyone who did? If you know anything, or any reason, you have to tell the gardai."

"No! Saints in heaven, no!" Her eyes became larger, darker, the corners pinched and white. "No, why would I? Like I said, he was paying me. And I don't know why anyone would kill him—besides the fact he was loathed in the townland."

"What a strange person he was." Blanche sat back in the chair and exhaled sharply. "Can you ever know what's inside someone's head? The sight of him must have been enough to drive you crazy."

"He wasn't that hard to read, Blanche. All he had to do was stand in front of a mirror, and you could see it. Declan's world. That was the extent of his range."

"And, here you are, linked to him in such a way."

"Like I said, he made the deposits. I mostly stayed away from Declan O'Brian," Mary said. "I didn't want to look at him, I couldn't. If I did, I know I would think he could have saved my child. *Our* child …" She looked down at her lap, wringing her hands. The cat gamboled about the room like it owned the place. It had found a beam of sunshine and a tassel and was having the delight of its young life.

Mary's head remained bent, her face averted. The sun shined on the white part in her dark hair; she smoothed a curl over one ear. Suddenly, she began to shake all over. Her hands covered her face. "God help me, I loved him, I did. *Why?*"

Blanche and Haasi exchanged a look of mild alarm. Blanche reached for Mary's hand. "I don't know what to say about that. Love is just plain crazy, now. Isn't it? How the hell can anyone explain it?"

Mary wiped her cheeks and laughed suddenly. "That about says it."

"I've been in love and done crazy stuff."

Haasi rolled her eyes. "Thank God, that didn't end in complete disaster."

Blanche turned to Mary. "We had a little hiccup in Mexico City, but things...*he*...is on the mend."

"Oh," said Mary. "Maybe it makes both of us feel better to admit it. Love is completely blind and *deef.*"

"Yup."

"I've held it in a long time."

Blanche wondered how long. Declan was older than Mary, and this odd relationship between them must have gone on for decades. For once, she didn't pry.

"Now it's out." Haasi whispered. "Mary, we'll keep your confidence whatever you tell us. And whatever you decide to tell the authorities may help to fix this broken mess."

"They'll find the payments. But I want you to know—"

"We're here," said Blanche.

Mary was silent. She patted her hair. Her face was flushed. "Ye might as well know the rest. He was going to stop paying me. I was glad of it. I'd come to rely on it, forgive me, and anticipate that little contact I had with him. But it was ugly money, it was. How I loathed him—and I loved him! But, yes, the payments were about to stop."

Blanche raised her eyebrows. "He was going to stop?"

"Yes, my choice. I told him no more. I'd come into a small inheritance, and the parish pays me some. I didn't need Declan O'Brian's pity, or his money. He'd already taken everything. He could never make it up. I wanted to be clean of him. If I could."

Blanche thought of her pain and losing her child to the O'Brians' maneuvering. Declan owned his fate, may have even deserved it, but none of it was any good—and it didn't make sense. The death didn't solve a thing, and Mary didn't seem to fit the scene. They sat, each mulling quietly the circumstances that brought them together. *Somewhere in all of this are answers.*

Blanche said, "I'm glad you told us. It's kind of a turning point."

"How is that?" she asked.

"Chipping away at secrets, I guess. There are an awful lot of them around." Blanche nearly choked on her words. She caught herself in the knowledge of her own secret. She'd been lurking around Declan O'Brian's house and hadn't said a thing about it to Mary. She was just as guilty of secrets as the rest.

"Yup," said Haasi. "The investigators should go over O'Brian's place real good. Especially over his records—his writings and journals—should he have any."

Blanche nodded. "Never know what they might find if they take a good look."

Twenty-Two

Say It in Ogham

"IT'S STILL EARLY, BLANCHE. Maybe we could drive over to the Dingle and have a look around. Some great scenery and pubs over there." Haasi had gone for a bike ride and then found Blanche in the library with a notebook and several volumes of Irish history she'd pulled off the shelves.

"Haas, you're just full of good ideas."

"I've been known …" Haasi flopped in an armchair. "What're you doing?"

Blanche slapped the book closed. "I can't help thinking about that Celtic cross we found in Declan's box of stuff. I wanted to look it up."

Haasi reached for one of the books on the sofa: *The Knot of Irish Legend: The Silver Cross and Other Treasure. The Secrets of Ancient Ogham.* "Well, look at you. What did you find out? And what the heck is ogham?"

"Ogham is an old Irish alphabet, each letter based on a tree and the like. It was probably used as a secret form of communication against invading armies in the fourth to sixth century, and possibly earlier. Look here, the 'M' means 'vine' and it's written like this." Blanche pointed to a slanted stick with a line through it.

"Well, say something in ogham."

"Very funny," said Blanche. "But you know that cross we found at Declan's? It had these weird symbols on it. I think it was ogham for "W" and "M."

Haasi sat up. "William McLoughlin."

177

"None other." Blanche sprang off the sofa and began pacing.

"Bang! Settle yourself down now."

"Didn't you see it, too? The symbols with the lines?"

"I did, Blanche, but I didn't think much of it." Haasi chewed her lower lip. "Until now, until you pointed it out."

"Think we should run by Maggie's? Just to say hello?"

"And have another look at that photo of William?"

"Great minds, Haas. Great minds."

"Is that what you call it?"

It was the middle of a misty afternoon in Ballycill when Haasi and Blanche set off on their bikes for Maggie's. There was not a soul on the narrow road. They pedaled side by side. "Do you think we should tell her about our visit to Declan's? Can we avoid it?" Blanche cast a glance at Haasi.

"No way around it. How else can we explain our question about the markings on this cross?"

"Right. We'll tell her. I'm sick of all the damn secrets. But we don't have to drag Mary into it. I'd like to keep her out of it, talk around it."

"The great circle of life, or should I say, obfuscation."

"In a word."

They rounded a bend, and the cottage came into view. The humid gusty breeze blew the fresh scent of the sea past them and made the fuchsia in front tremble in a wave of red and white. They parked the bikes. From out of Maggie's front door, the vocals backed by fiddle and pipes spilled the sad story of "The Long Black Veil."

The Irish: "For all their wars are merry, and all their songs are sad."

G.K. Chesterton might have been right about the songs—a lot of them went on and on about death and alcoholism. But Maggie's cottage was a wild contrast to the music with its scent of something good baking and its inviting warmth. Maggie herself smiled and hurried toward them with open arms. She stopped on the path. "Ah, here ye be then! 'Tis grand!"

"Thanks for having us," said Blanche. "Next time, please come over to the castle." She couldn't believe what she'd just said. *Come over to the castle?*

"Me darlin', been there and done that. It's lovely, and I might be after doing that, but for now, ye come into me parlor for a wee chat and a sip." The invitation was delivered with a great outpouring of welcome.

"Maggie, where do you get all the energy?" Blanche grinned at the octogenarian who radiated limber vitality. "What's your secret?"

"Well, now, I may write a book." She looped arms with Haasi and Blanche and waltzed them into the cottage. "I should say the secret of life is a clear conscience and fresh food. Maybe a tipple here and there."

Blanche noted the tipple on the table: a glass carafe full of liquor, plus the tea things and a pile of cakes. *The sweet secrets of life.*

They sat around the peat fire, which gave off a homey, smokey smell that seemed to pervade Ireland. The day was another temperate one, with less rain, and some sunshine. Maggie picked up a glass and the decanter. "Now tell me what yer up to. Or down to. I heard about the bog pit. What an awful thing to happen!"

"Thanks to Kevin O'Riley and his friend, Blitsy, we're intact," said Haasi. "It was a lucky stroke he came by."

"Ah, Kevin, then." Maggie stopped pouring into the glasses. "They say he's touched. It's a lucky thing he happened by. But then, in this world, nothing is luck, nothing is an accident. He was meant to save ye, and ye were meant to be saved."

Blanche would accept that observation and be done with bog pits. "Touched?"

Maggie handed them brimming crystal stemmed glasses and held hers up, a glint in her eyes. "By the spirits. Some of us know what to do and where to be and it's an uncommon thing for those touched by grace to miss a calling."

Haasi nodded. Of course, she did. Blanche wanted to know more, but the deeper she dove into Irish lore and custom and faeries, the further she shifted from reality and a sense of grounding. She'd just settle for Maggie's theory. *That's just the way it is.*

Blanche got down to business. "Maggie, we went to Declan's house. We broke in and found a bunch of journals. And a cross."

Haasi choked on her tea, and possibly a cake. Maggie's hand flew to her chest. "Did ye now. Well, isn't that a fine piece of news!"

"I couldn't wait to tell you."

"Apparently," said Haasi, who recovered from asphyxiation by tea, cake, and Blanche.

"Now, tell me about this find. Does seem of great importance to ye, but ye did take a chance there. Breaking and entering," said Maggie, her eyebrows drawn together in concern.

"It's kind of a long story," said Blanche. "We wanted to get to know him better?"

"Hmmm. Seems a little late for that." Maggie sipped her whiskey.

Blanche moved to the edge of her seat. "We found journals. His writing said things about his 'hobby' of seeking out the ladies. There were also records of payments, some of them strange. We're hoping the police get into all that. But what we really wanted to tell you about is what we found in a box. A silver cross on a chain." She glanced at Haasi. She vividly recalled the etching on the silver, the Celtic knots—the ogham marks.

"Well, my dear, he was the agent. They do keep records. And a Celtic cross is not so uncommon in Ireland, ye know." Maggie settled back in her chair at this anti-climactic announcement.

Blanche's voice went up a notch. "This cross had symbols. Ogham letters for 'M' and 'W.'"

Maggie sprang forward. "Did it now."

"Yes, the initials. But this was a special cross, antique silver. You could tell it was hand crafted," said Haasi.

She sank down in her chair, her hands to her cheeks. Her eyes dimmed as if she'd escaped to a memory. "Has to be our William's. I gave him that cross, and, yes, it had his initials. I thought it was lost with him in the terrible drowning." Then she burst out. "Ye found it? In Declan's things?"

"Yup. It's definitely unique—and antique. Special, and the symbols were strange. I looked them up. I feel certain it belonged to him." Blanche walked over to the photos on the table and picked up the one of William on his horse. "Like this." She held the framed black-and-white picture of William reigning in his horse, the cross dangling from his neck.

"How did Declan get it?" Maggie murmured. "I'd like to know."

"So would we," said Haasi.

Maggie was up pacing now, drawing her shawl tightly around her shoulders. She had a new spark that Blanche could only guess had to do with the revelation. "Well, we can't ask Declan. He wouldn't have told us anyway, the bloke."

"Who would know?"

"That's what me mind is pondering," said Maggie. "And one name keeps after me, loud and clear. Tony Costello."

"Blanche, I know you want to talk to him, but I think you should drop it." Haasi's legs pumped the pedals on the bike. Blanche had a hard time keeping up.

"I can't drop it, Haas. You know that. Tony and Declan must be connected, from all accounts. And somewhere in there, William McLoughlin is involved."

"A lot of personalities. This is beginning to sound like a Russian novel. Most of them dead."

"They're not all dead. I still want to talk to Tony."

"I know you do. I can only imagine where that will lead."

"Let's follow our noses."

"And keep our feet planted on terra firma."

"Oh, Princess."

Twenty-Three
Snoop It Up

THAT NIGHT, BARRETT'S PUB HOSTED A CEILI, a party with music, dancing, and lots of beer. Blanche and Haasi dressed in skirts, snug sweaters, and flats and went down to Ballycill to get a taste of the "local." The fiddle, flute, and accordion players were tuning up to "Molly Malone," a favorite tune about a fish monger by day and prostitute by night. Beers sweat golden beads and glistened up on the mantelpiece behind their heads in the low light, and the place smelled of soup and cigarettes. An assortment of musical instruments—framed drums, banjoes, pipes, and a guitar—hung on the walls.

"Are you ready to dance?" Blanche eagerly scanned the room where a makeshift plywood platform served as a stage. There was a buzz in the air, like a beehive ready to break open.

"Maybe."

"You know you are. It'll be fun." Blanche went to the bar.

Haasi was right beside her. "Since when do you *not* see fun?"

Blanche eyed the line-up of beverages. Jameson's and Paddy, Harp on draft. The menu on a blackboard listed bangers and mash, cabbage, and fish chowder. She read the choices out loud. The strong heady mix of hot food and booze wafting from the bar was intoxicating. The Irish knew how to feed the body, and the music certainly enlivened the soul—and told one story after another.

"Delicious," Haasi sighed.

"Yeah, I could get fat just breathing in here," said Blanche. "But, Haas, we just ate. Get that look off your face."

"Well, I suppose we could have a drink."

"How unusual." They burst out laughing.

The bartender was a young woman, ponytail high on her head, wearing a blue shirt that gave startling definition to her huge blue eyes. "Now here's a merry pair. What's the *craic*?" Her grin was open and friendly.

Blanche and Haasi looked at each other. "*Craic?*"

"What's new? How are ye? Hi!"

"We're great. How about you?"

"Grand! Ye must be the visitors from America. Come home, have ye?"

Home to Ireland. There it is again. "I guess you could say that. In a way. We're Florida Irish," Blanche said. "Good to be with you."

"A hundred thousand welcomes."

"Blanche here, Haasi, my cousin." Haasi nodded and smiled.

"Aisling McCarter. What will ye be drinking? Music is about to start."

And with that, a blast of pipes and strings nearly knocked them off the bar stools. Aisling set shots of Jameson's on the bar. They sipped and warmed up to the ear splitting jig.

Blanche couldn't help but move. She tapped her fingers on the bar, her feet found the floor, and pretty soon she was out on the dance stage, her arms straight at her sides, and the toes of her shoes pounding back and forth. She had company. The pub had started to fill, and the air became dense with smoke and laughter. Haasi sat on a bar stool, grinning and shaking her head. The music ended, and Blanche returned to Haasi and her drink.

"Bang, what was in that glass? And where did you learn to do *that*?"

"Something came over me." Blanche was damp, disheveled, and her face was hot. Her hair stuck to her forehead. "I used to watch the Irish dancing on TV. The wood floor at the cabin was perfect for practicing."

"That's a fine turn, Miss. Sean Callaghan's me name." He was tall, sandy-haired, with deep-set eyes, and a wide grin. He leaned over Blanche. He was a foot taller and long armed. Tight leather jacket and boots.

"Blanche Murninghan here." She nodded and smiled. "My cousin, Haasi Hakla."

"Ye must be the adventurers at the castle, then. Feck it! But ye can dance, too."

Haasi made a face. Blanche wasn't sure about this guy either, but she'd chance it. "We are that. Adventurers. Haven't had a whole lot of opportunity to dance, if you know what I mean."

"I do. So I hear. First, Declan O'Brian. And then the bog pit. I'm glad to see ye so cheery and about."

Blanche studied Sean: crinkles around the eyes, slightly slumped in the shoulders. He wasn't a young guy. More like late forties. "Did you know Declan?"

Haasi winced and sipped.

"Why, to be sure I did." He frowned. The shoulders slumped a bit more.

"And how is that?"

"Now I won't speak ill of the dead, but Declan and I didn't get on all that well."

"Duchess," Haasi murmured.

"Gee. It's so loud, I can hardly hear in this place," said Blanche, loud and clear. She leaned closer to Sean. "Why is that? You didn't get on with Declan?"

"A bit of a wanker, is all. We had our moments. But, in all, he did his business, and I did mine."

"How so?"

"Why do we have to talk about Declan? Come on now. Put it out there, lass…" He grabbed Blanche by the arm and twirled her off to the stage. The warpy plywood wasn't anchored to the floor, and the pounding of heels seemed close to blowing the roof off. Haasi slid from the bar stool, hands on hips. She swirled her whiskey and gave this Sean a twisted grin.

Blanche jigged around the edge of the stage. "Jump in, Haas. It's fine." The fiddle was deafening, and Blanche had completely gone back to her roots. She tugged at Haasi's arm while her feet were still dancing.

Haasi pursed her lips but then grinned at Blanche. "I don't have the Irish on me like you do. Enjoy it."

A short young fellow with a mustache approached her. "Would ye like to get a leg on?"

Haasi turned to him. "No." He drew back at her emphatic answer. "I have a leg on. I have two."

He laughed so hard, he spilled some of his precious Guinness.

"You're spillin' yer black stuff," a bloke said. He elbowed the mustache-guy.

"Haas, come on," said Blanche. "He means to have a dance with ye."

"OMG, Bang." Haasi tried not to laugh and climbed onto the bar stool. "Mustache" stood next to her. He'd simmered down to a chuckle, and he couldn't seem to take his eyes off Haasi's beautiful, though stony, face. His feet shifted, and he took a sip.

"How do you expect to dance with a glass of that?" Haasi finally asked.

"A practical woman, I see. I like that." He grinned but his glassy eyes did not have the sparkle of a sober person. In fact, most of the people in Barrett's were leaping, chugging, laughing, or yelling, up and down the scale. Most of them were *langered* already, and the night was young.

Blanche tugged at Haasi. "Come on. You know you love it."

"Oh, B."

The fiddle cut off, and the four ended up clustered at one end of the bar, the door open to the night. The sun had gone down, and dark shades of mauve and orange hung over the tops of the houses; the dusk seemed to hang on in Ireland, reluctant to give way to the night. Every so often, the door sprang all the way back, and a gust of fresh air cooled off the crowd. Blanche sipped a Jameson's neat.

"So. You been comin' here much?" Blanche had sobered up some on the dance floor, but she was pretty buzzed. Her limbs felt loose, and so did her tongue.

"Been weaned here, practically," said Sean. "Me dear ma was a cousin of the Barrett."

Now we're getting somewhere. The guy's been in town …

"And so you've known people. Hereabouts. Declan O'Brian. The McLoughlins?"

"Ye could say that," said Sean. "Willy Boy was after havin' a bit of fun. We tossed the ball around and such."

"Willy Boy? You mean William McLoughlin."

"A regular guy, despite his pony and the ladies and money and such. Liked the guy just fine."

"It's sad what happened."

Sean's eyes were glazed from the drink, the smoke—and memory? He seemed to lose focus; his sight narrowed. Just a little, but enough. He clammed up. "Yeah, 'tis sad, indeed. 'Scuse me." He turned to the bar and seemed to study the row of bottles on the shelf.

Blanche sidled up next to him. "And do you know a Tony Costello?"

"Ain't ye the one, makin' the rounds of all the blokes in town." He leered at Blanche.

She drew back and put her best smirk forward. "Why not? Do you know him, or not?"

"Sure I do. That's himself standin' in the far corner." Tony Costello hunched over his glass with his back to the music and dancing. His head was bent in conversation with a couple of stocky fellas.

"Who's he talking to?" Blanche peered at the dark corner.

"Ah, who knows? He's a dark one, he is. Always muckin' about." Sean took a hefty swig of Guinness and looked around. "What about tonight, ladies? Are you after comin' to a party later on?"

"Sure," said Blanche.

"No," said Haasi.

They laughed, with the exception of a subdued chuckle out of Haasi. Sean said, "Looks like the fellas will be playin' for a bit. Then we'll go down to Murphy's cellar. It's just around the corner, and over the patch at the baker's wall, and around the tool smith's. We'll walk ye there, then."

Haasi sipped, Blanche smiled. She whispered to Haasi. "Let's go. Just for a bit."

Haasi shrugged.

The boys finished their beers. Blanche wasn't sure she should have another drink; she was beginning to feel disconnected from her feet, which still twitched to the music, and she wanted to be alert to the details. As to what those details might be, she was even foggier. She checked out Haasi, who, of course, was placid and calm—but just a teensy bit wired. "OK, but we're not staying," she said.

They waved Haasi and Blanche to follow them out into the night, a misty, quiet one except for the barking and the put-put of slow, motorized wheels. After the smokey, boozy pub, the air felt good, and Blanche picked up her step next to Sean. "And who's having the party?"

"Our mate, Sammy Murphy. Good fella. You'll enjoy it, now." He winked. "A fine dancer such as yerself."

"We gonna dance?" Blanche doubted it.

"After a fashion." He let out a guffaw so loud it caused another round of barking.

Murphy's cellar was a damp place, smelling of earth and burned wood. It wasn't underground; it was more of a large open room built into the side of a hill in the back of a large frame house. Rough benches lined the walls. An odd tower of books at one end of the room, which Blanche saw at a quick glance, zeroed in on Irish history and tipped precariously. Sam Murphy stood next to a peat fire, smoking something that smelled vaguely of skunk. A guitar leaned against his leg. It was a cozy room, welcoming, like most of the living rooms and cottages and pubs Blanche had visited. *More than a hundred thousand welcomes. And secrets?*

"Yer here now. And brought the fine ladies, I see." He grinned ear to ear, a stocky fellow, short and hearty and friendly. And, obviously, ready to party. Musical instruments were at the ready. A tub of bottles and some glasses were set up in neat rows. Lots of bottles. Cushions and chairs lay about in seating arrangements that suggested the last group had just gotten up and left. *We're the reinforcements.*

Haasi stood at Blanche's ear. "Let's have a drink and get out of here."

"Why? It looks cute and cozy in here." She was swaying, just a bit.

"Oh, Bang."

The door burst open and in walked a pert redhead, her hair escaping from a blue headband. She wore tight black jeans and a sweatshirt that said "I ♥ Everyone."

A heavy-set man came in behind her. "Meet me new floozie, Peggie McBride." He laughed, raucously, his cap pulled down over his eyes. Peggie gave him a whack in the middle, and he reared back in mock-shock fashion. It was Tony Costello.

Blanche was still standing at Haasi's ear, "Well, this could get interesting."

"Or not," said Haasi.

"Now's my chance. To introduce myself."

"Hmmm. Be careful what you wish for. And stay clear of that Peggie." Haasi could speak without moving her lips.

Tony Costello opened a bottle of Harp with his teeth, a row of sharp-looking incisors that gave Blanche pause. He reminded her of a large dog.

"Hi, I'm Blanche." She stuck her hands in her back pockets and smiled.

"Well, howya, Blanche." He grinned. "What brings ye out this fine evenin'?"

"You?"

He laughed and put a meaty hand on his chest, which was sort of like a side of beef. *After all, he is a butcher.*

"Me?" He feigned surprise. "I hardly know ye, but I'd like to." He laughed again, this time his lips curling back with a leer. Blanche stepped aside, imperceptibly. His range was intimidating; he was a bully—she could see it right off. Blanche would not be intimidated.

"We've met. In the kitchen at the castle. The night before Declan was … murdered." Her tone was level, even soft and personable. "He'd mentioned you'd see me around. Well, here I am."

He took a swig of beer and then seemed to remember his manners— and that fateful night. "Oh, yeah." He pulled a bottle out of the ice, opened it in one fell swoop, and put it in Blanche's hand. She was grateful. Her mouth was dry, and so was her brain. *How am I going to do this? Very cool, that's how.* Blanche could sense Haasi not five feet away, chatting away amicably, with all ears open.

"Fergot about that night. Tryin' to ferget the whole thing, actually. 'Tis a shame." Tony Costello shook his head. Looked at the ceiling. Shifted his large sneakered feet. He returned to Blanche. "Are ye enjoying yer stay then? After all that's been said—and done."

"Sure. Ireland's lovely. Except for the murder and a minor inconvenience here and there, it's been grand."

"Can't say yer the worse fer it." He looked her up and down.

She ignored his obvious attempt to put the conversation on another plane. "I'd say Declan is the worst off. Sad what happened to him." She adopted the most empathetic tone with a melancholy lilt. She hoped she didn't break out in Irish song. "How well did you know him?"

He eyed her casually. He was a sly one, this Tony Costello. Blanche was sure she wouldn't get *jack* out of him. He sipped and looked off in the glowing peat. "Himself and me go way back. Ye must know that by now. Ye been snooping all over the townland, ye have."

Blanche felt a cold shiver. "Now, what makes you say that?"

"Ye know this place is full of secrets, and so it's a sieve of rumor and the like. Ye been talkin' up Declan in every corner."

"Maybe I have. He was the agent at the castle, after all." She could feel her backbone stiffen with each word. She did not like this guy, and she was not going to get a useful thing out of him about Declan—much less William.

"And yer a wee visitor on the lam and out of here before ye know it. Enjoy yerself." His gruff dismissal slammed the door. He slouched over to Peggie McBride and pulled her away from a fella who resembled a vertical snake and kept swaying into her.

"You handled that well," Haasi whispered.

"No, I didn't. Couldn't get a word out of him."

"That's what I mean. You're in no deeper than you were an hour ago. Let's get the hell out of here."

Blanche glanced over at Tony and Peggy and a couple of fellas. Tony pulled out a bag of white powder, another produced a mirror. Peggy rolled up a bill. Sam Murphy was nowhere in sight.

"Yup, I'd say so," said Blanche. "Time to go. We'll catch up with Sam another time."

"What? And thank him for the lovely party?"

Twenty-Four

In a Crack

BLANCHE COULD NOT GET TO SLEEP to save her life. Her eyes felt permanently glued open, and the moonlight filtering in the window did nothing to shroud her in dreamland. She was sick of the secrets and unfinished business, and she was sick of staring at the blue silk canopy over her head. *What is wrong with me? This place is gorgeous, and I'm complaining and moaning in this magnificent mahogany four-poster draped in blue silk? And, by the way, Blanche, who's listening?*

No one was listening, and that was part of the problem. Haasi wanted her to cool it, the police held her at a skeptical arm's length, and the people who might help solve this whole mess were too involved in their own personal dramas, or they just didn't want to be reminded: Tony, Mary, Una.

Well, that's just the way of the world, Gran would say. Or, she might add, in a less magnanimous mood, *They're all out for themselves.* Blanche couldn't blame any of them. She and Haasi had blown into town and created nothing but chaos in their wake. She wasn't responsible for Declan's death, and at once she felt a weighty responsibility to do something about it. Especially since the authorities still held her on the books as a suspect. And all the while, the ghost of William McLoughlin haunted her.

She threw the covers off and leapt out of bed. "I have to do *something*." Any reasonable person—Haasi—would have suggested she wait until the morning, at least until daylight. Blanche reasoned that it *was* morning—well, it was three o'clock. She pulled on a pair of tight black jeans and a black sweatshirt. She knew exactly what she was going to do and where she was going. And she'd better be quick about it. That seemed to be the operative—get in and get out and don't get caught!

She crept down the stairs and elected to leave by the front door; it was heavy, but she didn't want to chance running into staff in the back of the castle. Fortunately, the door hung nicely on its hinges and didn't give her away, like in a horror movie. She felt like she was the main actor in one. She hoped it ended happily. *Since when do horror movies end happily?*

Think positive thoughts, Blanche. You can do this.

It was only a short walk into town to the butcher shop. She had one tiny little mission in mind, and she hoped she didn't screw it up. She wanted to check Tony Costello's tires. She just had a hunch, and when one of those sat on her brain, it would sit and fester until she did something about it. *This is it.*

The early morning was fresh and heavenly. The walk along the narrow road, under clumps of fuchsia, was like walking through a cloud—which she'd never done before, but if she had, it would be just like this. She closed her eyes for a second and imagined the sea all around her. So freeing and endlessly strengthening.

The sign over the butcher shop swung lightly in the breeze. Even in the pre-dawn, she could make out the lettering for Costello's Meats and Comestibles. The large front windows with gold lettering were dark; not a sound came from the building or nearby. A path wound around to the back, and Blanche took it. She looked up. Above the shop was the flat. Attorney Flynn had pointed out Costello's place from his office, and Blanche had noted the arrangement of the commercial and residential floors at the butcher's. *So, Tony is probably at home. Up there. Sleeping it off.* She and Tony had had a less-than-friendly meeting at Murphy's, and she didn't want to continue the conversation in such a manner. She'd get her business done and be on her way.

Behind Costello's, an outbuilding—most likely for tools and vehicles—stood some twenty feet back across a small patch of yard. The tiptoes of her sneakers dug into the path. Her eyes adjusted to the early morning darkness. She wasn't exactly sure what she would find, but it had to do with the crunching of the gravel the night of Declan's murder.

That gravel. So fine, and unusual, almost as fine as large, even grains of sand. If anyone knew sand, it was Blanche. It had to have been a bike that made that sound. She was sure of it, and Mary and Maggie did not ride bikes, to her knowledge. Everything pointed to Tony.

She darted a glance at the top floor. Quiet so far. She walked carefully around the back building. Nothing. The yard area was neatly kept, with no stray items leaning or scattered about. A tall hedge hugged the back of the shed, and above it, a small dusty window peeked through the spikey leaves. Blanche had brought a tiny penlight. She shined it into the interior. More neatness, and lined up against the wall under a shelf of saws and hammers and such, was a bike. *Bingo. Maybe.*

She shut off the penlight and stuck it in her back pocket and pondered her next move. Obviously, she had to get inside the shed. She'd have to go around and go in the door. And pray.

A dog barked. She froze up against the wall of the shed and waited a full minute without moving. Quiet, again.

The door was open. It creaked, slightly. She didn't need to open it much; it was easy to fit her one hundred pounds through the crack. Her eyes adjusted to the dim light. She turned to shut the door behind her and heard feet pounding down the path.

"What are ye doing here?" It was Tony, and he didn't sound like the welcoming committee. She couldn't mistake him, except his dress was less than what he'd worn to the pub; he was in boxers and a sleeveless T-shirt, and his hair looked like he'd taken an eggbeater to it.

"Oh, hi," said Blanche. "What am I doing in here? Well, I'm looking at your bike."

"Why?"

"I like bikes? I need a bike?" Then it occurred to her, too late, he'd think she was stealing his bike. *Oh, great, Blanche. Think fast.*

"I like bikes, too. Especially mine. We need to call the police."

"Wait!"

"And why would I do that? I'm not waiting. I'm catching ye in the act. They need to haul yer ass off to the gardai."

She took a step forward, stood her ground. "I'm not here to steal your bike. Trust me. We have bikes back at the castle." That sounded pretty weak.

He shrugged, flapping his fat hairy arms at his sides. "Look, lass, I think we had this discussion before. Give it up. The snooping." He pulled a string and turned on an overhead lightbulb. She wished he hadn't. Now she could see the flushed, bloated face of Tony Costello. It was not a pretty sight. And he could see how freaking frightened she really was underneath all the bravado.

"I know, it is a problem. I'm nosey. I have to admit. I think it's an emotional problem, I've had these episodes …"

"Yer crazy, all right."

She decided that truth would out—maybe it would even get her out of this mess. Maybe a little distraction thrown in. "You knew my long lost relative, William McLoughlin? Willy Boy, as you call him."

"Yer not going to find him in this shed."

Keep talking, Bang.

"It's the funniest thing. I didn't want to bother you before, but I know you were there when he died, tragically."

"And?"

"Do you fish?"

"What does that have to do with *anything?*" Now he was doubly exasperated. Blanche could see it in the cheeks puffing out, the hands on the hips. He suddenly reminded her of a blowfish, and she tried not to burst out. He hadn't moved toward her, fortunately, but that didn't mean he wouldn't.

"Just interested in local sport, especially the kind of thing you and *Willy Boy* might have been up to. Do you hang out on the water?"

"Yeah, I like to fish."

"Where?"

"In case ye haven't noticed, we're surrounded by water."

"For sure." Gran had told her that the Irish threw lobsters to the pigs. Now, what did they cost a pound? Did Tony know that? Would he care? "But what about the river? Do you fish there? Now? And, say, twenty-five years ago?"

"Jesus, Mary, and Joseph. And the little donkey. *What is up with you?*"

Tony was blurry-eyed, and definitely hung over. Slow witted and slow moving. Maybe he didn't notice how Blanche had maneuvered her way around the shed while she talked, picking up a small bucket, a paint brush, a sheaf of sandpaper. *Why aren't there any tools for self-defense?* "Listen, Tony, it's been interesting, even pleasant, at times, chatting, you know. But I really have to run. Haasi is waiting for me ..."

"Not so fast." He leered at her, and it was all she could do to keep the half dozen beers and whiskeys from coming up. What a punctuation that would be! She was twelve inches from the door. The problem was, Tony's big, fat bulky presence took up most of the opening. She'd be bold, remembering the mantra: Be Quick. She darted around Tony Costello so fast he would have thought a bee or a mosquito had flitted by. She ran, and she didn't stop. And he wasn't chasing her. She could just imagine how this little adventure would end up. She just didn't want to go there. Again.

It had to be around five o'clock in the morning. It was still dark though the hint of a lightening sky promised a new day. That's what she needed. A new day, a fresh page—a way out. Blanche's heart was racing. She sat under a hedge and caught her breath. *Well, that didn't go well. And, damn, I didn't get what I came for.* She squinted her eyes shut. Something cold came over her, possessed her to follow through on this scheme. If he had appeared once, maybe he would not appear again. Maybe she'd tired him out and he'd gone back to bed? It was still way too early to be up and about and *butchering.*

Now she knew the territory. She'd be really quick this time. *That's what I said the first time.*

She sat crouched in a ball and concentrated on deep breathing. This position was not conducive to relaxation. She stood up and stretched. She'd learned a bit from the Buddha when she was in Vietnam, and now she would practice it: *Live in the moment, Blanche. Learn from the past, but move forward, with confidence and faith.* And don't forget to move quickly.

She crept back to the butcher's along the path and hugged the cover of hedges and tall grass. The shop was in the village, but it was surprising how rural the area was off the main street. She'd stayed away from the main street and taken the back route. The greenery grew like it was on steroids.

She made it back into the shed in less than five minutes. She took out the penlight, kneeled down next to the bike, and inspected the tires. Gravel. Special gravel. No question about it. She left the way she came.

Twenty-Five

Non-stop Snoopin'

HAASI WAS SHOVELING IN the fried eggs and bacon when Blanche dropped the news on her.

"Had a little adventure his morning," said Blanche, pouring yet another large cup of black coffee.

"Really? Did you go swimming in the Shannon? See a ghost? Commune with Willy Boy, as that tool Tony Costello refers to him?"

"Not exactly. But I did talk with Tony Costello."

"You've been saying that you wanted to. Was he out walking in the village?" It was now around nine o'clock. Blanche had showered, simmered down, and drunk three cups of coffee—waiting for Haasi to appear in the dining room.

"Let's just say I surprised him."

Haasi stopped chewing. Her wary look said it all. "OK, Bang. What happened?"

"I visited his shed at four in the morning? And he caught me snooping around in there?"

Haasi's face turned a blushy pink under her normally gorgeous golden glow. "What the hell, Blanche? What did you do?"

"It's what I didn't do the first time around. He wasn't really happy to find me there, but I talked my way out of it. Distracted him with talk of fishing and such. I swear he had something to do with William's drowning. At least, I know he was there. He looked about to grab me and throw me in the drink." She smiled, bravely, so relieved to get it all out on the table, so to speak. "Then I ran."

"OMG."

"So, then I went right back there to the shed. You can't blame me. I had to check out his bike tires. That's why I went in the first place. And guess what I found? Castle gravel in those tires!" Blanche's words ran together in an avalanche of discovery. "He could have been the one, Haas. Don't you see?" She sat back triumphantly and watched Haasi's face go from blush to stone.

"You have to tell Leary and company. Maybe that'll get you off the hook and place it squarely on the neck of Tony Costello. But, seriously, Blanche. How are you going to explain this piece of evidence? You were breaking and entering. *Again.*"

"I figure I don't have to give all the specifics of how I made this discovery. I'm going to tell them to check it out, and if they don't, they're missing the boat. What do you think?"

Haasi stared at Blanche. "All I can think is I don't want to miss my plane back to Tampa."

"Oh, Haas, it'll be over soon."

"That's what I'm afraid of, B. You may have disturbed a sleeping bear."

"No bears in Ireland. And no snakes."

"But there are butchers of all variety."

Garda Ian Handley tented his fingers and listened patiently. His head was cocked, his eyes narrowed at Blanche's every word. He wasn't on the team of investigators, but he was a garda with the ears, eyes, and brain of a police officer. She figured he'd be a good one to run this by.

"You know, sir, I heard the crunch of gravel outside my window the night that Declan was killed." Blanche sat on the edge of the chair in the front office of the garda station. She looked around the tiny space. It was barely big enough for Handley and Blanche. *Must not be a big call for criminals in Ballycill. Until I arrive.*

"We're aware of those sounds ye heard in the night, Miss Murninghan." His lips went right back to a tight straight line.

Blanche took a deep breath. "I found gravel—such as that we have in the castle drive—embedded in Tony Costello's tires. I've checked around a bit. It's distinctive. Imported from Italy, and not at all common in Ballycill."

Handley didn't respond, except that his eyebrows lifted, and his green-flecked amber orbs stared a hole right through Blanche. She flinched, slightly.

Handley cleared his throat. "And how did ye happen upon this gravel?"

"I happened to be in the neighborhood? I believe that bike is normally in full view. Most of the time. For anyone just walking by." She screwed up her lips. "It's worth checking out. Wouldn't the gardai think so?"

"Miss, Tony Costello is a delivery person to the castle. I expect the gravel would get stuck in his tires."

"But Tony delivered produce in a truck earlier that night. *Not* on a bike. He had large boxes he dropped off. Declan, Haasi, and I were in the kitchen. It's unlikely he delivers goods on a bike."

Now Handley looked genuinely perplexed. "How are ye puttin' all this together then?"

"A hunch?"

"And what *exactly* are the circumstances that drew ye to Tony Costello's bike?" Ian Handley was an especially thorough policeman, Blanche noted. She wished he weren't.

"A number of things … Do you want me to list them?"

"Let's focus on the bike tires. Again, how did ye come to this? Did ye ask the man himself?"

"Not exactly."

"I'll be pulling a tooth in gettin' ye to give me the full story here."

"I happened to be *around* Tony's bike. And I looked. I think that's all I need to say."

"Sounds pretty fishy to me."

"We did talk about fishing …"

He shook his head, slowly, his eyes still fixed on Blanche. A great deal of skepticism reflected there. He sighed. "It's a tip. I'll report it. Thank ye fer comin' in. But I'd say, stay away from Tony Costello and his property. And don't go anywhere near that bike."

"Oh, I won't," she said, merrily. She stood up and turned to the door, only a few feet from where she sat.

"By the way …" Handley continued.

"Yes?" She turned abruptly.

"Ye gave the investigators that tip about Declan O'Brian's writings. I thought it fair to let ye know ye had some good inside information there. I don't have me notes in front of me." Handley had nothing in front of him. His desk was a clean slate, probably as clean as his soul. Those empty white milk bottles from catechism class flashed through Blanche's mind; not a sin there, not even a few specks of venial sin. But someone was walking around with a very black milk-bottle of a soul, full up with the mortal sin of killing Declan O'Brian.

Blanche would share the glory of the found writings. "I believe Haasi and I suggested they look for Declan's writings, but Mary Fogarty was the one who told me about his … talent? Writers sometimes put their innermost thoughts and deeds into their writing." She shuddered. One of the joys of journalism was that she could hide, ostensibly, behind the aim of being objective. If she wrote poetry like Declan O'Brian, she wouldn't show her face. "Did they find anything?"

"They did indeed. I'm not at liberty to discuss it further, but I can say the man was prolific." Did Ian Handley blush—just a little bit? Or was it a reflection of that wire brush of red hair?

"He got around, I'm sure. Did they find anything *interesting?*" Blanche could feign innocence, if she put her mind to it, and she only hoped her deep frown and pursed lips got that across. She'd never been much of an actress; she wore it all on her face, so Haasi said.

"Boxes of volumes and a desk full of records. It's all been turned over for scrutiny. I understand yer a writer, Miss Murninghan. Wouldn't the writings give out a picture of Declan O'Brian?" He crossed his arms and sat back in his chair, a look of anticipation—and distraction—in his expression. "There are questions about Declan O'Brian. Always have been."

"I hope they give it a good look. I want to be out from under it. Completely."

"I can see how that would be."

"Ever the salesman."

"Sales? Not really. I'm not selling anything. I'm trying to get by over here. Lead the peaceful life, and keep the peace in the bargain." She believed him. He was still nodding and looking out the tiny window next to his desk when Blanche opened the door and scooted away before he asked her any more questions. She was fed up with the questions; she wanted to ask them, not have anyone ask her anything anymore. At least until they found Declan O'Brian's killer.

It was early afternoon when Blanche trekked back to the castle after meeting Handley. He'd offered to give her a lift. She'd declined in favor of a brisk walk, which she hoped would clear her head. She needed to think, but in this case, she was just about all *thinked* out.

The meeting had gone fairly well. It wasn't a great meeting, but at least she'd laid it out for him with tips to find the killer and get her off the hook. He'd seemed less than convinced.

The sky was blue, and the air was a soft, gray mist. It was almost enjoyable, if she could just manage to stay dry under her thin jacket. She hugged it tightly around her middle and picked up her step. The day might suddenly turn bright and sunny. It was supposed to happen this afternoon.

Haasi had said the day was fine enough for taking pictures. She was out and about shooting the landscape, the river, the topiary, the village; she'd taken a fancy to the bright-colored doors and the variety of dogs that mostly sat patiently waiting for someone to pet them or feed them. She wanted "atmosphere," and cloudy, ghostly, colorful Ireland owned it. She would provide the photos for the "travel" article Blanche was supposed to be writing for the *Island Times*. The newspaper planned to syndicate the story, and her boss, Clint Wilkinson, had said, "You're a damn good little digger, now get over there and dig. I want *color*." She visualized the headline: "Wearing of the Green Turns Red with Blood." She couldn't get her mind off the murder.

She walked up the drive to the castle—her feet crunching over the very gravel in question. She kicked it, pretty and fine and even, almost a pinkish-tan color. Must have cost a fortune to ship it here and line this drive—and provide a clue to a murder? That remained to be seen. The investigation seemed to be going in all directions, and they weren't telling Blanche much. Handley hadn't appeared to be convinced that the gravel had anything to do with it, especially since Tony made regular visits to the castle and some of them, possibly, were on a bike.

It was quiet when she came in the front portal. She decided she could hardly call it a door with its heavy carvings and brass trim and height of at least ten feet. In the entry, the light fell onto a crystal vase of pink lilies and branches of red berries. It was startling. The distinctive scent of the enormous blooms was something she'd always remember about the castle. "Lock it in," Gran would say. *Enjoy it.*

She guessed she was alone. Haasi was still out. Blanche intended to gather up her notebooks and get some work done. She tossed her bag onto the steps leading upstairs. Maybe she'd have a pot of tea in the drawing room with all the books and that beautiful view of the garden.

She started toward the kitchen, and stopped. The urgent sound of talking came from an alcove off the kitchen. It was Una, and, apparently, from the measured, one-sided remarks, she was on the phone:

"What do ye want me to do then?"

Pause.

"You're a perfect dolt, Tony. I'll not be after cleanin' up yer messes."

Blanche held back in the entry way and listened. The pot of tea would wait. *What is she talking to Tony about? What messes?*

The phone clicked firmly into the cradle, and Una shuffled into the kitchen. Blanche waited a second or two and walked in. "Hi, Una," she said, cheerily, "or should I say, 'howya.' Something new I learned."

"Miss Blanche." She laughed. "The English is a bit wonky now, isn't it? But we mean well."

"It's fun, a whole new vocabulary." Blanche looked through the rack of tea things, choosing. "Think I'll have a spot of tea. Maybe in that little room off the garden? I won't be in the way then."

"A spot of tea 'tis. I'll bring it around." She busied herself with the pot and a tray and the linen. She drew a tin of shortbread off the shelf and put the cookies on a tray. Blanche loved watching her sure, swift movements. If there was one thing she knew, tea was part of the culture, and it was practically a ceremony.

Now she couldn't hold back. "Una. I couldn't help but hear. Tony. You were just talking to him?" She meant to share her insights of the beefy butcher of Ballycill.

Una stopped midway between a spoonful of tea and the pot. "Now ye have been overhearing quite a bit, haven't ye. First the Declan business and now Tony. Yes, I was talking with Tony." She moved swiftly now, depositing the tea, pouring the boiling water.

"I'm sorry. I don't mean to be nosey. But you do understand I'm mixed up in all this, and I don't like it. In fact, I don't care much for that Tony. I've had words with him."

"Have ye now. Tony's all right, I guess. Pushy, comes on like something of a bully, but the lad has not had an easy life, ye know. I'd let him be." She picked up the tray with finality and settled a level gaze on Blanche. This conversation was clearly over. "Shall we?"

"Surely." Blanche followed her into the drawing room. Now she remembered. She'd left her notebooks there, and they were all piled neatly next to the volumes of Irish history she'd removed from the shelves. She had that feeling again; she was not alone, and everybody's secrets were in the wind. "Thank you, Una. Think I'll get a little work done."

Una smiled without a word and turned to go. Blanche picked up a cup and saucer. Her eye was drawn to the patio. She was sure the hedge behind the bench moved. But she let it go. The wind, again. Surely, the wind.

Twenty-Six
Gone Fishin'

BLANCHE SAT ON THE LOVESEAT in front of the fireplace, the hot tea and cookies on the low table in front of her, and the notebooks on her lap. She scattered them about the sofa and flipped to previous notes and clean pages and thought a bit. She clicked open her favorite pen. She intended to whip out the lede on this story and wax sublime about the lush green Emerald Isle, the warmth of the people and the pubs, the bucolic landscape and cozy towns overrun with fuchsia and goodwill and cows. *I need to be a little more specific about all these delights.*

Then the memory of Declan with a knife in his torso came to mind. She took a deep breath and a large sip of tea. Black and strong. It was soothing, and the caffeine went right to her brain. But it was no use. A large cement block sat between her ears.

Writer's block. Blanche, you need to stumble over this one and get on with it.

She gazed idly out the French doors, sipping tea. Now she was sure of it. The hedge moved again, and it wasn't the wind. If it had been, the whole line of bushes out there would have been dancing, and they were not. Someone was out there.

She got up and opened the doors. It looked pretty peaceful along the path. The hedges were tall and clipped short. Unlikely they'd *move*. It was all green and white and gray sky, but that was the problem. Everything looked peaceful, all the time, and it wasn't. She stepped onto the patio. She stood still, and breathed it in, warily.

Then she saw him. He was pretty hard to miss. He hadn't even bothered to camouflage himself with a dark shirt; a large, white-sleeved arm emerged from the enormous boxwood, and the rest of Tony Costello stepped out not ten feet from Blanche. She just didn't feel good about this little meet-up. He wore a leering grin that matched his sorry attire of dirty jeans, scuffed boots, and crummy long-sleeved shirt.

"What the hell are you doing in the bushes?"

"I should have asked ye the same thing."

"I wasn't in your damn bushes."

"No, ye were in my shed. Snooping."

"You're snooping now, so how about leaving."

"Not 'til I get what I came for."

"And what is that?" She put her hands on her hips and stepped back closer to the door.

"*You.*" Quite the emphatic pronoun. Now she almost leaped backward to get away, but he grabbed her arm. He was amazingly agile for someone so *thick.* Blanche was no match for his strength.

"Hey! Let go of me! What do you think you're doing?" He dragged her over the back lawn and headed for the edge of the property. A dense line of trees against a rock fence separated the castle grounds from a stretch of woods. She resisted but knew it was no use. She had no recourse; she started yelling her head off.

He stopped. "Now who do ye think is going to hear ye?"

"*Somebody.*"

"So sorry. They've all gone off to market, and that little sidekick is on the other end of Ballycill talking to a bunch of dogs and birds. *You* is fer the birds, and the fishes."

"What are you talking about?" She was making his progress difficult, planting the heels of her sneakers in the spongy grass—digging large grooves in the ground. She tried to bite his hand. He came around with his other and cuffed her on the side of the head. Now he was angry, and so was she. Blanche went immediately into the cool, calculating revenge mode. She needed to outwit this bumbling side of beef. "Where are we going?" She gave in, slightly, hoping to diminish his anger and aggression.

"Why, ye gave me the idea. Fishin', of course."

"Huh? Wait. Why don't we go get the poles and stuff. I know where it's all stored." She had no idea where anything was stored, but she hoped the suggestion would slow him down. Long enough for her to get away or trip him up. Her mind was going a mile a millisecond.

He laughed, uproariously, his revolting lips and pink tongue making her nearly gag with disgust. "Ye won't need no poles, lass, where ye be goin.'"

She did not like the sound of that. She tried breaking from his grasp. She twisted her arm until she thought her skin would burst, but he held on.

The river gleamed ahead, beyond the wide stretch in front of the castle. *The demesne, they called it. Well, la-de-da.*

Blanche looked all around. There was not a soul, not even a cow. Tony picked up his step and quickly dragged Blanche along like she was an awkward sack of goods. That was how she felt, pretty awkward, and useless. *I need to get my bearings. And maybe I need flippers.* She had a premonition about what he was going to do; she was both relieved, and terrified.

At least she would get away from him.

They crossed a narrow road at the bottom of the hill in front of the castle. It was only a short distance to the river now. "What do you think you're doing?" Her voice screeched; gone was the cool, calculating Blanche.

"Whadayathink, lass?"

"I think you're nuts, that's what I think." The sweat skin-to-skin had done some good. She wrenched her arm out of his grasp and took a step back. She thought to run, but it wouldn't help to try. There was nowhere to run in the tall grass at the edge of the river. The ground was slippery, and her shoes were caked with mud, weighing her down into the muck. He came closer. She raised her hands, palms out.

"Wait. Can't we talk?" She looked him directly in the eye. "It won't matter anyway." It was a chilling thought, and also a delay tactic.

He looked away. "Ah, well, I have all day. I'm just gonna enjoy this." He planted his boots wide apart and crossed his arms, nearly toe-to-toe with Blanche. "Ye been snoopin' and wantin' to talk to ol' Tony, so here I be. Himself." He chuckled, a low venomous rumble with his mouth closed, thankfully.

"Why the river? What did I do?"

"Ye done enough, stirrin' things up. All good McLoughlins deserve the best."

"What the hell does that mean?"

"Willy Boy. He drowned in them waters." Tony yanked his head in the direction of the fast-moving current.

"Did you ..."

"After a fashion, I guess. We'd been playin' ball with Declan and the lot of us and later Willy Boy went in. Thanks to your man, Declan. He weren't no fan of the fancy man."

"Why? What did he do?"

"Nothin'. That's just it. Nothin' at all. Willy was after playin' with the women and ponies. He was a right chap and all but ..." Tony stopped and scratched his head. "Case of jealousy? I don't know. Declan wanted power, control. That's it."

"What do I have to do with all this? Let me go. Declan is dead."

"He's dead. We made sure of that."

"*We?* What do you mean by *we?*"

"Now I'm talkin' too much, should be fishin'—if ye want to call it that." He laughed and lunged at Blanche. She dodged.

"Wait!" She leaned down and smeared mud on her arms. Nice and slimy.

"What're ye doin'? Ah, well, what'll it matter. Yer goin' in the drink." He went after her again, and missed. "No more of yer snoopin' about me bike tires and the records and such. No more of yer damn questions."

"As long as this is it, tell me. *Why Declan?*"

"'Cause yer man weren't payin' no more to shut me up about the drowning. He was about to ruin me business. He wanted it all ... That was Declan's problem. He wanted it all. And the whole thing was unravelin' and yer no help to it." He was tired of talking. That was obvious. Blanche glanced at the water. An escape of sorts. And she did know how to swim. *What am I thinking?*

She didn't have time for it. He yanked her out of the mud by the back of her shirt with one hand and flung her across the short stretch of bank and into the river.

His aim was good. She was well away from land, and the water was moving fast. It was deep and cold. It carried her.

I will not panic, I will not panic.

She managed to keep her head above water, barely. She saw him standing there, watching. Making sure he'd done his damndest. But then he was gone in a flash. She was whisked away.

She knew this much: *Don't fight it.* There's no force stronger than water, and she was no match for it. She stuck out her arms and spread her legs and flew down the river. It was wide here, but the surface was relatively calm; it was the current underneath, concealed and dark, that ripped along faster than the devil. Deadly, if she didn't go along. She went along. The water had been cold when she went in, but now she was used to it. Only trouble, among many, was it drained her. She didn't know how much longer she could go.

Haasi tromped into the castle entry. She was happy and eager to share some village vignettes with Blanche. She'd had a good day of it, getting photos and talking to the villagers. For a place so gray, it had a lot of color—the cobalt-blue and tomato-red doors, the flowers of every kind, the redheads and apple cheeks, and the delicious displays in the outdoor markets and bakery windows. She liked Ireland just fine. She wished Blanche could have been with her.

Una was in the kitchen, alone. She appeared to be writing a list. Bundles of potatoes and onions, loaves of bread and cheese wrapped in cloth were arranged neatly on the marble counter. "Hi, Una. Looks like dinner!"

She looked up. "Miss Haasi! It is, indeed. And how was yer day about Ballycill?"

"Grand! Lots going on, lots of photos. Where's Blanche?"

"Now, that's a good question. I been to the market and back. Left her in the drawing room with a pot of tea. But I see it's gone cold. Her notebooks and such are there, the door to the patio was open a crack. Maybe she had a walk about?"

Something colder than that tea swept over Haasi. Blanche had been snooping since they arrived; the insatiable curiosity of that girl. Haasi didn't like the feel of it.

"All right then." She checked her watch. It was after four o'clock.

"Guess I'll have a drink in there. Go and look her things over, see where she went."

"I carried off the tray. But if ye like, a bite or some ice or even tea? I'll fetch it."

"No, no, that's fine, Una. You've done enough." Haasi said, hastily. She was agitated, and she wasn't sure why. "I'll go then. See you later for dinner?"

"Some fine salmon fer ye. From the river. Since ye loved it so the other day. About eight then?" She smiled.

"Oh, yes, thank you." Haasi had already turned toward the drawing room. Sure enough, Blanche's notebooks were there. And her favorite pen. *Open.* She always closed that pen. Haasi was a stickler for details. And the notebooks. She'd left them in the middle of something. They were all opened and scattered about the sofa, Blanche-style. She'd definitely been carried away from the work.

Haasi looked to the doors. They were closed. Una had probably shut them when she picked up the tray. Haasi went out onto the patio. The hedge, oddly, had a disturbed, bare spot. And that was all. Everything else looked undisturbed.

A dog barked; a cow mooed. Haasi's eye wandered down the path, following the source of these mundane sounds. Then she saw it. Scrapes on the ground. And, further, drag marks as if a shoe had been digging ruts in the grass. She followed them to the property line. They were headed in one direction.

She raced back to the castle and to a phone.

"What do you have here, Una? 911? To call the gardai? I need them. *Now.*" Haasi turned to the door and back to Una. "And tell them to get down to the river."

Una was clearly alarmed. She picked up the phone. Haasi ran off to where she saw the marks in the grass, leading directly to her worst fear: the banks of the River Shannon.

Twenty-Seven
Pretty Far Gone

A BEND IN THE RIVER floated into Blanche's line of sight, and in the bend, a branch of a fallen tree extended out over the water. Her face above water, she gasped for air and steadied herself, and then she swam and swam. She lay flat and stayed close to the surface, like a water bug, going toward the branch with all her might. Haasi's warning in the bog echoed in her brain: *Don't resist, lean horizontal.* It was easier said than done, but she struggled and concentrated, and somehow she made progress toward shore.

A leafy twig shimmered from the branch. Tantalizing. She snatched at it and pulled away the dead leaves, and reached again, and finally she had it in her grasp. She pulled herself forward. She looked back at the stretch of river behind her: desolate gray-green and white frills on the wavey surface. She breathed deeply and hung on, pulling and pulling herself along the branch, closer to the bank. The muddy underwater slope was slippery, but she was almost there. She relaxed now and used the last of her reserve. Her fingers wrapped around a root growing in the mud, then her hand sought an outcrop of rock. She swung her leg onto land and collapsed in a wet heap on the grass under a tree. The sky had never looked so blue, well, gray-blue, the leaves overhead, so green. And fresh. Alive.

I'm alive. Exhausted, afraid. But alive.

She must have dozed with relief. How could she? She was freezing, but the high, soft grass sheltered her. She wasn't a damn fish. She wasn't meant for it, to be thrown in like that. The heat of her anger, the surge of relief, warmed her, and she dozed off again. She lay there. She had no idea how long. *Time has no edges to it, it flows around us, and we swim in it. And try to survive it.* Where had she heard that before? Emilio! How she missed him. How she wanted to see him. Now she would because she hadn't drowned in the damn river, no thanks to Tony Costello. She didn't want to move, so happy she was to be alive.

This other feeling? The nastiness with Tony Costello? I'll think about that later.

She dropped off again, numb and drained, and woke up shivering. She had to get up and get going, but she didn't have the strength. She closed her eyes and drifted. Drifting on land, the lapping of the river safely moving along without her.

Dogs. She dreamt of dogs. And Haasi was there with her camera, taking photos of dogs and birds and the doors of Ireland. No, this was no photo shoot. The barking was close at her ear. Her eyes popped open to the thrashing through the grass. A male voice. Handley! Then, Haasi! Blanche struggled to sit up. She forced the sound from deep in her chest and gave out. "*HEY!*" she yelled.

They all fell on her at once, and she was never so glad for a welcoming committee. Haasi's face was a wreath of smiles, and relief. "Blanche! What did I tell you about swimming in the Shannon? And how did you get here? I saw the drag marks in the grass …" Her words ran together in a confusing mishmash of happiness and annoyance.

"Will you remind me to listen to you?"

Ian Handley crouched down on the ground. His cap was pulled low, but she could see the green glint in his eye. "Let's get ye back and dry. And then ye be tellin' me all ya know." He *winked.* "Gotta say, yer one fine detective."

"Please. No encouragement." Haasi sat back on her heels, hands on her hips. She cocked her head at Blanche. "I guess you just can't help it, girl. But I wish you would."

"Oh, Crikey. Give me that blanket. Let's get out of here." She could hardly walk, or talk, for once.

Ian Handley wanted to take Blanche to the local clinic for a check-up. She declined. "I just want to be clean and dry."

"And then we can talk. I expect a bit of debriefing when yer up to it." Both hands were on the wheel. His lips were set as the police car took off down a narrow road near the river.

They drove back to the castle over a bridge and through the village in the police wagon. People were clustered on street corners, watching the garda drive past. "It's not a usual sight, ye know," said Ian. "They're curious. Since ye visitors have been here, there's more than a wee bit of interest in the doings at the castle."

"I guess. The sooner things are fixed, the sooner we can go home, and you can get back to normal," said Haasi, looking out the window. Waving to Aine, the baker, and Paulie, the general store manager.

"Who you waving at, Haasi?" Blanche managed to lift her head.

"My peeps?"

"Your new friends? Still want to go home?"

"I left my heart in Ballycill. I almost left sister-cousin in the Shannon. Yeah, I think it's about time to go home."

Ian swung around to the front door of the castle and jumped out. He waited while Blanche and Haasi climbed out of the back. Blanche smiled at him and stumbled into the entry, her strength slowly returning. "Come on in. Una can get us some tea. I'll just be a minute, and then we need a chat." She dragged herself up the stairs to the shower and dry clothes, leaving Haasi and Ian Handley standing there shaking their heads.

"Well, all right then. Let's go see who's in the kitchen," said Haasi.

Ian Handley didn't move. He twirled his cap round and round in his big hands, awkwardly shifting boot to boot. "I guess I'll just wait for Miss Blanche to come. We need to talk. 'Tisn't a tea party, ye know."

"You can say that again," Haasi scoffed. "What craziness. Come on." Handley followed Haasi into the kitchen. Una and the staff were nowhere to be seen. Haasi called out. No answer. She went about heating water on the stove and drawing down the pot and cups for tea.

"Why don't you have a seat there while I fix the tea and we'll take it into the drawing room. Blanche can meet us there."

"Now, ye don't have to go to all that trouble." He was still twirling the cap.

"Nonsense. An Irishman turning down tea? That's sacrilege."

"Ah, ye Americans. Yer a trip all right. Hard to turn down a cuppa."

They went into the drawing room and took seats in front of the fireplace, Handley sitting stiffly on the edge of the sofa, surreptitiously taking in the room. "'Tis a grand place, 'tis." He whistled softly. "Now look at those grounds. Such a fine landscape, I see."

"Yeah, well, that's where I found Blanche's heels dug into the path and all along the boundary toward the river. A good thing, too." She had an idea about that, but she'd wait for Blanche. She poured the tea and gave him a dash of cream and two lumps. "That sweet enough?"

"Quite." He sipped, eyeing Haasi over the rim of his cup.

They both looked up as Blanche walked into the drawing room, fresh and clean, her hair wet. She glanced, skittishly, at the French doors, then skipped the tea and went right for the whiskey. She poured herself half a glass, clutching it in two hands, and sat on the edge of the armchair. "Wow."

"I should say, and alive. Blanche, how did this happen?" Haasi eyed Blanche. Her knowing look said it all; Haasi knew her sister-cousin well.

"Yes. Suppose ye tell me how ye ended up on the banks of the Shannon, Miss Blanche." Ian Handley produced a notebook and studied Blanche. His focus was cool, his tone business-like.

"Believe me, it was not the place I wanted to be. Tony Costello threw me in the river." She tossed off half her drink and welcomed the warm feeling all the way to her toes. More than she usually did. She had no idea whether or not Ian Handley would believe her, and, at this point, she didn't care.

He shot to his feet. The look of disbelief and confusion turning his face red. He sputtered, "For the love of God and Jesus and Mary…Why didn't ye say so?"

Haasi was also on her feet. "Yeah, Blanche. What were you saving this news for? The *Island Times*?"

"Will you stop? There's a lot more to all this. I needed to catch my breath."

"I see that ye have. Now, we'll be after picking up Tony Costello." He pulled the radio out of his jacket and after a great deal of static and back and forth, the garda instructed the station to send out a car and find Tony Costello. "Get back to me when ye do."

"There's more," said Blanche. "A lot more."

They all sat. Handley snapped open the notebook. "Let's look at the disaster at hand. He threw you into the river with intent to kill ye?"

"Well, yes, I'd say so. And what's more, he killed Declan. He actually said *we* killed Declan. It doesn't stop with Tony."

"We'll pick him up now, and there'll be questions, for sure."

"I don't know who he meant by 'we.' But it was *shocking*. They need to find out—that team of investigators—who the 'we' is."

Handley's expression was stern, his gaze riveted on Blanche.

"Further," Blanche said. "Both he and Declan had a major part in the death of William McLoughlin. I don't know if they drowned him. But they could have saved him. I'm almost sure of it. Tony Costello told me about it and the game they were playing. And everything he said pointed at Declan's jealousy and greed for control."

"Ah, they say the nephew was not a swimmer, and it certainly must have been a factor in his demise."

"You'd have to be a swimmer to survive the current in that river. That's something Tony Costello did not know about me. I swim in the Gulf of Mexico. I have a healthy fear of water, but I can mostly cope." She drank off the rest of her whiskey. "I was lucky."

Ian Handley cleared his throat. He lowered his chin and looked from Haasi to Blanche. "I may as well tell ye, now that we've come thus far. There seems to be corroboration in Declan's writing that the two indeed aided and abetted the death of William McLoughlin. They could have saved him, and they didn't. What ye say, Miss Blanche, backs it up."

This sad corroboration was a jolt of reality, one she'd have to accept. She'd suspected it, and now it was fact. "Did you find records of payments to Tony?"

"Now how would ye know about that?" Handley sat back, the pen poised over his notebook.

"A hunch? I suggested the investigators look through his things and writings and such. Not that they wouldn't." Blanche struggled to keep a lid on and as cool a tone as Ian Handley maintained.

Haasi's eyes went from one to the other. "Garda Handley, you must know we are now friends of Mary Fogarty. We visited her, with the help of Peter Flynn, and she came to the castle for breakfast."

"She dropped off Misty Pumpkin," said Blanche, with finality.

Handley looked perplexed. "Who?"

"A cat, an adorable cat." As if on cue, Misty Pumpkin appeared and jumped up on Blanche's lap. She rubbed her head on Blanche's nubby sweater and burrowed under her arm.

Handley picked up his cup, his eyes not leaving Blanche and the cat. "Well, there are a number of actors involved. Yes, I suppose Miss Fogarty was a help in describing Declan O'Brian, his faults and deeds and such." He colored up, again. It was getting easy to read Handley. "All of it is under investigation at present. Miss Fogarty is an unlikely suspect in the murder."

"Why?" Blanche couldn't help but burst out.

"B!" Haasi shot her a look. "Really?"

"Oh, I don't mean Mary." She was flustered, just the least little bit. "But Costello said *we* when he talked of the killing of Declan. Don't you want to know who the *we* is?"

"We certainly do, and we will."

Twenty-Eight
Cooked

IT HAD BEEN AN EXTREMELY LONG DAY since the visit to Tony's shed. That dip in the river had almost done Blanche in, but her nerves hummed. It had something to do with adrenalin—and getting her Irish up? When Blanche got excited, or angry, it was *up*. Tony Costello was in custody for trying to kill her, and she hoped the sorry bloke was cooling off in a cell at district headquarters. Ian Handley had left them. He had a call from the gardai, and the next morning the Dublin office was coming for a visit.

"I think we're about to end this thing, Haas." They sat in the dining room with the remains of dinner, candles burning to the quick, and an empty bottle of pinot noir.

"I sure hope so." Haasi crossed her arms on the table and leaned toward Blanche. "I'm glad you're all right. Had me worried, but you've got more lives than Misty Pumpkin."

"I think I've run through a few. Haasi, how did you know to head to the river? Had to be you. Handley wouldn't have found me down there on his own."

"A hunch?"

"Thought only I got hunches."

"Nope, not fair. You are never alone, B. I saw the drag marks in the grass and along the property line. Those sneakers did a good job. Like leaving breadcrumbs."

"I'll have to remember that."

"No, you won't, because you are going to be good and not get yourself into these messes. Anymore."

"Hah! Life, Haasi. Life."

"OMG." Haasi's hands shot to her cheeks.

"Now what?"

"I forgot to tell Handley about the marks in the grass. Tony's footprints, and yours, have to be there." They both looked toward the window, darkened in the early evening with a downpour. "Oops."

"They just have to believe me. How else would you have found me? And how else would I have gotten into the river?"

"You slipped on the bank?" Haasi played the devil's advocate.

"Oh, sure." Blanche slumped. Defeat slinked into her thoughts. "They better believe me, dammit."

"The other thing, B. You mentioned 'fishing' a number of times. That Tony is a dunce, but he picked up on it, and it probably gave him the idea to throw you to the fishes. He's really a sick-o, but he got sick of the snooping. It got super dangerous for him, in case you didn't notice."

Blanche diverted. "We'll find out more tomorrow. By the way, have you seen Una?"

"No, have you?"

"No." They silently sipped the last of the pinot.

Tony Costello was langered, knockered, many sheets to the wind. *Ossified*. He sat in a dark corner of Barrett's Pub with several Guinnesses and a few shots under his belt. John Barrett had already warned him off. "Time to call it a day, Tony. Enough of the black stuff, and the *uisce beatha*."

His head hung, lolling back and forth, his shoulders hunched as he babbled on with his cronies. They'd been talking football and the pony races, but the more they drank, the more the small talk heated up.

"Whatcha doin' at the meat counter, Tony, me boy?" One of the lads lifted his glass and the rest of them laughed at the double entendre. Tony had had a falling out with Peggie McBride, and it was well known. What wasn't well known in Ballycill about the butcher, the baker, and all the rest of them?

"Shut yer gob er I'll stick this glass up yer festaris." Tony's words slurred, mightily. He cast an evil look at Sean Falloy who'd taunted him. Peggie was one of several women in the townland who had dumped Tony Costello, and he wasn't proud of it.

"Ah, Ton, now we're just jibin' a bit. Ye know the ladies love yer meat counter."

They all laughed. Tony's face turned red. He stood up and threw the glass against the wall. He might as well have called out the Pope. It was against the rules to show disrespect to the patrons and upset the calm and sanctuary of the pub. A few snarled at Tony. He swayed and sat down abruptly, his head in his hands. Silence hung about the table and flowed to other corners of the bar as heads turned and the spigots paused. John Barrett fetched a broom and the words he would use to kick Tony Costello out of the pub.

Tony looked around, his face even redder, his jowls and bristles a sweaty sight. He fell back into his chair and slammed a fist on the tabletop. "I done it; I killed her."

"*What?*" It was a cry in unison from the lads.

"I trow-ed her in da drink, I did." He was barely seated and swaying badly now. His mate grabbed the fleshy arm and righted him. They stared at Tony Costello and hung on his words. He looked around the table. It was a void that needed filling.

"That little bitch, the American, always snooping around, asking questions. I caught her in my shed. I should have done it then. But I waited."

"Fer feckin' sakes, Tony. *Is she dead?*"

"Yeah, she's dead. Good riddance."

The timing of this announcement couldn't have been more fortuitous. It was out of the lads' hands, and John Barrett's. The pub owner stopped sweeping a few feet from a pile of broken glass, the broom suspended. He would not need to find the words to eject Tony Costello from the pub. Ian Handley was standing in the door right behind John. The garda planted his feet in front of the men. "Tony Costello, you need to come with me."

It didn't take Tony Costello long to open up. He spilled it all, fairly gushed with the details, and he wasn't going down alone.

Inspector Myles Flannigan of the Dublin murder squad was back at district. It had been little more than a week since Declan O'Brian was killed, and the police had moved swiftly, searching the victim's property, going through his records and journals, and putting together the pieces.

The new development with Tony Costello was one more piece.

Blanche had pleaded to sit in on the interrogation, and Flannigan had denied her access. She talked them into letting her sit in an ante room to await details. She argued that they might need to call upon her. And, after all, her relative had drowned in full view of the suspect's negligence, and she had been the one to insist on searching Declan's belongings. Tony had tried to kill her. She'd promised to stay out of the way for which Haasi drew a sigh of relief. She declined to have any part of it—except to celebrate the outcome with confirmed plane reservations.

"The charges are piling up, Mr. Costello." Flannigan's twitch was non-stop, but his eye focused steadily on Tony. His lawyer, a public defender, sat back with a look of consternation and a tight lip. "You're accused of attempted murder of the American visitor, Blanche Murninghan, just yesterday."

"She slipped," said Tony.

"No, don't think so. There were drag marks, and evidence of scuffling. It rained, but we found them. It all backs up Miss Murninghan's story. Besides, that area where she went in is flat. She couldn't have slipped," said Flannigan.

"Oh, all right then. So I *helped* her into the river. She's alive, isn't she?" His head was bent over his thick knuckles, squeezed into a fist. "She's not dead." He avoided mentioning her name. The breathing was audible in that room. The space seemed to shrink, by the minute, or was it the pressure? His head felt like it was in a vice. He thought he'd explode.

"Yes, Miss Murninghan is alive, no thanks to you. You'll mostly likely face attempted murder." Flannigan nodded at Costello who remained quiet, except for an occasional whimper.

Flannigan cleared his throat. "And now to other matters. There's evidence your bike was used to visit the castle grounds."

Tony glanced around the table. "I visit the castle grounds often."

"So we hear. But you usually drive the truck. What were you using the bike for?"

"Just a bit of a go-round? It's a pretty place, ye know." He sat back and slapped his hands on his knees, defiantly. He avoided eye contact with Flannigan.

"Could you have been having that go-round the night Declan O'Brian was murdered?"

The detective didn't put the brakes on when Tony jumped to his feet. "I didn't do it … alone. I'm not taking the blame for the lot of it."

"So we understand." And Flannigan laid it out:

"Declan O'Brian did in fact like to write. He wrote a lot. You were blackmailing him since the drowning of William McLoughlin. You both had a hand in that. It's unclear that Mr. McLoughlin was shoved, or *helped*, into the water during a particularly rough ball game, and the two of you did nothing to get him out. You knew he couldn't swim. Declan O'Brian was quite gleeful, and specific about the details. And he named you as an accomplice."

"It was a long time ago," Tony whispered.

"Declan O'Brian had an important job here in Ballycill as the castle agent, and he didn't want any more trouble about his past talked about. Lately, he was going to stop paying you. You threatened him."

"So? That doesn't mean I killed him."

"We think you did, and you had help."

At that, Tony Costello turned from red to pale. His mouth dropped open. "*Who?*"

"You know who because you planned it together. That suspect is now in custody. Talking her head off. You're in the soup. It's only going to help you if you start talking."

Tony looked up. The heat of bodies in that small room was stifling. It served a purpose. Tony was cooked.

"Declan O'Brian planned to kill Una. He was going to pin it on

Blanche Murninghan. He'd had her pick up the kitchen knife earlier in the night. On purpose," Tony said, almost petulantly.

"Yes, we know that," said Flannigan. "There were witnesses to that. And, like I said. Declan O'Brian kept notes, a journal." Here he nodded at Costello, waiting for that to settle in. "Thanks to Miss Murninghan's suggestion, we did thorough searches of Declan's property, and we turned up plans. Deeds. He was meticulous about what he'd done, and what he intended to do. He wanted to get rid of Una Mullins."

Tony looked at Flannigan askance, as if he were sizing up the inspector. Tony did not measure up, and he knew it. "I didn't care about the old lady," Tony snarled. "I used her. She wanted Declan gone, and so did I. She was afraid of him. He'd threatened her a number of times. I guess it all came down to that night … Una set up the time for me to come into the kitchen. He happened to have that knife at the ready. It was perfect how it came together."

"Perfect? Not quite. Except for the facts coming together," said Flannigan. "It does seem perfectly tied up."

Twenty-Nine
The Good-Bye Gift

"I DON'T THINK YOU'LL SEE UNA AGAIN." Peter Flynn sat behind his desk, fingers tented. "They've taken her to Dublin, and she's under investigation for her part in Declan's murder."

It was chilling, and sad. Blanche had such mixed feelings, but that's the way she'd felt about the entire experience of this visit to Dunfaedan. Ireland was funny and beautiful and dark and sad, too. Haasi sat next to her, hands between her knees, her head inclined toward Blanche.

"To think we were so close to all of it," Blanche murmured. "What'll happen to her?"

"No telling. There are some mitigating factors. Self-defense, perhaps. He did mean to kill her. Most likely right there in that kitchen, but she got the jump on him, after all. And Tony was there. We aren't sure who exactly put the knife to Declan O'Brian. The point is Tony and Una had a play in it."

"So odd, how everything collided," Blanche said. The room was quiet except for the hiss of the low fire in Peter Flynn's fireplace. "I don't think she meant to cause me so much grief. Do you?"

"No, she didn't. She didn't know about Declan's plot to frame you, but it became clear soon enough, the more police pressed you about your involvement. Your fingerprints, and words with Declan that Tony overheard. She tried to keep you out of it. She thought it would just go away."

Haasi was perplexed. "Why couldn't he just let it go? He had a lot of control over the management of the estate. His father set it up that way."

"But his father was dead, and the bank was pulling away from Declan. And he knew it." Flynn shook his head. "Greed. He wanted to get rid of Una and have more control over managing the castle. The McLoughlins had been specific about her legacy, that she would stay on and be cared for and continue to be house manager. Then, Declan certainly did not like Blanche appearing on the scene as yet another person with her hand in the estate."

"He could have said something. I've always been a reluctant owner. We could have *talked*."

"I know, but, again, the greed and power. They get in the way of talking," said Flynn. "The colonel, and the nephew, had given a lot of power to Una. It grated on Declan and led to the disintegration of whatever good working relationship they'd once had. He figured pinning Una's murder on Blanche would deflect from him and get rid of you, Blanche, and Una. Staff and townspeople knew of the rift between Declan and Una. He had to think of something.

"In other news …" He cleared his throat and dropped his folded hands on top of the desk with emphasis. "In the meantime, the board found major discrepancies in the castle's financial records. Declan and his father had embezzled funds that were meant to run the estate and benefit the people of Ballycill."

"And it's just coming out now?" Blanche was incredulous at how matters could get dusty, and inertia could keep the worst rolling.

"The tip-off happened when we looked into a glut of visitors leasing the castle—including some rock bands who had broken the beds and furniture and then paid handsomely to fix and replace everything. Declan had padded that income and other rental and taken it for himself. He had plenty of hush money for Tony Costello, Mary Fogarty, and wherever else he chose to spend to prop up his ego and cover his transgressions."

"We came out on the other side, and I gotta say, no small thanks to you, B." Haasi smiled, and shrugged.

"Maybe. But what's wrong with me? I just can't seem to let go." She sat back and looked from Flynn to Haasi. "I gotta thank both of you for staying with me through this mess."

"And the village of Ballycill thanks you, Miss Blanche. The gift of your inheritance back to the village will be much appreciated. You can't tell it much, because they put such a good face on it, but times are tough here, and that donation will add to the rents and upkeep of the grounds. As you know, proceeds benefit Ballycill as well as the castle, per the colonel's instruction."

"I can't say I won't miss it here," Blanche said. "We'll come back and visit." Haasi rolled her eyes.

"There's a bit more business to come out, but I'll see you before you go," said Flynn. He stood up, glanced out the window behind his desk. "It's a fine, fine place. Ballycill. I hope you won't have hard feelings."

"How could I? My family lived here. We made good friends here. We had good *craic*," said Blanche.

Flynn pounded the desk and laughed. "That you did."

The staff at the castle was not in disarray. Nancy and Mae were long-time staffers, and they knew how to keep things going. According to Peter Flynn, they would run things until the board—made up of bankers, accountants, two schoolteachers, and a priest from the county—stepped in and set up new arrangements. The board had already contacted Flynn after Declan's death to help straighten out the matter. They hired the lawyer to oversee the local details until they could find another agent and manager.

Haasi and Blanche arrived back at the castle after the meeting with Flynn, and Mae and Nancy greeted them on the landing out front. "Oh, Miss Blanche, Miss Haasi, 'tis a great thing you're safe and home again." Mae clapped her hands, her face flushed pink, and her hair escaping from the blue velvet headband.

Nancy stood back a bit. She'd always been reserved, the quiet one, working, working, working. But now she was smiling. Big time. "It's hard for the little one to contain herself," she said, casting an eye at Mae. "She's been a wreck with all the news. Now I'm so glad it's done with." She left the part about Una unfinished. Her fate hung between them.

"Una's gone to Dublin, and they'll decide. She had a rough time of it. I don't think she meant any cruelty to any of us. She was in danger. The officials will take that into consideration, I hope," said Blanche.

"That is the word about. Mr. Flynn called here, and the board will be contacting us about the operations," said Nancy. "But for now, yer hungry, no doubt, and we've got a lovely colcannon and some chops with mint. It'll be ready when ye are."

Blanche couldn't hold back. She rushed up the step and hugged Nancy, then Mae, who both looked about to faint with the outpouring of gratitude. "You are the best. Both of you. Always thinking of us, trying to make us comfortable, when you've probably been going through hell with all this."

The two looked down on the ground and shook their heads in unison as if Blanche had pressed a button. Then Nancy met Blanche's eye, pure calm relief in her expression. A strong woman of good character and obviously resigned to the changes. "'Twas a desperate situation and all, but let's move on with our hats in our hands and the clothes on our backs … "

"and the wind beneath our wings while the road rises to meet us." Haasi finished it. They laughed together and the sound of it pushed every dismal thought aside. At least for the moment.

"Ah, it is good to laugh. It's the music we need to hear," said Mae. She turned and hurried back into the castle, presumably to do one more thing to make Blanche and Haasi feel right at home.

Nancy lingered. "And the village is turning out to meet ye at Barrett's later on—for some good craic. Maggie McLoughlin arranged it, the fiddle will commence at ten, and she says ye better be there for the send-off. Miss Fogarty even promises to be there. They'll all be happy to see ye!"

"I'll be happy to see them. Bet they'll be happy to say good-bye," Haasi said under her breath.

"Oh, princess," said Blanche. She turned to Nancy. "Can't wait!"

It was a loud craic. Haasi and Blanche rekindled all their acquaintances in Ballycill, some closer than others. Most were glad that the rude, unruly Tony Costello was gone though they hated to see one of their own guilty of such heinous acts. They'd suspected Costello's involvement in William McLoughlin's demise, but it was never confirmed. With Blanche's bad luck and Declan's murder more or less pinned down by authorities, they could rest easy. And celebrate. That didn't take much prompting. Blanche's Irish jig came back in full swing, and even Haasi gave it a whirl with a tall, mustachioed, dark-haired fellow who swung her around like she was the queen of Ballycill. Blanche whispered to him that she was the "princess of Ballycill." The whiskey flowed at Barrett's. The music raised the roof. Garda Handley looked the other way when closing time rolled around.

Blanche's face was hot and glistening when she hugged Maggie at the door. "I'm about jigged out," said Maggie. "But ye go on. And on." She laughed then, and the resemblance to Maeve Murninghan was so startling that Blanche stood back, her hands on Maggie's shoulders.

"Cousin-Auntie Maggie, I'll see you again."

"O shite and onions," she said. "Ye know I'm with ye. All the way. Wherever." She hugged Blanche, mightily, for one so elderly and small, and she turned down the road. The purple wings on that cape flapped under the lights of the pub sign. Her white hair in the night was the last Blanche saw of her. She almost ran after her. It was the ghost of Maeve Murninghan if there ever was one. *Or maybe it's the Jameson's.*

Blanche slumped down on the bench in front of Barrett's. The music thrummed through the walls and into her heart. "I've come home again." She looked up at the cloudy dark sky, down the lovely quaint street of Ballycill, and locked it in. It was home, but all she could think of was Santa Maria Island and the cabin and the sunset.

Epilogue

BLANCHE WAS HOME, still drifting over thoughts of Ireland. It was weeks now; Haasi was off on a charter to St. Kitts, and Blanche was eagerly waiting for Emilio to come up from Mexico. His visa for the fellowship had finally come through, and they planned to celebrate.

It was good to be back on her island, to have two homes, really. The Irish were right; once ye had the auld sod in yer soul ye couldn't let it go. Ha Ha. She sat on the porch with a package in her lap. It was covered with stamps picturing Irish harps. She eagerly ripped it open: a note wrapped around a small box. From Maggie. Blanche read the note quickly:

> Dear One, Cousin of Mine,
>
> Come here to me, I miss you already, for at last we met, and it was hard to say good-bye. What a time of it we had! You came out of it rosy, you did, and may the saints preserve us. Please plan on a return trip, and we'll have a brilliant run of it. We'll go down to the sea and have a ceili or two at Barrett's, and we'll discuss every book on my wall—with nary a murder on the agenda! Ha! It was grand to meet you and the lovely sister-cousin, Haasi, and please be sending me love to her, as well.

I must catch you up on things. After you were cleared, and Tony Costello's tongue run like a torrent, Una's culpability come out a bit clearer. When phone records were put to her, she admitted setting up the little meeting between Declan and Tony the night of the murder: Tony rides up on his bike and comes into the kitchen, for sure, and Una is standing in the doorway. Declan has the knife—the very one with your fingerprints upon it—and he come after Una, dead set on putting the blame on you, Blanche. Nancy, the cook, stood witness to the yelling amongst the three of them and the scuffle, well, most of it anyway, before she covered her ears and eyes and run off to her bed. She finally come forward, she did, but it weren't much. Tony sunk them, one and all. Oh, what a fine kettle it was!! Again, I'm sorry for the lot of it, and that you got stuck yourself with any taint of the affair. Well, God rest the scamps as well as the saints.

Tony still swears that Una was as much to blame as he, but then, we'll never quite know, ever, what's in the minds of the people we think we know so well.

I know one thing. You're a fine one, Blanche Murninghan, and it is good that you are carrying on the McLoughlin-Murninghan line. I hope one day you have a handsome son and a lovely daughter to tell the stories to. Well, most of them anyway. You can leave out the part about the bog and getting thrown in the Shannon and the murder! Mercy!

You must know, Mary Fogarty and I have become great friends. What you're doing for her, helping her search for her child in the adoption chain, is admirable. Only God and the Virgen know how that will work out, but your contribution to the agencies involved is much appreciated. The awful hospital is closed, but there are good people around who might help. Perhaps one day she will meet her child, but, if not, you tried. God bless you, Blanche Murninghan...

Blanche glanced at the back bedroom. The stash under the floorboards was not calling out to her in the creepy language of Edgar Allen Poe anymore; the rest of the money was happily laughing and singing, *Let me out, Blanche! Let me help find Mary's child!*

Blanche smiled. Gran had written it—*Ireland*!

She went back to Maggie:

Ah. But I'm getting carried away. The box, herewith, in this packet. Have a look now. Was returned to me from the district superintendent himself, part of the possessions of that Declan O'Brian, possibly ripped, sadly, from the neck of the beautiful William on the banks of the Shannon one fateful day. You must have it. Wear it fondly and remember your home.

Love to you, dear little cousin. Come again to us.

Yours, Maggie.

Blanche opened the box and inside was a small, enameled case. Lined in satin. A silver chain coiled into a nest and a silver Celtic cross on top. She lifted it out, held the shiny Irish silver up to the sunny Florida light where it caught a beam. *From heaven, surely. God rest ye, Cousin William!*

THE END

Acknowledgements

MANY THANKS to you, my readers, for sticking it out with Blanche on another adventure. Hope you enjoyed it. A lot of great memories inspired the setting for this story:

In 1981, we stayed at Glin Castle in County Limerick for three weeks. It was stunning, and I tried to make the castle come to life in A Deathly Irish Secret. At Glin, Desmond Fitzgerald and his wife Olda were charming hosts, their staff were like family, and we enjoyed more than the comforts of home—priceless antiques and books, salmon fresh out of the Shannon, scads of vegetables and flowers and herbs from the gardens, and cows roaming the demesne chomping on the topiary. I just had to go back, so I sent Blanche. Castle Dunfaedan near the village of Ballycill is all invention, but I couldn't help drawing on those memorable weeks at Glin for the book. Blanche needed that soft landing while she bounced off accusations of murder and mayhem.

I couldn't have negotiated the intricacies of Irish policing without the unbelievable patience, insight, and experience of Malachy Daly, a garda and detective in the service of Ireland for more than thirty-five years. He helped me clarify some of the boundaries that Blanche was bound to push, and helped me straighten out some of the procedures that involve murder in Ireland (which, by the way, is pretty rare, comparatively speaking).

Bill Murphy's incredible knowledge of Irish history was invaluable. Bill has a doctorate in Irish history from the University of Chicago and has visited the auld sod at least a dozen times—how lucky that he agreed to read the manuscript and point out details that corrected my ways.

Any misinterpretations, exaggerations, and license in the telling of this story are my doing; sometimes my mind runs off and it, stubbornly, won't come back.

My beloved friend, Maggie Fitzpatrick, who spent some wonderful days with us at Glin, died during the writing of this story. I acknowledge her for her support and love. You're with me always, Magathy.

I'm eternally grateful to Judith Horner, reader and editor, for her steadfast grasp of the story line—I couldn't do without her input on all the Blanche adventures. She makes Blanche look real good—as does the wonderful staff at Light Messages/Torchflame Publishing! Thank you to my editor, Jori Hanna, and to all the Turnbulls, Elizabeth, Betty, and Wally.

And, thank you, Mom and Dad, for Glin. I hope that wherever you are you're enjoying martinis among the heavenly topiary.

About the Author

NANCY NAU SULLIVAN is the author of memoir, mystery, and a novel. She began writing in high school and college for the newsppers. Later, she worked as an editorial assistant at New York magazines and as a print journalist throughout the Midwest.

Nancy was born in San Francisco, grew up outside Chicago, but often visited Anna Maria Island, Florida. She returned to the island with her family and wrote an award-winning memoir, *The Last Cadillac*, about the years she cared for her father while her children were still at home--a harrowing adventure of travel, health issues, adolescent angst, with a hurricane thrown in for good measure. She went back to the Florida setting for her first cozy mystery, *Saving Tuna Street*, creating the fictional Santa Maria Island for the Blanche Murninghan mystery series, now in its fourth installment with *A Deathly Irish Secret*. She also wrote a novel, The Boys of Alpha Block, based on the years she taught in a boys' prison in Florida.

Nancy, for the most part, lives in Northwest Indiana. She is a graduate of the University of San Francisco (San Francisco College for Women, Lone Mountain) with a double major in Spanish and political science and holds a master's degree in journalism from Marquette University. She also attended the University of Florida in English and education.

Follow Nancy at:
nancynausullivan.com
Twitter: @NauSullivan

Saving Tuna Street

Saving
Tuna Street

A BLANCHE MURNINGHAN MYSTERY

Nancy Nau Sullivan

WHEN HER DEAR FRIEND IS FOUND MURDERED in the parking lot of the marina, Blanche Murninghan begins digging into his death. With her friends Liza and Hassi by her side, she stumbles into a pit of greed, murder, drug running, and kidnapping. Blanche has survived her fair share of storms on Santa Maria Island, but this one might just be her last.